Just Like a Woman

Jill Gascoine

CORGI BOOKS

JUST LIKE A WOMAN
A CORGI BOOK : 0 552 14442 8

First publication in Great Britain

PRINTING HISTORY
Corgi edition published 1997

Set in 11/13pt Monotype Plantin by Kestrel Data, Exeter.

Corgi Books are published by Transworld Publishers Ltd,
61–63 Uxbridge Road, London W5 5SA,
in Australia by Transworld Publishers (Australia) Pty Ltd,
15–25 Helles Avenue, Moorebank, NSW 2170
and in New Zealand by Transworld Publishers (NZ) Ltd,
3 William Pickering Drive, Albany, Auckland.

Reproduced, printed and bound in Great Britain by
Mackays of Chatham plc, Chatham, Kent.

*To Barbara, my stepmother, for her courage,
tenacity and love,*

and

*To the memory of my Dad, for the memories
and the laughter, I'll miss him for ever.*

Acknowledgements

Thank you: – Dr Seigler, for the medical advice in Daisy's story, and for making me laugh when things looked black; my brother, Wayne, who lives in Idaho; my darling Colette, who pushed and pulled me through the year and fed me with jello to keep up my strength; my husband, Fred, and my sons, who propped me up with tireless love; to Judy, my agent; and once again, Diane, my editor, who always discovers the things I leave out.

Chapter One

Daisy knelt on the tiles in the restroom at the back of the diner and laid her hot, flushed face against the cool plastic lid of the toilet bowl. It was the third time she'd been sick since she'd woken at five that morning. After a few moments, without even glancing into the mirror above the basin, she stood to wash her hands and splash her face with cold water. She knew, without looking, that the small blood vessels in her face had broken, as they always did, after she'd vomited. The pale and fragile look that came so often with sickness had never been hers, even in her youth.

'Are you OK, honey?' Dorrie's usually harsh Southern voice from outside the bathroom door sounded concerned, and much softer at that moment than when she was bitching about a difficult customer in the diner.

Daisy opened the door and smiled weakly, the way some people do when they want to apologize, and there's nothing to be sorry for. 'I'm fine, Dorrie. I think I must have eaten something. Do I look dreadful?'

'Dreadful.'

Daisy laughed. 'That's always been your most endearing quality, Dorothy Danson. The way the

9

bullshit just rolls off your tongue when it's needed!' She moved behind the counter of the by-now thinning out diner, followed by Dorrie.

'Don't you walk away from me like that, pretending it's nothing,' Dorrie muttered. There were still a few customers left in the restaurant at the end of the breakfast rush. 'That's the third or fourth time you've been sick this week alone. If I didn't know how old you were, I'd think you were pregnant!'

'Don't be daft – it would be a miracle.'

'You mean an immaculate conception?'

'No!' Daisy tried not to laugh. Dorrie could be embarrassing, even after all these years of friendship, with her way of just coming out with things without thinking. A customer had already passed the counter and raised her eyebrows at the words. 'Bob and I do get it together sometimes you know,' Daisy whispered out of the corner of her mouth, busying herself by wiping the necks of the bottles of ketchup that lined the counter like little red soldiers, 'in spite of ma-in-law lurking outside every door.'

At the end of the counter, across the cruets and relishes and sugar bowls, a customer at the other end of the counter tapped the side of his empty coffee cup and smiled for her attention.

Daisy moved towards him, coffee jug in hand. 'Sorry to keep you waiting, Sam. My legs don't seem to be moving so fast these days. Must be old age, I guess.'

'Get outta here, Daisy Francken! I remember

you at twenty. When you first stepped off that boat from England. All eyes and no tongue in those days. Wasn't that yesterday?'

'Feels like it, Sam. Some days it sure feels like it.'

He drank his coffee, paid his bill, chuckling at his memories. She watched him as he walked out, and through the steamy, half-curtained windows of the diner, followed his progress as he stopped and chatted to everyone and made his way down Main Street and back to the hardware store he'd worked in and owned for the last twenty years. It made her feel safe, that special comfort of living in a town where everyone knew you, and had watched you grow older through the years, along with themselves. 'You don't get that in a big city,' Bob was always saying. 'You don't even have to lock your door round these parts, honey. Never did.'

She looked at the clock above the counter. Nine a.m.; it always ran ten minutes slow, had done for years. Been repaired hundreds of times, but always went back to being ten minutes slow. 'Got a mind of its own,' Daisy had once grumbled after it had made her late to pick up the children from school one day, 'like all the other Franckens.' It had been in the family for years, Bob had said once, came over with the very first Francken, apparently.

Breakfast was almost over. The people from the insurance office would be in soon, picking up morning coffee and doughnuts. The door opened to more customers and she could see, as well as feel, the cold air swirling around them. She shivered. Thanksgiving was less than a week away. Winter was coming. They expected a hard one this year. It had rained a lot that summer, and a lot of the farmers grumbled about the crop ruin, between themselves, when they brought their families in for dinner some nights. Not that Daisy was working that late these days. She helped out in the mornings quite often, when she was needed. Dorrie was always there, and it was from her that one heard all the gossip.

Daisy turned to brew another pot of coffee. At her shoulder suddenly, startling her, Dorrie hissed in her ear, 'Go home, honey. I can manage this lot. Jan'll be in about eleven for the lunches. I'm off at three, so I'll come over and see how you are.'

Dorrie had no children, just a husband with a bad back, and no employment, unless he did old Sam a favour sometimes and helped out at the store when they got too busy. 'Injured at work,' he said when people asked about his disability. 'What work?' Dorrie would complain to Daisy over many a mug of coffee in the early evenings, sitting on the Franckens' front veranda, old Mary in her usual chair, and the two of them in the swing. 'Always been a lazy bum, even when he was young. Now he's round my feet all day. Just sits there. Reads the same paper over and over. Reads, eats and complains about my cooking. Mind you, never says anything till the plate's empty!'

They'd been married since the day after they graduated: high school sweethearts. Too young of course, but no-one could stop them. 'No kids,' Dorrie had once said sadly. 'Not for the lack of trying, I can tell you. Back in those days, anyway.' She was four years older than Daisy, and had been her friend since the young and frightened English wife of the Franckens' only cherished son had trembled into town.

It was the year Daisy had arrived in Wellington, along with two-year-old Marjorie, who hadn't seen Bob since she was a year old, which was when he went home to Idaho, in 1946, back from the war in Europe, back to Boise, where he'd worked before the war in crop insurance. He'd sent for his young wife and his small daughter a year later, and settled them both with his parents in the old house in his home town of Wellington. He travelled the seventy-five miles home each Friday night after he finished work, staying until dawn on the Monday, when he drove back to Boise, while Daisy watched from the bedroom window, praying the week would go quickly, praying her mother-in-law would stop making those awful jokes about Englishwomen having no spirit and doing nothing but weep in their bedrooms when there was so much to do about the house and garden.

Daisy would count the hours until Friday night and the return of a husband, smelling of the city when she hugged him, but she could never find the words to explain why she was so unhappy and afraid when he was not there. She had watched her own daughter pull away from her, lean towards the over-indulgent grandparents, listened while the small, fair-haired girl lost the English accent she had when they first arrived, and became, before her mother's eyes, the quintessential American child, made to look like a real live copy of 'our very own Shirley Temple' by a grand-mother with a passion for the movies. In next to no time, she went from Marjorie to Marje.

From the beginning, Daisy felt like an outsider. Bob didn't understand, couldn't understand. She'd always been shy, he knew that, even from the first moment he set eyes on her at that dance the Red Cross had arranged for the GIs. The English girls filled a gap and helped the swarms of young Americans forget the girls they'd left behind. Falling instantly in love was part of a young man's nature in those dreadful, delightful days, especially when he was thousands of miles from family, hungry for everything, anything, to stop him thinking of home and all he'd left behind. Stolen kisses to shut out disillusionment.

Bob had been thirty then, and a major in the US Army, handsome in his well pressed uniform, so charming, so full of ease when he spoke to a girl. He knew how to flirt, how to make her forget any of her home-grown sweethearts who might be stationed somewhere in Europe, somewhere that was even worse than the bombing, and the ration books, and the black-outs, that were then part of Britain.

Daisy was an innocent, who lived with her parents, and was brought up with loving and strict Catholic moral values. Then the Americans arrived. Bob was stationed at the camp across the bridge from where Daisy had lived since she was born. Her mother and father believed firmly in reaching out with friendliness to all these young men who had at last become their allies in a war that had to be won. Daisy met Bob, and they had welcomed 'Yankee' Bob and his tins of ham (almost a forgotten luxury) into their home with a kind of Victorian idea of hospitality. They were no different from thousands of other British hosts at that time. And neither was the outcome. Daisy got pregnant: a good Catholic girl who told her parish priest everything, including her undying love for the American who had arrived in her uneventful life, and persuaded her so eloquently to abandon the innocence of her upbringing and 'go too far'. 'Well, at least he's Catholic,' were the words her mother murmured to Daisy's bewildered and distressed father.

When she was six months pregnant, Bob got permission from the Army to marry her. This he did, despite the anger of his mother reverberating across the Atlantic into his sleepless nights. Not for him a forgotten child in a foreign land. He knew what was right, no, more than that, what he *wanted*, because he had loved Daisy, and his mom would grow to love her as well. He'd go back to Idaho as soon as the Army allowed; Daisy and little Marjorie would follow when he'd settled again.

It had taken a year before they were reunited. A year before Daisy tore herself up from her roots and went to live with a man she suspected would have become almost a stranger since he'd gone home. He was now a man out of uniform, an ordinary man who sold insurance, and whose pockets were not crammed with candy and nylons; anyone in America could buy those sorts of things for themselves with dollars of their own. He was a man she would have to learn to fall in love with all over again.

It had taken years for her to settle, to stop feeling homesick, to embrace small-town life in the state of Idaho. But small-town folk are friendly. At first suspicious and wary, they eventually came round, especially once young Robert was born in 1949, quickly followed by Gary a year later. Three children to cope with, young Bob away in the city all week, leaving his English wife in his parents' house. 'And,' the townsfolk gossiped, 'Mary Francken was always a little difficult, specially since her husband bought the diner on Main Street after managing it all these years. Didn't take much to make Mary get above herself!'

Daisy worked as a waitress in those days. The extra money helped them save, although her own father-in-law wasn't exactly generous, believing that the young didn't need much money, not as much as their elders, anyway. 'Time enough when yer old to buy new dresses and take vacations,' he'd say. 'And the young should stand alone, be independent, strengthen their character, build their family. It's the American way – what made this country great!' Mary Francken cared for her grandchildren while her daughter-in-law waited tables, and Daisy watched helplessly as her children were influenced more and more by an upbringing that had been so different from her own.

Waitressing in the diner was fun at first. Dorrie wasn't there in those days. She'd worked in the next town as a hairdresser, and she and her husband Billy rented a small wooden house with a front porch opposite the Franckens. When Bob gave up insurance and moved home to help his dad in the diner, he and Daisy rented a house two streets away from the big house. Just for them and the kids. Those years had been good. Daisy had felt like a family at last.

In the late fifties, Bob's dad died after a long battle from cancer. He'd refused quite emphatically to give up smoking, and his wife was only a heartbeat away from saying to him on his deathbed, 'I told you so.' But she was furious after he'd gone. Blamed him for dying on her for the rest of her life. Bob inherited the diner, and he, Daisy and their three children gave up the small rented home she'd loved, and moved back into the big house on the hill. 'To keep Mom company,' Bob said. Daisy hated it, but said nothing. An optimist at heart, she felt that all her mother-in-law really needed was understanding.

Her silence over that decision was only the beginning.

Everywhere had become busier in the sixties, and some of that had spread even to the small towns. The older folks hated it. But then the whole world was changing so rapidly since the end of the war, and even the rural areas were driven to catch up a little. The farmers were still there, of course. They would remain always as far as most people could tell. Their German ancestors, like Bob's, had settled there generations before; they'd handed their ways, their morals, their prejudices and their farms down from son to grandson, and so it went on.

When they'd first arrived as immigrants, Bob's ancestors realized there might be more potential in the new country than just tilling the land. After a few years they had gone into shopkeeping: supplies, groceries. People would always eat, they reckoned, even in the bad times people would still get hungry. It stood them in good stead two generations later, when the Depression was upon them. The farm became smaller and smaller over the years, and soon it supplied only the family and the shop. In the thirties, Bob's father turned the shop into a diner. Labour was cheap. Many men would work merely for their food and a shelter to sleep in. So the family prospered, albeit from the desperation of men who worked to keep from starving. The diner was built with this labour. All through the Depression, itinerant workers came and went. The Franckens stayed put: a hard-nosed family to marry into, it could be said, but one that stayed together when so much else in the world was falling apart. After the war, the small farm was sold. The diner would expand as more women worked outside the home, and more meals were eaten out.

Over the years, Daisy had settled finally into a way of life that was easy for her to deal with from day to day. She succumbed to other people's desires. It made her life peaceful at least. Even made herself believe she was happy. And if it ever crossed her mind that her marriage had turned out unfulfilling and disappointing, as indeed was the complaint of many of her women friends, she was reminded constantly by her mother-in-law, who counted the depressing rise in the statistics of divorce in a country that was built on family values, that she lived with 'a good provider, a home-based father'. And even if Bob did occasionally stray, which Daisy often suspected, at least he had the good manners to keep quiet about it.

And so their marriage bobbed along – like most, if you leave all stones unturned. That way no-one sees the maggots lurking underneath. A quiet life was a happy one.

It was in 1975 when the trouble started. They were doing well. The diner, gift shop and gas station flourished. The children had grown and left home.

That November morning, six days before the holiday, Daisy, still feeling bad, took Dorrie's advice and drove straight to Dr Hart's before she went home. 'I've no appointment,' she said when faced with the surprised look on the face of the girl behind Reception, 'but it might be important.'

'It's OK Mrs Francken, he'll see you as soon as he can. Do you need another prescription?'

'I've no idea what I need Carol! He'll probably tell me it's nerves again. Isn't it always that? Though heaven knows what I've got to be nervous about.'

The girl laughed. She liked Daisy Francken. A lady right down to her well polished shoes. Daisy sat and waited, flicking through old magazines, realizing after a few moments they were the same ones she'd donated to the surgery only a month ago.

After thirty minutes Douglas Hart put his head round the door. 'Come in Daisy, my dear. Whatever it is you've got, if it isn't a cold which all my patients today are insisting is life-threatening 'flu, you'll be a welcome relief!'

After the usual enquiries about Mary, 'Everyone is always so preoccupied with her,' Daisy thought, 'she'd be thrilled if she knew!' Douglas Hart said, 'Now then my dear, what's your problem?'

'I don't know Douglas, except I'm more tired than usual, and I've been throwing up a lot. Specially in the mornings.'

Douglas raised his eyebrows. 'Perhaps your Robert's young wife is handing out pregnancy symptoms in the hope she'll fall for the real thing. Poor girl seems desperate.'

'I know. Every month she cries for days, Robert tells me. It's all she thinks about.'

Douglas Hart scribbled something down on his prescription pad.

'I won't take them,' Daisy warned grimly, 'whatever you're prescribing, that is. I'm too busy. All I need is a tonic. Something to perk me up, give me more of an appetite, stop me feeling queasy all the time.'

'Off your food completely?'

'Just certain things.'

Dr Hart thought for a moment, then, 'Put on one of those nasty green examining gowns of mine, Daisy my dear. Let's have a thorough look at you.' He left the room while she undressed and then eventually came back in with his nurse. He took her blood pressure and temperature. 'Both a little higher than usual,' he said.

'Perhaps I've eaten something that disagreed with me,' Daisy smiled brightly.

Douglas said nothing. Then, 'I'm going to give you an internal, my dear. I know you hate them, but Terri here will hold your hand.'

Daisy laughed. 'Oh dear, maybe my mother-in-law has been right all these years. I really am a wimp. Even my doctor knows it.'

He examined her in silence. She could hear the small travelling clock on his desk ticking loudly underneath Douglas' measured breathing. When he finished he frowned, pulled off his gloves, said something softly to the nurse, and then turned once again to Daisy. 'Get dressed my dear. I'll be right back.' He left the room abruptly, leaving her alone with the ticking clock and the beginnings of a headache.

She began to worry for the first time since she'd started to feel so unwell. 'Is it cancer?' she blurted out when Douglas came back. 'One always thinks of things like that when you get to a certain age, or am I just being a neurotic silly old woman? Post-menopausal and all that?'

'Nothing like it,' he smiled, sitting down behind his desk. 'You're not ill. Quite the opposite in fact.'

'What d'you mean?'

'How old are you Daisy? I've forgotten for the moment.' He began to glance through the pages of her medical history laid out before him on the desk.

She answered quickly, 'I'll be fifty-one next June. What has that to do with anything?' Then, sitting there in that tiny room, listening to the rain beginning to pelt down on the roof and window, she knew. 'Tell me Douglas,' she said, then, 'no, I don't want to hear. I can't hear. Let me delude myself for a little longer.'

He reached across and took her hand. 'You're pregnant, Daisy. There's little doubt in my mind, you're about seven, probably eight weeks pregnant.'

Daisy stared. At last, 'How? Whoever heard of a woman of my age giving birth? How can it happen? I don't believe I've menstruated for almost a year! How *can* I be pregnant?'

Douglas Hart smiled. Reached across to take her hand. Comforted, Daisy thought she could have stopped time at that moment, have no future to think of, no husband to render speechless at dinner that evening. She just wanted to sit there in that room and listen to the rain and hold on to the smooth and placid hand of a man who gave this kind of news to a variety of ears, but seldom to one who had no idea of how to react.

Douglas said, 'It's rare. This occurrence, I mean. Rare, but not unusual. You will be the first post-menopausal pregnancy that I've personally dealt with, but your position is not unheard of. We can deal with it in two ways. We can take extraordinary care of you while you carry the child to term, but you can talk it over with your husband, and I doubt if I will have any problem getting you a perfectly legal abortion. One day, women in their fifties will no doubt find it almost commonplace to have children, but we're not quite at that point yet. The decision must be yours and Bob's.'

She sat staring at her hands clutched together in her lap, trying to stop them shaking. She said at last, 'We're Catholic, Douglas. An abortion is out of the question. But what are we going to do after the baby's born? There's my mother-in-law, and Bob is not getting any younger, none of us are. How will we take care of a small baby?'

'I suppose your church would tell you that the Lord will tend to those problems.'

'Then it's a great pity He's not around to sort

23

it out now, if it's His mistake in the first place.'

'Daisy dear, talk to Bob, then your priest. Exceptions are made, I'm sure. In circumstances like this, common sense, as well as a reverence for life, must prevail.'

She stood, holding on to the prescription for a tonic in her hand, a list of the vitamins she must take, the food she must eat. 'I know all about this, what I have to do and all that,' she said ruefully, quietly. 'I've been this way before, remember. Three times to be exact.'

'But this time you must do it properly. And is it any good at all telling you to rest more?'

'I doubt it, Douglas. You've known me long enough.' Daisy managed a smile as she went to the door. 'God knows what my mother-in-law's going to say about all this, let alone the children.'

With one arm about her shoulders as they stood by the open door, Douglas Hart lowered his voice. 'Don't tell the rest of the family until you've spoken to Bob. If you both decide to terminate, there will be no reason for anyone else to interfere.'

'Let's hope we both come to the same decision.'

'It's your child, Daisy dear, you're the one who has to shelter it for the next seven months. It's your strength that matters. Think hard, have no regrets, but think as quickly as you can. Another few weeks and it will be too late for an easy termination. Do you understand?'

She nodded. Shuddered. Not only from the cold blowing through the open door.

'Call me at any time,' he said, 'don't hesitate.'
'Thanks Douglas.'

She sat for a long time in her old pick-up outside the surgery. 'If I decide to go through with it,' she mused, 'I must buy a car. Can't be thrown around in this for the next seven months!'

She must have sat there for even longer than she realized. A sharp knock on the window startled her, and, looking up, she saw the smiling face of her daughter-in-law. Robert's wife, Sharon, was standing shivering in the rain in only the short thin overall she worked in. The beauty salon, where she worked as second chief stylist six days a week, since graduating without the best of grades, was located directly opposite the doctor's.

Daisy opened the passenger door for her to climb in. 'Goodness Sharon, you'll catch your death. What are you doing without a coat, child?'

Sharon leaned over and kissed Daisy warmly on the cheek. 'You sound so English when you call me "child"; after all these years, still so English!' They both laughed. Sharon said, 'I saw you through the window of the shop. You've been sitting here for ages. Is something wrong? Why were you at the doctor?'

'Oh, just to renew a prescription. Nothing to worry over.'

'I could have done that for you! You should have called the salon. It's Friday, remember? Robert and I'll be up for our dinner tonight, and I'm sure Gran still wants her hair done. What about you? I could give you a trim if you like. Save you coming in next week for Thanksgiving. Shall I bring anything tonight?'

Daisy had forgotten, for the moment, the Friday ritual. The last thing she wanted to do was cook for five people that night. Fish, of course, with two kinds of potatoes, mashed and french fries, and lots of corn and home-made coleslaw. It had been the same every Friday as far back as she could remember. Her heart sank. She felt nauseous again at the very thought of the evening ahead.

'Oh dear,' she said, 'I forgot to get fish.' The way she'd been feeling lately had left her no time to stock the freezer.

Sharon said, 'You look all grey in the face suddenly. Would you like me to bring something in tonight for a change? You look so worn out. I could pick up some pizza, or fried chicken if you like. Just this once?'

Daisy smiled at her gratefully. Sharon was a sweet girl, with seemingly boundless energy. Married five years and no sign of a baby. She was the only one at any of her class reunions who was still childless, and Sharon hated to be pitied or to come in last.

She said out loud, 'D'you think my mother-in-law would eat pizza even once?'

'Not likely!'

Daisy put her hand out to touch her daughter-in-law as they smiled at the words. 'Sharon dear, are you sure you wouldn't mind bringing the food?

It would be such a relief. I am very tired. I'd be so grateful.'

Sharon kissed her. 'Don't worry. I'll try and get fish sticks for Gran. That might shut her up a little!' And she was gone. Shivering her way back across the road to her next customer, pleased as punch to be doing something as important as taking over the Friday night at the Franckens.

Daisy went home. The rain was coming down faster than ever, and old Mary would be complaining about the damp in the house, forgetting it had always been the same. Daisy would light the old stove in the corner of the living-room, then let it go out when Bob came and complained of the heat and the waste of logs and it wasn't even the end of November yet. And Mary would just sit there, warm as toast by that time, and shake and nod her head at her son's words, as if the lighting of the fire had never been her idea in the first place.

Daisy heard the television blasting out as soon as she opened the back door. It did little for her headache, and she wondered if there was any aspirin in the house.

'Is that you Daisy?' her mother-in-law called from the family room.

'Yes, Mom. D'you want some tea?'

'You're home early today!' Mary somehow managed to make it sound like an accusation.

'I'm feeling under the weather. Dropped in to get a prescription from Douglas. Left the diner early. The morning rush was over quickly today.

People gone into town for Thanksgiving shopping, I expect. They've got that new market open just a few miles down the state highway.'

'No-one left in our town if that goes on,' Mary grumbled.

'D'you want the stove lit?' Daisy said as she tried to make her mother-in-law more comfortable against the cushions in her old chair.

Mary looked surprised. 'Bit early in the day isn't it? Not that I can't feel the damp, mind you. You get to eighty-four, you deserve to get damp in your bones!'

'Shall I bring the fire down from the bedroom then?'

'Don't you dare! If you want to be generous with those logs all of a sudden, who am I to complain? It's just not like you to suggest.'

Daisy was appallingly tired. She thought longingly of bed and a hot water bottle against her aching back. The ironing waited for her in the kitchen basket. She could see it in her mind's eye. 'What on earth d'you mean Mom? I'm not the mean one in this house, and well you know it.' Daisy knew it would probably have been more diplomatic to have used the word 'careful' instead of 'mean' when she was talking about Bob. He was still, even at sixty, his mother's blue-eyed boy.

'My son's careful with his money,' Mary said crossly, 'it runs in the family. Always has. How else d'you think we've raised ourselves from the farmyards?'

Daisy had heard it all before. She could have

28

joined in the words. She felt sorry at times for the old woman in the chair. Everyone hopes there'll be someone around to take care of you when age finds you out. Sneaks up and gets inside your body one day while you're busy living and wishing your life so foolishly away as you yearn for better things. She bent down again and made to plump the pillow at Mary's back.

'For God's sake girl stop fussing! If you want the stove on, do it! But I didn't ask, don't forget that. What are you after with all this fussing? Something must be up. I might be old but I'm not senile.'

Daisy's compassionate thoughts disappeared even faster than they'd arrived. 'I'll get the logs,' she said. 'And yes, you're quite right. I'm the one who's cold, and I'm the one who can feel the damp in my bones today. I've been up since five this morning; I feel dreadful, and I look worse! Sharon said she'd bring food in tonight. I don't feel like cooking. And I think I'll go to bed early.' And with that she threw her coat across the room and onto the sofa and stomped back into the kitchen to sort out the logs before Mary could reply.

Two at a time, she carried them back in, wary of the life inside her. She took her time, listened with only half an ear to her mother-in-law's conversation.

'I'll not eat pizza,' Mary said. 'I don't like foreign food, and you know that. I used to cook every night when my men came home. No matter how I felt. Even when I was carrying! Probably why I lost two of them. Only ever known hard work.'

Daisy looked sharply at her mother-in-law, wondering if the remarks about her own miscarriages had been instigated by that extraordinary old woman's ageless instinct. 'Maybe she really is a witch,' she thought, watching while the logs started to catch, knowing that soon the room would be as warm as toast, and not even Mary's sharp tongue could stop her feeling cosy. It was the best thing about the Idaho winters, the abundance of logs to make their houses warm. Shivering around the coal fires in England was, by now, just a depressing memory. She remembered chilblains as a child, rushing to sit on the school radiators during morning break, warming and drying one's feet and socks after a snowy day's hockey lesson. How the English revelled in the cold, testing their stamina, building their character, taking cold showers, trying to fall asleep in cold bedrooms. Daisy shivered, then smiled at the memories. Winters and hockey games were amongst the things she didn't miss.

'If you're so ill, Miss Daisy,' old Mary's voice cut across her thoughts even more icily than the English damp, 'if you're really that ill, what, may I ask, are you smiling at? You look quite mad sitting there gazing at that open stove. Shut the darn thing for goodness sake, and boil some water for that tea you promised. And while you're at it, make sure there's enough hot water for my hair tonight. It ran cold on me last time. Goodness only knows what I could have gone down with.'

'I'm beginning to feel like Cinderella,' Daisy muttered as she stood up. She got as far as the door.

'If Sharon's only bringing pizza what will I eat?' The whine and challenge in Mary's voice was clever but well practised.

Daisy turned. 'She's promised to try and find some fish. You can have that with mashed potatoes. You know it's your favourite.'

The afternoon finally drew to a close. Darkness fell along with the rain. A blustery wind rattled the windows, making Mary start up from her chair, waking her from a slumber she would never confess to indulge in, and disturbing the stillness in the old house that was such a rare joy to Daisy.

Bob came home along with Robert. Sharon had their car and would be along with the food later. Tonight would be a difficult time to break the news. Maybe tomorrow. Bob enjoyed his Saturdays. There was sport on the television, and not even his mother's complaints would mar the day. Daisy pottered in the kitchen, preparing for Sunday and the traditional roast dinner she'd brought from England, and cooked for the family all their married life: beef and Yorkshire pudding. Delicious. Everyone in the town had the recipe after all these years.

It had been a good week, thought Bob. Robert ran the gas station at weekends. At sixty, Bob had earned his Saturdays and Sundays. He had started to plan his retirement. Him and Daisy. If the good

Lord would smile on them and take his old mother to His bosom, then life would be even better. A wicked thought, but for a man who believed there was a better place we go to after death, there was hardly a reason to cross himself when wishing for an old woman's gentle demise.

'I'm home, honey!' he called.

And this well-contented man took off his cowboy boots and went into the warmth to greet his mother and his wife, to read the local paper, and wait for his Friday night dinner with his family. There was little else a man could need to fill his stomach and his heart.

Chapter Two

Mary sniffed. Petulant. Derisive. Her fork probed the food placed by Sharon in front of her on the kitchen table.

They only used the dining-room at Thanksgiving, Christmas, baptisms and funerals, when the kitchen was too small, and the whole family, Franckens from everywhere, were present. At funerals, especially. Funerals were big with the Franckens.

Mary sniffed again. 'What exactly am I expected to eat?' she said. 'What is this, Sharon?'

'Fish sticks, Gran. Have you never had a fish stick? You'll love 'em. No bones. Not a piece of skin even. Do you want ketchup?'

'Yes. Thank you, dear.'

The ketchup was passed. The television blasted in the other room. There were just the four of them. Daisy had by this time gone to take a bath, declaring herself not hungry.

'Are you sickening?' Bob said, not looking up from his pizza, smothering his french fries with ketchup.

'It's only a cold, I'm sure.'

'Made you see Dr Hart, though,' Sharon said.

Bob looked up at his wife. Funny for Daisy,

33

bothering the doctor about anything. She was seldom ill. 'That old quack? What did he have to say?'

'Nothing much,' said Daisy quickly, one peeved glance at her daughter-in-law, who continued eating her salad, innocence written all over. 'Well, no-one told her it was a secret,' Daisy chided herself.

'It's just a woman's thing,' Daisy went on, 'you know.'

'Oh. As long as it's nothing serious.'

He went back to his food. Daisy to her bath. 'Typical,' she muttered to herself, watching the hot water pour out and foaming up the bath gel she'd thrown in first, 'Isn't that typical? My, oh my, is he in for a shock.'

After too hot a bath, her skin damp at once with sweat, and feeling light-headed, she put on her night-gown and robe. Thoughts of that hot water bottle urged her back into the kitchen, where Sharon was loading the dishwasher and waiting for the coffee to brew.

'Thanks for doing supper, Sharon. I'm sorry for being such a depressing object and disappearing to bed so early. Can you cope with Mary?'

'Sure. I'm setting her hair. Giving her a new style so she'll get over the sight of those fish sticks! She went on as if I was poisoning her.'

Daisy smiled. 'Are the men OK?'

'They will be when I give them apple pie and ice-cream.'

Daisy, the hot water bottle already warming up

the feather bed, thought she'd try to catch her husband's attention enough to settle him down for a talk. It wasn't the best of times. They were showing *All in the Family* on one of the networks. Bob's favourite.

'I need to talk, Bob.'

'Can it wait honey?'

'Tomorrow then?'

'Sure honey. Get some sleep. You don't want a cold for Thanksgiving. Sharon's looked after us like she was born to it. I told her she'd have to watch herself, she might steal your job from right under your nose!'

It was a delightful thought.

'Didn't like those fish things,' sniffed Mary. 'Who's ever seen fish with such straight edges? Probably not real food.'

Robert punched her gently on the arm. 'Shut the noise Gran. Sharon did her best. She's been working all day. You always complain you can't taste anything anyway. 'Night, Mom. See you Sunday.'

' 'Night, all of you. 'Spect I'll be better tomorrow. Don't wake me when you come to bed, Bob. I'll leave your side light on, then you won't stumble around in the dark.'

It was the end of another day. One with news that was hungry for sharing, but time and place had not been on Daisy's side. Bob would be home all day tomorrow. She would maybe bake his favourite pie, and find a private place for them to talk. Lying in bed, she touched her belly, smiled.

'I mustn't get too attached,' she muttered to herself, 'Bob may disregard his principles, and then an abortion would be arranged, and no-one but us would ever know.'

Secrets. Families are full of them.

But Saturday turned out to be a day of disasters. Robert, alone at the gas station, hurrying to a customer who was in some great haste and wanted a full service, slid on some oil lurking on the forecourt, left over from the night before, and sprained his ankle. Bob went down to take over, while Sharon came to take her husband home and call the doctor. Robert could look forward to a weekend of being comforted, and Sharon could look forward to no Sunday lunch with the family.

So Bob was cross that his weekend was ruined, and Mary was furious about missing her usual Sunday dinner, the routine of meals being of the utmost importance to her, because roast beef would be silly with just herself and Daisy there to eat it. Bob decided at the last minute not to spend the day alone with his wife and mother, and took the opportunity to visit some friends in Boise, seeing that this particular Sunday, without Robert or Marjorie and John, would not be a real family day after all.

So Bob, seeing it would most likely be quiet at the gas station as it was the weekend before Thanksgiving, and the weather was rough, decided to close the station for the day, due to illness he said, and drive into Boise as he'd planned to look at some new pick-ups he'd seen were up for sale at a good price. He said, 'I could meet up with the old gang, stay the night, and drive back early the next morning. It'd be crazy to try it at night. I'm bound to have a drink in me. Remember the old gang?' And he laughed. Daisy looked at him keenly, until he turned away from her. She heard him on the telephone, making arrangements, wondering what he was getting up to in that head of his; it irritated her, knowing it was all an excuse not to spend the day with his mother, knowing that Sharon and Robert wouldn't be there to ward off Mary's acid tongue, and his wife unwell.

Daisy sighed. He had always loathed her being ill. And it would have been such a good time to tell him her news. She should have insisted, put her foot down. Instead, she packed an overnight bag for him and waved him goodbye, promising to take advantage of all that free time to herself, then went inside, lit the stove in the middle of the day, and put two pork chops on the grill. Mary loved pork, and it would keep her happy for hours. The thought of spending the next twenty-four hours with her mother-in-law made her feel even more tired, and she cursed the selfishness of men.

And the infuriating thing was, the whole of the following week became just like that: never a moment, it seemed, to get Bob on her own, being asleep when he came home at night. Then suddenly she had to call in the doctor for Mary, who had developed a dose of the 'flu bug that was going around.

Dr Hart spoke to Daisy while he was writing

out the prescription for the old lady. She looked tired. Douglas told her so, said she must rest, especially if she and Bob had decided against the termination. 'I'd like to speak to you together,' he said, 'put all the pros to you. You must let me know as soon as possible. Don't let this thing drag on, whatever decision you've both come to.'

'I haven't told Bob yet.' Daisy raised her hand to silence his protests. 'I know, I know. I can't seem to find the right time. He's always a bit elusive just before Thanksgiving. You know how men hate all the upheaval these holidays cause. I promise I'll try tonight.'

Douglas left. Daisy went for Mary's medicine. Apart from the sickness in the morning, and the extra weariness that hit her at the end of each day, Daisy was bearing up quite well. She hated being unable to drink tea because it made her feel nauseous. But that was merely irritating for an English soul, having no hot, sweet and milky tea to soothe away the ravages of life.

Then there was the shopping that week, of course, and the careful choosing of the turkey. A wreath of fir cones and berries went on the door, and some lights appeared, strung up outside across the front porch. 'There's more decorations at Christmas of course,' Mary would tell her friends with the excitement of a child when they dropped by to have coffee with her in the mornings. Gossipy and rather fractious old women, but Daisy liked them coming. It brightened Mary up no end.

She'd told Bob she would not go into the diner the last week before the holiday. Dorrie would manage, and the new girl seemed to be working out real well. So, all at once, it was the day before turkey day, and Bob was still unaware what was going on with his wife. He suspected nothing. Most women seemed to get cranky at that time of year. All that extra shopping and cleaning, and endless preparation. Make even the most sainted of them irritable.

And then, on the Monday of that week, Gary called from California. 'Hi Mom! Got a surprise for you. Are you up for it?'

'Gary! Oh my goodness, what a delight to hear your voice, son. It's been so long since you called.'

'I know. And I'm sorry. Just like always.'

It was easier to forgive her younger son more than anyone else in her life. She waited.

'Mom, I'm coming home for the holiday. I need to talk to you.'

'How wonderful darling!' Too wary to expect much, she kept the excitement out of her voice. 'How long for this time?'

'I'll be there on the day. Some time in the late morning. Well in time for turkey.'

'Are you driving?'

'We're leaving Tuesday, Mom. I'm dropping a friend off who lives in Boise. I'll stay with him Wednesday night. Don't want to keep you up all night waiting for me.'

Daisy's heart sank a little. She knew he lied, knew that staying under his father's roof for just one night would be uncomfortable for all concerned. They didn't like each other, Gary and his dad. Never had. There was something in the atmosphere when they were together that had never been aired. Daisy missed her favourite child. Missed his wit, his openness, his laughter. But she said nothing. She would have him there at least for the day. It would have to be enough. At least he would be there to hear her news. They all would. The thought unnerved her for the moment.

And then it was Wednesday. Time for the stuffings to be made, the house to be decorated, more cookies to be baked: the ones with peanut butter and chocolate chips. Gary's favourites. She laid the table in the dining-room, ready for the next day. Maybe at bedtime that night would be the last chance to tell Bob on his own. Mary had been difficult all week, more demanding, unless Daisy was imagining it because of her own weariness. On Wednesday night, the old woman sat downstairs by the stove making ribbons to go round the napkins for the big day. Mary loved Thanksgiving, went on and on about what it had been like down the years. How they always had at least twenty sitting down at the table, how all the women brought desserts and salads, how it had all changed since the war. 'That's thirty years ago, Mom! The world is different now. Families are spread. Neighbours keep themselves to themselves.'

Mary said the same thing every year since her husband had died. 'Don't have to tell me, girl!

40

Everyone moving into the state from outside, that's what done it. Marrying strangers instead of your own. Didn't do Idaho any good. Never will, you mark my words.'

Daisy repressed a deep, impatient sigh, thanked Mary once again for making such beautiful ribbons for the table, and resisted the impulse to remark that it probably made for a better and brighter community when people married strangers instead of kin. She fed her mother-in-law her favourite smoked sausage for supper, laid out her best dress and jewellery for the next day, and put her to bed early, letting the fire die out so she could give it a good clear out before she lit it again early in the morning.

She sat alone, waiting for the flames to die down, the door of the stove open, staring into the last of the warmth, hoping Bob would be home before sleep seduced her and she would miss their last chance alone. But Bob was late. It had been too much to hope that he would forgo his usual holiday drink or two at the local bar. She didn't blame him. In the home, the night before Thanksgiving was for women only. They needed the space, and the men needed that breather before the family descended. Daisy had always believed that neither Thanksgiving nor Christmas would have gone on being celebrated year after year if it had been left to the men. They loved it all when the day was done, but the preparation? No thank you! Daisy smiled as she got into bed on her own that night. She didn't blame them. They quite obviously had the right idea. Every day, after the event, after the quarrels and the disasters, she and millions of women like her would mutter, as they cleaned house, and husbands nursed hangovers, 'Never again! Next year we'll eat out!' And then, come early November, it would all start again. 'This year will be even better! I'll bake all my own cakes this time.' And so on.

So Daisy fell asleep, alone in the big feather-down bed, holding her secret close and placing her hands over her stomach, hot water bottle between them, as if to keep the child even more comfortable and safe where it was. 'Your first Thanksgiving little one,' she muttered, as if she'd already made up her mind that the child inside her was to stay, and there would be many more turkey days to anticipate with joy or dread. She dreamt of babies that night, and woke at six the next morning full of hope for the future, and whatever decision was ahead. But it was done: the child was settled, had already become a part of her. Only Daisy didn't realize it then, didn't face it, as she crept from the bed, kissing the open mouth of Bob as he snored gently in his sleep.

'Don't stir yet, dearest. I'll bring you coffee when it's brewed. And light the stove. We can sit up in bed and talk. I've something to tell you.'

Something in her voice made Bob open one eye. 'Now? You need to talk to me now? Can't it wait until tomorrow?'

'No. We should probably tell the rest of the family, and I want you to digest the news first.'

'Christ. You sound like your mom.'

Daisy smiled, kissed him again, and left the room.

It was the extra strong coffee she brought back into the bedroom thirty minutes later, along with a big bowl of creamed, sweetened oatmeal, or porridge as she always called it, harping back to her growing up in England. The things that Bob loved best for breakfast.

'Hey! What's this Daisy girl? Did I do something right for once?'

She smiled broadly at him as he sat up in bed and took the tray.

'Maybe you did,' she said. '*You* tell me.'

'Get on with it, honey. Mom'll be awake and yelling any minute.'

Daisy turned her head to stare out of the window, searching for the first words, trying to ignore the way he always slurped his porridge, because this particular morning it made her nauseous. 'I'm pregnant, Bob.' So much for the gentle approach. There was such a long silence, she eventually turned her head back towards him.

He sat, open-mouthed, with the spoon of porridge that had been halfway to his mouth dripping its contents on the clean sheets. 'Christ Daisy, tell me this is your idea of a joke. Tell me that and I'll forgive the limey sense of humour for once.'

She shook her head. Her eyes still fastened on his face. She took the tray from him. Left the spoon in his hand. He scratched his head, leaving porridge in the hairline. Just a fraction. Enough for her to put her hand out to wipe it away and take the spoon from him.

'How can you be?' he said. 'How can you be? I thought we were past worrying about that.'

'So did I. And Douglas.' She took his hand. 'I need you to tell the kids. If we keep it, that is. Should we keep it? The baby. Our baby.'

'Kids? Baby? What you doing to us, Daisy girl? I'm sixty for Christ's sake. What am I going to do with a baby at my age? There's a mistake been made here. Must be.'

Once more Daisy shook her head, and as she felt him pulling his hand away from hers, she said quickly, 'Do you want me to have an abortion? Is that what you want? I'll do what you want Bob. Just make this decision for me. For us. I can't do it honey. I can't do something like that on my own.'

Bob pulled away from her and swung his legs out of bed. Sitting there, naked as he'd always slept, still a fine and strong figure of a man, on the edge of the bed with his head in his hands. Not looking at her, the smallness of her as she sat there, waiting for his answer. He was afraid she'd touch him, or hold him, or want something from him that he could no longer find in his heart to give her.

'Bob?' she said, afraid to raise her voice, hearing Mary stir upstairs.

'Well, that's the holiday ruined,' he said. 'Any more surprises before the rest of the kids arrive?'

'Don't!' Her eyes filled with tears.

'Don't cry, woman. For Christ's sake don't cry.
I can't think when you get all teary on me.'

She said again, 'What do you want me to do?'

Bob stood up. 'I don't know, girl. It's out of
my league, all this. Maybe Marje'll know. It's
woman's business, this.'

'You'll tell them then? Today?'

'Christ.'

Daisy heard Mary on the stairs. 'I'll go help
Mom. Stay in here for a while. I'll bring you more
coffee.'

'You do that.'

'I'm sorry darling. I'm sorry.'

She wondered briefly, as she closed the bedroom door, what she was apologizing for; the
joy she'd felt before she fell asleep last night was
a forgotten emotion as trepidation and disappointment filled the space.

Gary was the first to arrive. Daisy heard his voice
from the yard, talking to his father, who was
outside creating a lot of fuss about the state of
some of the logs he was stacking, to bring in for
the dining-room fire. She could almost hear the
anger in him with every throwing down of each
unburnable piece of wood he encountered.

'They're soaking wet!' he yelled to his wife.
'Why are they always so goddam wet?'

Daisy didn't answer. Merely shook her head as
she basted the turkey, which was beginning to
sizzle nicely, lying there in the oven, fully stuffed

and bacon-covered. She knew it wasn't the logs he was angry with this year. All morning he'd not mentioned their earlier conversation, and she was too fearful to bring it up as the preparations for the family took over in priority from what was uppermost in both their minds. Besides, it was the same complaint every time when it was Bob's responsibility to keep the fire going in the dining-room, chilled as it was from lack of human heat for most of the year. He always forgot that he'd bought so many logs when the weather showed signs of changing that there was never enough room on the porch for them, and yet another twelve months had gone by without him fulfilling his promise to build a separate and larger shelter.

Daisy threw the back door open and held out her arms to her youngest son. 'You're so early,' she smiled, and when they hugged she remembered once again how good he always smelled, how handsome he always looked.

'Let me in, Mom, it's freezing out here! The heater in the car doesn't work.' He laughed, hugging her, pulling and pushing her into the warm kitchen, slamming the door behind them, and turning up his nose to soak up the familiar home-cooked smells of the season.

'I thought the roads would be busy,' she said, touching his face, reaching up to push back his hair. Gary had never minded being touched as he grew up. Not like his brother and sister, with their embarrassment in case their friends saw. After Gary was born, Marjorie was too often left to mind

Robert on her own, and she was a little girl who had never really been tactile in her emotions. It wasn't long before Robert, adoring his 'worldly' sister in those days, became like her, shunning his mother's 'babyish' cuddles, when in reality his mother's arms were all he wanted. And Daisy was too busy to notice. And even if she did think her middle child was sometimes looking a little sad, it never occurred to her that she was the cause. 'He's just growing up,' Bob said brusquely, 'becoming a little man. You'll see.'

'I've brought your Christmas presents,' Gary said, and then, 'You look tired, Mom. I mean more than the usual holiday weariness.'

'I'm OK darling. I'm fine. And you look wonderful.'

Holding him at arm's length, her eyes alight, her face could hardly contain her joy at seeing him. 'It's been almost two years this time. What are we to do with you?' She was laughing, unreproaching, knowing he was sure of her love, even in his absence.

'I want to talk to you about that, Mom. It's why I got here early. Before the ritual begins. Before the beers get drunk, along with the rest of us. Before the tongues get loose and unwise.'

Daisy shook her head. 'No, darling. Dad's promised this year he'll behave himself. And you must do the same. I'll get some coffee. We can sit in here so that I can prepare the vegetables.'

They sat, Gary looking quickly at his watch, wondering how long they had before the madness, wanting his mother to himself in the same way as he'd always done, pulling her away in his childhood, separating her too often from his father, her friends, and his brother and sister.

Daisy saw the look, recognized the memory, unable to forgive herself, even now, for the tentative but real pushing aside of Robert. 'You've got about fifteen minutes before your gran appears,' she said. 'I gave her breakfast in bed this morning, actually sent her back to bed after she'd got up! But she needs to be downstairs in her favourite chair before the rest of the family appear. You know what she's like, and it's too late for anyone to change in this house.'

'That's what I'm afraid of. With what I have to tell you, that is.' He took her hand, spilling his coffee a little as he did, then restraining her before she could rise to wipe it clean.

'I've news for you as well,' she said, 'but mine must be later. When everyone is a little mellow.'

'If you can recognize that moment and give me the nod, before the meanness kicks in, I might even share mine!'

'Oh hush. They're not that bad. They just shout a lot when they get excited. Makes your dad sound angry. He's like his German granddad. He means no harm. He gets excessive when all the family are together, brings out the patriarch in him, sitting at the head of the table and all that.'

They smiled at each other. Sharing old memories without the need of words.

'What is it, son? Is it bad? Don't worry about your dad. I can tell him later.'

Gary threw back his head and laughed. 'That might even be worth staying the weekend for.'

'For goodness sake, Gary, spit it out. I'm beginning to believe you are suddenly going to tell me you're going to be married and settle down or something. That, and the girl in question is totally unsuitable. To your father, anyway.' She squeezed his hand, speaking quickly, confused for no reason she could think of, laughing and frowning, the words coming heedlessly.

'I've always had the feeling when I told you this that it would come without any surprise,' he said.

She waited. His hand was hot in hers.

'It's not a drama, Mom. You're right. Well, sort of. I have fallen in love. First time, I guess. It must be. We've been together for almost a year now. It's good. It won't go away. And I needed to tell you.'

'Of course.' She smiled at him.

'It's hard to find the words,' he said. 'LA seems centuries ahead from Idaho. Don't say anything – I realize Dad likes it that way. But I sometimes think you really have no idea how different the city of angels actually is. It's less provincial, more tolerant.'

'I know that, son. Not in those words exactly. Your dad uses rather different adjectives, as you well know! Anywhere away from the middle of America is filled with degenerates, child abusers and druggies, according to him! I've never

49

believed him. Just couldn't be bothered to take him to task about it. He's terrified of anything foreign or anyone that votes Democrat!'

'What about you, Mom?'

'Oh darling, I've voted Democrat ever since I became a citizen. Just don't tell your dad. Every four years we go through the same ritual. He takes me with him to vote, since the beginning I mean, and says as we drive home, "Well that's another two votes those limp-minded liberals won't get!" And I never correct him. Why make him mad? He won't change, and neither will I.'

'Is that out of fear or laziness? Not telling him, I mean. Not once as far as I've ever noticed, have I or anyone in the family seen you getting your own way, doing what you want, even going to a movie you want to see, or eating the food you like best.'

'I'm all right son. What started out of fear – of all the Franckens, it seemed – changed to something else after the first few years. I gave in because I couldn't be bothered. Laziness, like you said. It suits me. We rub along nicely, me and your dad. He's a good man. You're just not like him, that's all. We're not all like our parents, you know. It's not written in stone that we even have to like them very much. It just saves a lot of heartache if you don't confront it. Sounds very English doesn't it?'

Gary smiled at her. Took her other hand. 'I'm gay, Mom. That's part of what I've wanted to tell you for ages, and why I'm telling you now, at

Thanksgiving. I've always suspected you knew, somehow. About me, I mean. I just never got round to telling you. I should have done. The second part would be easier then. Didn't seem necessary until now. Now I want you to know. Maybe both of you to know. If it alienates Dad, it can't be helped.'

Daisy remained quiet for a long moment. She realized very quickly she had probably always known, always believed there was something different about him, something she couldn't put her finger on, something she wasn't going to understand. Now she knew that what it was, what took her by surprise, even without understanding it, was her lack of shock. Not surprise: shock. All she wanted to know about was his happiness. She wondered where and when she'd become so liberal-minded. Homosexuality wasn't anything she'd confronted since she'd arrived in Wellington. She remembered that, as a teenager, she'd lived next door to an elderly widow and her forty-year-old only son. Mrs Crumpet and Howard Crumpet. Their names had caused much mirth in her own family. Her dad used to say, 'What a name, for God's sake! For God's sake what a name to go home with! Why didn't they change it, I wonder? To something like "bum", or even "dick"!' And her mother would giggle and shush him, and try hard not to laugh when either Howard or Mrs Crumpet came for tea. There had been something weird about that forty-year-old bachelor, something she could never put her finger on. Something that would throw everyone off-balance in suburban Surbiton before the war. Her mother once muttered under her breath as both Crumpets left after tea one day, 'I'm sure he's queer. You know: a nancy boy. Or even something worse. Maybe even a child molester. There's a funny look about his eyes that I can't put my finger on.'

'Maybe he's both,' her father had said later that same night. The war was on by then, and they'd been discussing why poor Howard had no friends, and hadn't even joined the home guard. Such a lack of patriotism was frowned upon. At sixteen, and going through her love-of-all-mankind phase, Daisy had been offended. 'It doesn't necessarily follow, you know, Dad!'

Now here was her son. Her handsome, tall, California-bronzed son, a young man most girls would have on their available list. In Wellington, they would more than likely name him the town's most desirable bachelor. Maybe if he'd stayed close to home he would have married his child-hood sweetheart, the one he took to his junior prom. He did take her, didn't he? Daisy had forgotten her name. When had he known what he was? Did he choose it much later? Daisy longed to ask him, longed to condone and understand. But things were different while she was growing up, different when she came to America. And in Wellington, and in the Franckens' minds, little had changed in the last twenty years. The sixties had been about Kennedy, Cuba, and finally Vietnam.

The sex revolution had passed straight over their heads, and skirts stayed where they belonged – on the knee and no higher. At least until the girls went away to college. But that didn't matter. Not really. Not to Daisy. If she found his way of life hard to accept, it made not a jot of difference to the way she loved him.

She smiled gently at this man who would never give her grandchildren. This man who now would be an even greater disappointment to his dad. Her favourite child. 'I think I *have* always known son. As long as you're happy. Are you happy?'

'Enough to make a mother relax,' he grinned. Then, 'His name is Jason, Mom. You'd like him. We have an apartment. Been living together for the last six months. It's good. I'd like you to meet him.'

Daisy said, 'Darling, do you really think it's wise to tell your father? Need he know?'

'If we're to visit, yes. He'd die of shock if I just turned up with Jason one Thanksgiving. You know that.'

'Well, you can't do it then. Not just like that. But you could always say that,' she paused, then, 'you could say that Jason was a friend. A good friend. Was just a friend. Would that be so hard?'

'Well then, Mom, we couldn't even hold hands for the whole day!'

He was teasing her. It was hard to smile at him in her confusion.

Gary went quiet. Looking down at the floor, afraid to pull away from her, meet her eyes, searching for words. The right words – without the anger and sadness that was beginning to grow in him. He looked up at her again. 'I won't do that, Mom. That's what I wanted to say. If Jason and I can't come into this house and be who we are, then this will likely be the last family holiday I can spend here. I'm sorry. I'm not that much like you, Mom. I won't be like that. I won't appease other people's feelings. Not when those feelings are ignorant and bigoted, without giving something they don't understand a sliver of a chance. Jason is like family to me now. I won't sit at Dad's table any more unless he can accept us; I don't expect him to condone our relationship, that would be too much to ask for, but just to accept it. I won't sit and joke and put up with all the shit like you do, not unless I can bring the man I love.'

All she could do was stare at him, and fight to understand.

Then the rest of the family arrived, all together, kissing and hugging, forgetting the quarrels of the year before, determined to make this day, this year, the best yet. After all, couldn't everyone, for at least one day, pretend they loved being together? Daisy had – for years. And her suspicions of her daughter's coldness could be pushed under the carpet for this one day. And Marjorie promised herself she wouldn't show her irritation with her mother, her impatience with Mary, and her very strong dislike for her brother's silly, vain and tastelessly dressed wife.

Daisy liked John, her son-in-law. His ways were quiet. His smile gentle. His sense of humour about the vagaries of life obvious. They embraced. She thanked him for the beautiful flowers he'd been clutching to his breast when he and Marjorie arrived. Why did she know immediately that bronze and yellow chrysanthemums were his choice and not her daughter's? She smiled on the way to the kitchen to dig out a vase. Sharon had brought Mississippi mud pie, a dessert too rich to be eaten after the turkey, too exotic and sickly for at least the older members of the family. It was the same every year: Sharon brought the dessert, and it was always the same one. She had never seemed to notice that she and Robert were the only ones who so much as tasted it. But Daisy cooed over it as usual. Decided once more that next year she would remember to say something before her well-meaning daughter-in-law prepared it again. But now, as always, it was placed in all its splendour in the refrigerator, by the side of her own fruit salad and the covered bowl of cream. 'You'll make us all fat, Sharon. What am I to do with you?'

Mary sat in her same big chair, 'the one my dear husband always sat in,' and Bob opened some beer. 'Do the ladies want wine yet?' He was pleased as punch once more now that all the family were together, one arm round his daughter's shoulders.

'Not yet, Dad. Too early for me on an empty stomach. John and I will have coffee,' Marjorie said, smoothing her new red dress over her skinny hips, liking the feeling of her concave stomach against her hands, pleased with her good taste and her well-tuned body.

'I've some ready,' said Daisy, going back into the kitchen, followed by the two girls.

Marjorie called over her shoulder, 'Stay in here John, I'll send out the coffee. Tell Gran about your latest book.' Then out of earshot, 'She loves the kids' stories. I wonder why no-one writes for the old: an open market, I would think.'

Drinking coffee with the two of them, testing the turkey, putting the vegetables on to cook, Daisy felt safe and comfortable while Sharon and Marjorie chatted. She let them whisk the cream, find the serving dishes, put the finishing touches to the table she'd already set in the dining-room – shouting through the door for Bob to keep his eye on the fire. Bob was swearing under his breath so that they could hear, enjoying all the familiarity of a family tradition, right down to pretending to be annoyed as he put on some more logs, feeling them to see if they were dry, warming some fresh ones from outside by the side of the stove in the family room, complaining about women who kept men from their beer, and Robert opening more cans and trying to push one on Mary ('No, no, son') Bob shouting over his mother's protests, 'She'll be asleep before we sit down!'

It was almost as if he'd forgotten Daisy's news. She was waiting to spring it on the family, praying for their mellowness when they had been well fed and soaked in alcohol. She watched him all the time, out of the corner of her eye. Bob was carrying on the same as every other year, and she joined in the jokes, laughed too loudly. She didn't see John frown as he watched her being amused at things she had never found funny.

Some years the teasing got too much for her, and she would run away into the kitchen to find peace in the clatter of pots and pans. The Franckens were not the gentlest of families. She remembered again what it was like when she first arrived, the way she couldn't speak for the first two days, only tremble, until Mary had whispered to Bob's dad, had their son married an idiot?

This year she stuck it out. Wondered for the umpteenth time how someone like John coped with it all. It had to be said, he often seemed more at ease with women than men. 'On account of his mother dying so young,' Marjorie had explained years ago, when she'd brought him into the family. 'They were very close.'

Daisy smiled at him as they began to take their seats in the dining-room, and he took the bowl of mashed potatoes from her and cleared a space on the table. Bob stood at one end sharpening the carving knife, despite the fact that Daisy had already done that in the kitchen, and she carried in the turkey while everyone 'oohed' and 'aahed'. Mary sat at the other end of the table. The rest of the family had left an empty chair either side of her. Daisy said nothing. Everything was as always. She sat beside her mother-in-law and John

57

sat opposite, winking at her when she pulled a face at him. Then Bob carved, and Marjorie put on the candied yams, the green beans with bacon, mashed buttery potatoes, corn, and finally the gravy.

Daisy couldn't face any wine. The sweet white Riesling made her feel quite queasy for once, when she took her first sip. 'Anyone else want water?' she asked on the way out to the kitchen. She brought back in a big iced pitcher, just in case. Robert and his father drank beer.

Going into the kitchen as they started on the desserts, Daisy knew they would have to break the news soon, while everyone was full of beer and wine and good, heavy Thanksgiving food: too full to move, or even quarrel, or shout. She'd been trying to catch Bob's eye for the last thirty minutes. It seemed he was avoiding the whole issue. She put on the coffee, listening to the murmur of voices coming through the open door, and decided she'd have brandy with her coffee just this once. Maybe it would stop the queasiness.

She took the bottle in with the coffee, John scraping back his chair in his haste to take the heavy tray from her. She'd had her first brandy by herself in the kitchen, and it had hit her emotions almost immediately, making her feel hot and excited, and angry as well. Seeing her husband, cigar in mouth, holding court at his end of the table, ignoring her, shrugging off all responsibility, she realized he was never going to speak up. 'What does he think?' she thought, filling up her brandy glass once more, caring little for decorum as she felt her face get hotter and hotter. 'Does he hope it will all go away without himself being involved?' And hating his weakness, she got angrier and angrier, until she felt John's hand on her arm as he leaned across the table towards her. Across the sleeping form of Mary, shrunk down in the big chair, farting quietly to herself while the family grew louder and louder around her.

'Are you feeling OK?' John's voice was concerned.

'I think I'm drunk.' She smiled. 'And it's making me angry.'

He squeezed her hand, and she thought how smooth his hand was, how clean his nails were, and how gentle he would be with Marjorie when they were intimate. And, shocked at herself, she pulled away abruptly and sat up straight.

Sharon suddenly said, 'We forgot to join hands and say what we were thankful for! We should have said it after Grace. Let's do it now.'

And then it was the right time, suddenly. And Sharon, of all people, had opened the right door. Daisy stared at Bob so hard that he was forced to look up at her. He shrugged. And in that moment she knew it was up to her to break the news. She was grateful for the warmth the brandy was giving her, and the false courage with which it had filled her. She waited tremulously for her turn, and in the silence before she spoke, she opened her eyes, and found them all staring at her. Except Bob, who was twiddling with his coffee spoon, his eyes lowered.

Mary snored loudly suddenly, and then farted violently, waking herself up briefly. 'Wind's up,' she said, and closed her eyes again. The table exploded with laughter, and for a moment Bob and Daisy's eyes met.

'Tell them,' she mouthed across to him.

'I can't.'

The words came out aloud, and Marjorie turned to him. 'Can't what, Dad?'

'Fart as loud as Gran, I should think!' Gary shouted in glee. And everyone laughed again.

Daisy looked sadly at her husband, and took the matter into her own hands. It was the first big step she'd taken for the last thirty years. And even if it was thanks to the brandy, and the good humour all around her, at least she'd taken it.

Chapter Three

'I have some news for you all. I mean, your dad and I have some news for you. It's just that it seems to have fallen to me, so I hope I don't make a pickle out of it.'

Across the table, John smiled. Daisy looked at her husband. She pushed her chair back and went to stand by him, her hands resting gently on his shoulders, the same shoulders that had once borne much to marry her, this man who had done his best to love *all* his children, even if that love was less than unconditional. She bent to kiss him quickly on the side of the cheek.

Robert, very drunk, said loudly, 'Looks like you're on for tonight, Dad!'

Sharon giggled.

'What is it, Mom?' Gary said, and then, 'Get on with it – we'll be round this table till doomsday at this rate.'

Daisy said, 'We must apologize for breaking the news today of all days, but we needed you all to be together, not to make the decision for your dad and me, but just to stand by us whatever we do. We're still family, even though you're grown and making your own lives.'

'What's she going on about?' Mary, awake

again, afraid she was missing something, tapped John vigorously on the arm as he sat by her.

'Daisy has news for us,' he said patiently.

'Well tell her to get on with it. I'm nearly asleep here. I need another coffee. She always takes too long to talk. There's more in my life than listening to her.'

'Not now, Mom,' Bob said from the other end of the table, furious at his fractious parent.

'We're going to have a baby,' Daisy said quickly. 'No, that's wrong. What I really meant to say was, that I'm pregnant.' She held up one hand, as if someone was going to interrupt her, as if anyone could find anything to say that would cut through the stunned silence of the room, the sheet of astonishment that seemed to fall at that moment with such a clatter, the widening of many pairs of eyes, the intake of much breath. Daisy went on, taking advantage of the silence, 'And before you ask, yes, I have seen the doctor; I'm not imagining it, and though it's unusual at my age, it's not unheard of. And don't ask how. It was obviously conceived in the usual way.'

The quiet continued. Then Gary began to laugh, and, to everyone else's amazement and Robert's consternation, Sharon began to cry.

'For God's sake Gary, act your age!' Marjorie's voice snapped across the table. 'And Robert, take your wife to the kitchen and splash some water on her face.' Sharon's tears were rapidly turning to uncontrollable sobs. 'She's had too much wine, she's almost hysterical. It's not the time or the situation.'

Robert put an arm round his wife's shoulders and glared at his sister. No-one moved. As Marjorie seemed the only one with a voice, she felt it was her duty to ask all the questions that each and every one of them would want to know. 'How pregnant? Do we need a second opinion? And for God's sake Dad, have you never heard of the rhythm method?'

'Don't speak to your dad like that Marje,' Daisy said, 'it's quite natural to believe that when one turns fifty there's no need for precautions of any kind. Not that that has anything to do with you or anyone else, for that matter. And it certainly cannot be blamed, if that's the right word, on your father.'

'I hope to hell you don't mean that, honey,' Bob said, hoping to lighten the situation. The humour fell on deaf ears. But Daisy squeezed his shoulder. She knew he was trying at least. 'Perhaps we should talk to Father Harris?' Bob looked up at his wife, the thought only then occurring to him.

'For Christ's sake Dad, talk sense!' Marjorie's sharpness had slipped quickly into irritation. 'Neither of you step inside that church from one Christmas to the next. None of us do. It's quite obvious Mom should have a termination. It's perfectly legal these days. Dr Hart can organize it. No doubt he'll be glad to. It seems a better alternative than carrying round a growing foetus at Mom's age.'

Daisy winced. She hated her daughter just then. Hated the abruptness and chill of exasperation in her voice. Daisy wondered what on earth she had done to rear a girl so casually unfeeling, and she was beginning to feel a little queasy from the brandy as well as the unaccustomed feeling of power that had swept over her. She put her hand to her forehead. This seemed to be turning into rather a nightmare. Her timing had been appalling after all.

By this time Sharon's tears had stopped, and nobody except Daisy saw her shake off Robert's arm from round her shoulders and sit stiffly away from him, her fury locked tight into her body language, the corners of her mouth drawn down. Robert watched carefully from the corner of his eye, defeated, afraid of something, but of what? Daisy had no way of knowing. She looked round the table. John's head was bowed, his eyes blank towards the floor, only glancing up once to attract his wife's attention. Marjorie ignored him.

Gary interrupted his sister as she started again about the best way out of what suddenly seemed to have become her dilemma, and not one that belonged to her parents. 'I say leave it to Dad and Mom to make up their own minds. Why is everything taken at such a personal level with you sis? Cool it for once.'

'Fuck off Gary! You opted out of this family by choice years ago. Don't butt in now.'

'Marjorie!' Suddenly, Bob was furious. He sat

up straight in his chair, pushing Daisy's hands from his shoulders, throwing away their moment of intimacy, afraid more of her gentleness than anything else. 'You'll give your grandma a heart attack with that language. And your mother. Keep your mouth clean in this house. It's my home. My rules. I don't care how smart you think you are. You weren't brought up as some sort of low-life. Big city talk!' He turned to his wife. But Daisy had gone. Allowing him, thankfully and at last, to take the reins into his own hands.

Driven by fatigue and sickness into the bathroom, she sat wearily on the side of the bath and put her head against the cold marble of the wash basin. She could hear from the dining-room the raised voices. Her daughter giving her apologies loudly to her dad, thinly disguised anger in her voice at being treated like a child again. All their voices fighting to be heard above the arguments, a slamming of the front door, sure it was Gary going into the yard for a cigarette, knowing he was already regretting his decision to be here for the holiday; Sharon's tears again, then the beginning of an argument between her and Robert. Daisy couldn't hear what any of them were saying. She had waited for Mary's input; dreaded it. Perhaps the old woman had fallen asleep again. She did that. Could sleep the sleep of a baby when the loudest cowboy movie that had ever been made was blaring away on the television, and if Daisy tried to lean across her to turn the sound down, she'd open her eyes and glare at her. 'Leave it!'

she'd say, scaring the living daylights out of her daughter-in-law.

'I'm sick of them all,' Daisy muttered, when she stood at last and splashed her blotched and puffy face with cold water. Feeling dreadful, she opened the bathroom door and went quietly into the kitchen. No-one noticed her as she passed the open dining-room door. She stood at the sink and watched Gary through the kitchen window, standing under the bare trees and taking deep breaths to quieten his rage. It was a familiar sight.

She had let others dictate to her for too long. It was time to smarten up, live her own life. But her mother's early advice was still faint in her ear: 'Don't make waves, Daisy. Better keep your opinions to yourself. Men don't like women that are too clever. Stay quiet. That makes for a good marriage and a peaceful life.'

'More a bloody tidal wave,' she muttered to herself. She smiled grimly. 'That's it then, Mother. All your good and silly advice down the drain. I can just hear Dad, "You've gone and done it now girl. By heck you have." I have a strange feeling the peaceful life is over.'

'Are you all right, Daisy?'

And she turned from the window to see John come into the kitchen and close the door behind him. She realized his kind of gentleness was the only thing she could have stood at that moment. What others saw as weakness and lack of ambition, she saw as quiet strength. John Maverick was the only person she could have borne to be giving her

66

comfort. She guessed that they were alike, she and her thirty-five-year-old son-in-law. Both reluctant to make a fuss about their lives, even though he seemed to have actually done something with his, which she felt was more than she could say for herself. She seemed to have always been a vessel for other people's desires, and had no-one to blame but herself. She felt cheated, as if the way she'd lived her life up till then had all been a lie in order to fulfil others. Husband, parents, in-laws, the church, and now eventually, even though they were independent adults, even her children wanted her to plan her future with their ease in mind. Damn them all. When was her turn? What did she want? Just one, as yet unborn, child to be only hers?

And even though she had scarcely seen John put his foot down about any decision important to him and Marjorie, there must have been a time somewhere, anywhere, when he didn't feel like embracing his wife's ideas or pleasures. Being moderately successful as a children's story teller seemed to Daisy a wonderful thing to have achieved. What a shame that neither he nor Marjorie wanted children. She smiled at him.

'I'm fine, John. Thank you. Sorry – I seem to have ruined what was turning out to be quite a merry Thanksgiving for once. My timing has been terrible, I'm afraid. Never was my strong point. Always doing something at the wrong time for everyone else. It seems no-one under-stands that it wasn't done on purpose. It might have been easier if it had come from Bob.'

'That's their problem, Daisy. You have enough ahead of you as it is.'

She looked at him carefully, sipping a glass of iced water to ease the raspiness of a throat sore from vomiting. 'My God, John, can I detect an edge of anger in your voice? It's taken me by surprise.' She said it teasingly, gently, warming to the compassion in his eyes.

'My wife, I'm afraid. Sometimes she makes me angry. She's inclined to speak without much thought sometimes. Unusual for an attorney. In private life she rather prides herself on speaking her mind, which usually turns out to be the truth as she perceives it. I apologize on her behalf.'

'You don't have to John. I know my own daughter. I'm not always that proud of her, I'm afraid. She terrifies me! Has done since she was about five. The boys were much gentler.' She turned to put the glass in the sink. 'I don't believe I've done that good a job at raising my family after all. I'm not sure I'd better try again. Not at my age, anyway.'

Before John could answer, Gary came in through the back door, shivering with the cold. He went to kiss his mother, his mouth and nose chilled with the sleety rain that had just started outside. 'All right Mom? All right as you can be after all that? I did my best to be good. More difficult than I remembered in this family. Christ it's freezing outside! I'm too used to Hollywood weather. Got spoiled I'm afraid.'

Daisy said, 'I'd better go back in. Will you two boys come with me? I feel the need for two pairs of strong shoulders.'

Marjorie met all three of them as they walked back into the dining-room. 'I was coming to get you, Mom. We all seem to have come at last to the same understanding. Have you been sick? You look pale.' She turned to her husband. 'John, go and get Mom the stool in the family room. It's the brown one by the stove. She'd better put her feet up. And Gary, make yourself useful for once – make some more coffee. Grandma's just beginning to wake up. Just like her, opening her eyes when we finish yelling! And bring in that cream thing that Sharon brought with her. Gran can't remember eating any dessert. She says she's still hungry.'

She pulled her mother away from the two men and into the room, back to the vacated chair beside Mary, who peered at Daisy through red eyes.

'I'm still hungry,' the old woman grumbled, 'I had no ice-cream.'

Daisy said, 'Gary's bringing Sharon's Mississippi pie from the refrigerator.' She couldn't be bothered to remind her mother-in-law she'd had dessert already. The wine and rich food had given Mary her usual indigestion. John put the stool at his mother-in-law's feet and she thanked him, smiling. Mary glared at her. Daisy thought, 'Oh well, you'll soon know what's going on, you poor old thing. I wonder how you'll deal with it.'

When Gary had come back in with fresh coffee,

and Robert and his grandmother had each taken a bite of the rich dessert, Marjorie leaned across and took her mother's hand. Daisy stared at her, surprised at her daughter's damp palms. She'd never thought of Marjorie having sweaty palms, or sweaty anything, come to that. Funny the thoughts that went through one's head at important moments in one's life. Irrelevant. Irreverent even.

Marjorie's voice had an impressive amount of quiet understanding in it when she spoke at last. It would have fooled anyone except her mother, and probably her husband. 'Look Mom, we all seem to have come to the same decision, even Dad. It'll be upsetting, we know, but the alternative would be disastrous.'

Daisy frowned at her, then looked down the table at her husband. Why wasn't he here, by her side, instead of slumped at the other end of the table facing an empty glass of beer with an abstracted look of bewilderment hovering around his eyes? Why was he letting this daughter of theirs speak for him? Bob didn't, or wouldn't, catch his wife's eye. He sat looking down at the table, rubbing some salt into a patch of what looked like spilled red wine. Daisy wanted to say loudly, 'That never works, Bob. Look at me. I need your attention.' But, of course, she didn't. She was on her own. Or so she felt at that instant. As if all this, all these people, the aftermath of the turkey dinner still sitting on the dresser behind her, the fire dying slowly in the fireplace, neglected by Bob as usual, had nothing to do with her. She only watched it all in a peculiar kind of detached way, her hands across her stomach, warm against the life growing within her. She was on her own. Or rather they both were. She and this child. Daisy smiled to herself, and she saw Marjorie frown at that smile as she looked at her mother.

'Go on,' Daisy said loudly. Defiantly. Beginning to enjoy herself. 'What have you all decided would be best for you?'

'Best for you, Mom,' said Robert quickly. Sharon lit a cigarette without asking anyone around her. Mary glared at her and screwed her nose up.

Daisy said, 'Do you mind not smoking, Sharon dear? It's bad for Gran, and I'm afraid it makes me quite queasy these days.'

Sharon crushed the remains of the cigarette viciously into her coffee mug and threw her body back into the chair with a furious look on her face, pushing against the pine struts with a hard anger that made them groan at the strain. Daisy winced. Robert glanced sideways at his wife, but said nothing. Daisy was surprised at the behaviour. Her daughter-in-law had always been so pleasant, perhaps too much so; the act was slipping, and the look on her face as well as her posture obviously made Robert uneasy. Daisy hoped they'd stay friendly until they were back in the privacy of their own home.

Marjorie went on, 'You must have a termination as soon as possible. Dad will phone Dr Hart in the morning; it could go ahead when they were ready.'

'Termination?' Daisy looked surprised. 'You mean an abortion. It's an ugly word isn't it? I've always thought so. Not that I've ever considered it. I believe it was mentioned once or twice when I discovered I was carrying you. Not actually abortion, mind you. Not that exact word. It was illegal then, you see. But I believe your grandmother mentioned once or twice across the Atlantic something about "getting rid of the brat". Something other girls were doing at the time, I believe.' She regretted the words as soon as they left her lips. Hated herself, her obscene cruelty at that moment, which had taken her suddenly by surprise.

'What're you saying?' Mary nudged her fiercely with her elbow. Daisy rubbed the spot but didn't answer. 'She's sitting right next to me and I can't hear a darn word she's saying,' the old woman muttered as she sank back into her chair. She looked as disgruntled as Sharon.

'Mom, be sensible.' Marjorie was assuming a certain patient tone in her voice, but it was peppered with too much irritation to be a good performance. 'Neither Dad nor you can cope with another baby at this time of life. Dad will retire in a couple of years. You've talked about going back to the old country for a long time. Gran's sister is still alive, and Dad hasn't seen her since before the war. You've both been looking forward to it for ages. Having some time to yourselves. And apart from that, there's Gran to take care of. What will she do with a small child in the house? We're right aren't we?'

The question was asked without expecting an answer. Daisy had searched for the pain in her daughter's eyes at the viciousness of her mother's previous words, but was met with mere blankness. No-one could have that little feeling, Daisy thought.

'It's not *my* old country,' Daisy said loudly, taking them a bit by surprise with the aggression in her voice. 'My country is England. It's always been England. Even though I married a Francken, it didn't make me German, you know. That's not how it works. And it's your father that wants to go. He's the one. Silly really. My Englishness is much more in me than any German is in him. I don't know why he goes on and on about it so much. He's third generation, for God's sake. Didn't feel like that during the war. Seems he was on my side then.'

'What's she going on about? Isn't anyone going to tell me?' Mary banged on the table with her wine glass.

Daisy went on quickly, taking advantage of the silent surprise that had settled on the rest of the table, 'And while we're on this track, I've no desire to go to Vegas either, although your father has wanted to for years, and has always presumed it was my choice as well. I don't necessarily like everything he wants. Same with you kids. My desires have often been very different. I just have never voiced them, that's all.' She wondered if she was still drunk, and whether she'd regret all this in the morning.

'What's this leading to Daisy? Get on with it, honey. You've sobered us all up mighty fast.' Bob came out of his confused sloth suddenly and reached across the table and poured himself a glass of wine.

Daisy noticed his hand was shaking. 'Don't drink that, Bob,' she said, 'it always makes you ill.'

'There's no more beer.'

Gary said, 'Come on Mom. You've mentioned getting what you want. Tell us. Not a word will be said. Well, not on my part anyway, I can't speak for the rest of the siblings, or their other halves.'

Marjorie sniffed. 'Shut up Gary. You're such a facetious bastard at times. Just button it.'

Everyone was looking at Daisy. It was quite extraordinary, being the centre of attention. Gave her quite a 'zing'.

'I want this baby,' she said. 'I'm going to have this child. And if that means going to bed for the rest of the nine months, then so be it. What you all do is your concern. Now you have *my* plans.'

Mary's voice rose in fury. 'What do you mean, girl? How can you be having a child? At your age? Whose child is it? Does my son know?'

Daisy began to laugh. Then Gary joined in, and then John and Robert could not contain their smiles.

74

Bob said, 'Shut up Mom. You heard right. There's no need to be silly.'

Mary turned her head from staring at Daisy and glared at her son. 'If your father was here he'd show you his belt for speaking to me like that! And I've a right to know what's going on in my own house. It's not yours yet son. Don't forget it.'

Bob shrugged his shoulders, shook his head, and muttered something that sounded suspiciously like, 'Jesus Christ woman, I'm sixty years old!'

Daisy said quickly, 'I am having a baby Mom. At my time in life it'll be tough. Everyone in the house will have to do their share. It's not that difficult. And you might enjoy another baby. Look how you loved having the others around when they were small.'

Mary stared and stared. Eyes darting from one pair of averted eyes to another. What was this Englishwoman saying now? After all these years? Just bringing more trouble into the family. That's what comes of marrying a foreigner. Her confusion was getting worse, her sense of past and present leaping around her as she fought to find the words that remained elusive in a brain grown old and unused. Finally, 'Kick her out son. It's not yours. I've said that all along. She was always out to get you. After all these years. Too sly and quiet for my liking. Not the American way. You must marry Mary-Anne. She's waited all these years. Get rid of her. And the little bastard. Send them home, boy. Send them home!'

Marjorie, still smarting from her mother's remarks, the pain pushed into denial by the anger rising within her, cried, 'For God's sake Dad, take Gran to bed! Put her in her room.'

Daisy said quietly to Marjorie, 'Forgive me child. I've hurt you. I was cruel.' Her daughter turned to her. Her eyes told Daisy nothing. 'She's lost to me,' Daisy thought. 'She's been lost to me for years. And I've done nothing to try and get her back. I've been a dreadful mother.' She looked across at Gary. 'You too son. And you Robert. I'm sorry.'

Both her sons looked at her, confused, neither of them sure exactly why she was apologizing.

She said, 'But I'm having this child. You'd better think again, all of you. I love you all very much, and whatever you've come to believe over the years, that has never changed. I should have told you more often. I assumed you already knew. Maybe I never learned how, or maybe I was too wrapped up in my own fear and laziness. You'll have to forgive me and get on with your own lives. But none of you will tell me what to do or not to do ever again.'

It was Marjorie who eventually took Mary to bed, telling her it was almost ten o'clock so she didn't feel she was missing anything. They could all hear the old woman muttering as she disappeared down the corridor. Bob came round and sat by his wife at long last. Conversation fluttered. Sharon remained silent. Thanksgiving was over.

Daisy wanted her bed, longing for them all to

go, yearning to be alone with all her fear and excitement. It wasn't just about the baby – it was hard to put an image to the child yet – but the feelings of courage within herself, the way they'd so quickly arrived, the terror that they would disappear again before she could find lasting use for them. Marjorie came back. She'd made Mary's hot water bottle and turned on the television in her room. Everyone wanted to go to their own homes. Nobody wanted, or even knew how, to make the first move.

It was John who said at last, 'We must be getting back, Marjorie. This sleet could turn to snow. If it settles we'll have to stay the night.' He went for his wife's coat.

Robert said, 'Are you ready Sharon?'

Daisy smiled up at her daughter-in-law, who seemed to have calmed down a little, and looked now nearer to tears than anger. 'I'll phone you tomorrow, Sharon dear. Perhaps we can have a nice long talk.'

'I'll come by after work and pick up my dish.' The girl had never sounded so subdued.

Daisy's heart went out to her. It seemed to be so hard for even the ones who had married into the family to show or articulate what really made them hurt. They hid it behind tight smiles and angry eyes. And when they did manage to explode, any of them, it quickly became a farce, with obscenities and half truths making up for the reality that was kept secret. And then they were gone. Cheeks now resistant to family kisses.

Marjorie would call the next day and speak to her father. Maybe he could talk some sense to her mother.

John smiled warmly at Daisy, squeezed her arm, whispered, 'You're doing a great job, Mother-in-law. Keep it up.'

Daisy wanted to hug him on the spot, but Marjorie pulled him away. Robert promised to open the gas station in the morning. His father could stay in bed.

'You can both have a good talk.' He nodded at his parents. 'Sort things out.'

Only Gary was staying the night. It was too cold and snowy to brave even the beginning of the long drive home to LA. Daisy could see his restlessness, knew he was thinking of Jason, wanted the safety and sanity of the man he loved. Maybe he was the only one to have found something, someone, whose presence in his life would lift him up and away from the mundane. 'For after all, isn't that what love is supposed to do?' Daisy thought, as she watched her younger son. 'And why aren't we told that from the beginning? Love, relationships, whatever you want to call them, don't only function to produce children. That's not just what we're here for, surely?' Daisy envied him. There was something in Gary's eyes when he spoke Jason's name that belied all the rules set down by church and state. She was glad. At first, she'd been dismayed at his news. She realized that now. She'd felt that Gary's problem was her fault somehow, that even her favourite child she had failed. But now she knew that first thought of hers had been wrong. Gary had made his own life, and to him it was not a failure, nor would it ever be. It had nothing to do with Daisy.

'I'll do the dishes, Mom. You talk to Dad.' And Gary winked at her, counting the hours before he could leave.

But neither she nor Bob knew what to say, or how to say it even if they had known. She hugged her husband, left him to clear the remains of the burnt-out fire, took her hot water bottle, and murmured something like, 'We'll talk tomorrow. Everything will be just fine. You mustn't worry.'

And before she could finally come to terms with the day's events, she went to bed and fell immediately to sleep, before she could even ask God if He would mind if she said her prayers that night with her tired and swollen legs wrapped tightly round the heat of the covered water bottle which she'd placed between her thighs. Just when prayers were more than usually needed. Ah well, her relationship with the Lord had always been a little ambiguous, especially while she was growing up, when she had been taught about the anger of the Lord if she didn't follow His commandments. The idea of this invisible Father watching her constantly, even when she went to the bathroom and used more toilet paper than she should, terrified the wits out of her when she was a child. Under constant surveillance from an unseen, all-seeing eye was more than she could comprehend. There was no way even to hide her nakedness when she had her Friday night bath, or, horror of horrors, when she discovered masturbating for the first time, alone under the rain cover of her aunt Betty's hammock in Guildford. She had never wanted to go to heaven in those days, prayed she'd be sent to hell instead, thinking it would be more fun.

Thanksgiving was over. There would never be another one quite like it. And next year there would be another child to celebrate with them. If they could celebrate anything as a family ever again. The baby would take Gary's place at the table: sad, but inevitable. She smiled with that sadness in her sleep. And her husband, coming noisily to bed in the small hours, wondered at the serenity on her face, and what on earth she was finding to smile about when nothing but trouble lay ahead.

Chapter Four

Then came that strange four weeks before Christmas descended upon everyone. There was more snow, unusually early that year. January was usually the real herald of their formidable winters. But they almost had a white Christmas. Sadly, the snow vanished three days before Christmas Eve, and didn't appear again until early February – Groundhog's day, actually. It was a custom that Daisy had encountered almost immediately after she arrived in the country. 'How does it work?' she'd asked Bob.

'They dig the groundhog up from hibernation and hold him out. If he sees his shadow we have another six weeks of winter. If not, we're in for an early spring!'

'I like that.' And she had cheered up considerably at so quaint a custom. The eccentricity of it reminded her of England. 'How d'you know if he sees his own shadow?'

Nobody could tell her. Bob had laughed, enjoying her logical thinking. When Robert was four, he'd asked if the groundhogs took it in turn to put themselves in the place where they knew they would be found and wakened before it was time. Perhaps it was a form of punishment for a groundhog who'd been naughty that year? Then Daisy had laughed, thinking how like her he was. All that literal thinking.

Somehow they got through Christmas. Daisy wanted so often to talk things through with Bob, discuss the baby, make plans for a time in their life which might be far from easy, but which could bring them both much joy. She wanted him desperately to be as pleased as she was beginning to be, but he couldn't. Marjorie had talked for a long time to him the day after Thanksgiving. Daisy was not told of the advice, if any, she had given to her father. But after that, Bob seldom mentioned the baby. It was as if it would all go away if it was ignored. Close your eyes and no-one will see you. But he never said a word when there was no dinner on the table, and the remains of a pizza that had been sent out for stood with a note attached when he came home from work or the bar, or indeed anywhere he chose to disappear to in those early days of the new year. Daisy tried and tried to sound out his feelings as the days went by, but it drove him even more out of the house.

On Christmas day, Bob took advantage of the lack of snow and drove his wife and mother into Boise for Christmas lunch. The conversation over the meal was sparse and stilted. It was obvious that Mary had been warned to keep her mouth shut about what was happening in their lives, not to pressure Daisy with silly and irrelevant statements about whose baby it was. Therefore all she'd done for the weeks before that was stare at her daughter-in-law with bewilderment, curiosity and indeed, fury over the turmoil she'd created suddenly in their lives, turmoil that had put that sullen look on Bob's face, and had them all pussyfooting round her, afraid to say anything, while they hung around with baited breath, hoping she'd change her mind about the baby. As if she could, or even would. Too late now.

John and Marjorie had gone to Aspen for the holidays that year, for the first time, and at the last moment joining friends from Marjorie's office. Daisy didn't blame them. Another day round that dining-room table with the rest of the family would have been unbearable to them all. Even Robert and Sharon had gone to her parents' house in the next town. Gary telephoned from time to time, more than usual in fact, and asked her how she was doing, and to let him know if there was anything he and Jason could do, knowing all the time, before Daisy even said it, that 'There's nothing, son. I'm managing.' And then she'd go on and lie through her teeth about his father being wonderful and suchlike, knowing Gary didn't believe her for a moment, trying to convince even herself. In reality all she could see was Bob withdrawing more and more, either into himself or the bar in the town, beer and pals becoming desperately important to him. It was too ridiculous for him to dwell on. Becoming a father again at his age? A grandfather would have made more sense. Someone who could give the child back when it started to scream, or teethe, or mess its nappy. The baby was still an 'it' to Bob, afraid as he was to even discuss names, let alone gender, responsibility, or ageing fatherhood. He couldn't face the fact that he prayed most nights that Daisy would never carry the child for the nine months. After all, Douglas had said she would have to take special care.

Bob was amazed how far she took the advice. Just one single, tired morning, and she would take to her bed for the day. She watched her diet, her blood pressure, the weight of everything she carried, even leaving the heaviest of necessities to Bob, for when he came home. They used the oil heaters and left the fire until he could find the time to leave a good and lasting stack of logs by the stove. Mary hated being without the fire so often, and complained bitterly to her son about the smell of burning oil and the force-feeding of convenience foods to her. 'I'm too old and sick to change my habits now! I need home-cooked meals, son.' Daisy had to wait for Bob to come home before she could be helped in and out of the bath. Douglas had said, 'Rest, rest, and more rest.'

Bob drove her to Boise to see the gynaecologist, who had wanted to talk to them both, but Bob saw her into the waiting-room and went off, muttering something about 'having a few things for the gift shop to look at.' Daisy was disappointed, but said nothing. Every day she hoped for a change of heart to come upon him, that he would begin to look forward to the forthcoming child. But she longed in vain. Bob went on secretly praying it would all go away, that he could have his wife back, the fire lit at night, and Sunday dinner with the family, like always. But Daisy began to put on weight, her face took on that especially serene look that happened so often in pregnancy, and soon the news got round the small town. Once Daisy gave up and broke the silence she'd imposed on herself while waiting for Bob to accept it all, she had Dorrie in for tea and told her the news. She knew perfectly well that her friend would find it impossible to hang on to such news, and in a matter of days the whole town seemed to know. It saved Daisy several telephone calls, although she was willing to confirm the news when several friends called her. At that time, Bob didn't mention the reaction of the guys in the bar. She wanted to ask, but whenever she tried he looked so haunted that she dropped the subject.

By this time she was almost five months pregnant; she couldn't let herself believe he wouldn't come round when the child was born. Believing the dangerous first three months were behind her, Daisy ceased to be so strict with herself and got back to cooking and shopping and lighting fires again. It was a long, hard winter. Round about the same time, her mother-in-law, seeing her son's wife more like her old self, began her complaining again, loud and irascible as always. But this time she had a different Daisy on her hands, a woman with a dream that was beginning to become a reality.

The child inside had begun to stir. Experienced as she was with childbirth, she recognized that fluttering in her stomach one day as the first quickening. She flushed with pleasure. 'Oh my God,' she whispered, and folded her hands tenderly across her belly, as if to tell the baby she was safe where she was. She had convinced herself it was a girl by then. That was what she longed for. A little girl she could have all to herself this time. She willed it to be a girl. Believed it.

The clinic at the hospital she attended told her from the beginning she would be their oldest mother ever. It made her feel like Abraham's wife, which made Dorrie laugh. Daisy tried to share the joke with Bob, but the humour of it failed to touch him. Instead, he looked quite embarrassed, and shuffled out, saying he had something important to do in the garage.

'What is it?' Mary said, 'what are you whispering for?'

They were taking tea in the afternoon and waiting for Dorrie to bring home Daisy's groceries for the coming weekend. At least, Mary was taking the tea. Off coffee as well by then, Daisy had developed a taste for chocolate milk.

'What is it?' Mary said again. 'You've got a silly look on your face. Are you feeling bad?'

'No, Mom.' And Daisy stretched across to take her mother-in-law's hand and tried to place

86

it on her own stomach. 'Can you feel it?' she said.

'Feel what, girl? Is that child coming out now?'

Daisy laughed. 'My God, I hope not! Not for quite a while yet.'

Mary pulled her hand away. 'I think you're making the whole thing up, girl. Bob never mentions it. Nobody does. Not even Sharon. What's the matter with you? 'Fraid no-one will pay you attention unless you go and do something like this?' The words had come out sharply, held in for so long as they were.

Daisy could feel anger rising up in her. Tears of frustration filled her eyes. 'For God's sake Mom – what do I have to do or say? The girl, the baby, will be here in four months. What will you do then? Ignore her? Not speak? It's not just me who's having this baby! It's Bob's as well, you know. And yours. Your blood, for Christ's sake.'

'Nice language for a woman of your age. Nice goings-on as well. It's all been a terrible mistake.'

Daisy stood, her eyes flashing, her hand in a tight grip now on Mary's arm. 'What d'you mean, you silly old woman? What d'you mean with your stupid remarks? Do you mean my marriage? *Our* marriage? The good one that Bob and I have had all these years, in spite of you?'

Mary squirmed under Daisy's grip. She whimpered, her mouth drawn down at the sides. 'What's the matter with you? You're hurting my arm. What's got into you these days? My son'll put an end to this. Take your hands off me. Go on. Get out!'

Daisy let her go, the sudden anger turning to fear as she felt a dampness between her legs. She held herself, walking towards the door and to the bedroom.

Mary called, 'Don't just walk away. I've wet myself again! You've made me wet myself! All that shouting. Come back here. I can't sit like this. I'll catch my death of cold in all this damp.'

'Sit in it, Mom. You'll have to sit in it.'

And Daisy closed her bedroom door, sat on the bed, and peeled her pantyhose and underwear away with trepidation.

She could hear the old woman call out to her again, the voice tearful, alone. But Daisy saw only blood coming from her, and nausea that was merely panic swept over her. 'Sweet Jesus.' She propelled herself gently back onto the pillows and lifted her legs to stretch them out in front of her. She reached for the telephone by the side of the bed.

'I need to speak to Dr Hart, please. It's Daisy Francken.'

'He's with a patient, Mrs Francken. I can only disturb him if it's a matter of life and death.' It was not the usual receptionist. A different, almost cold voice with an east coast accent.

'It is,' Daisy said, trying hard to keep from screaming, 'a matter of life and death, I mean.'

'Would you like to give me the details, Ma'am? I can tell Dr Hart when he's through.'

Daisy took a deep breath, controlled her trembling, and her unwarranted immediate dislike at the coldness in the girl's tone. 'I have to speak directly to Dr Hart,' she said. 'I was told to tell him at once if this happened, and he would come straight away. I've been his patient for a long time, and these are unusual circumstances. Please tell him at once. I'll hang on.'

'What exactly shall I tell him, Mrs Francken? Can you give me the symptoms?'

'Goddam you,' Daisy felt the tears begin to run down her face, felt her cheeks reddening with anger, 'I think I'm losing my baby. Tell him Daisy is losing the baby. I need him. I don't know what to do.'

The receptionist started to say something else, but Daisy slammed down the telephone and burst into tears.

Mary was standing outside the bedroom door. Daisy could hear her breathing heavily. Expecting her mother-in-law to at least say something eventually, she quietened her tears and waited. After a few moments the old woman shuffled away without speaking.

Daisy picked up the telephone again to call her husband, hoping he would be still in the gas station or at least on the way home.

She heard Mary's voice on the extension in the family room. She was talking to Bob. There was a tone in her voice Daisy had heard quite often over the last few months. The voice of the much martyred. 'Bob? Son? There's something going on here. I've had one of my little accidents. It's not my fault. Your wife is frightening me. She was ranting at me like a madwoman. Now she's shut herself in her room. Crying. The way she used to. What shall I do? I need you to come home. You have to talk to her. Tell her to stop all this nonsense. I can't change myself, and I'm standing here without my underwear. You know I mustn't catch a chill. At my age, I could catch pneumonia. Certain people in this house seem to have forgotten I'm an old woman.'

'What did you say to Daisy, Mom? I told you to leave it. I've told you and told you. We have enough going on right now. Let me talk to her.'

Mary began to sniffle, small self-pitying murmurs. Daisy felt quite sorry for her. The old woman was confused. One wanted very little else except a quiet life when one grew old. She put the telephone down by the bed, leaving mother and son to resolve it as best they could. The bleeding seemed to have stopped, but she remained where she was, putting her head back once more on the pillows and pulling the bedcover over her.

She must have fallen asleep. When she heard the doorbell, she opened her eyes and it was already dark. Five o'clock. It was Dr Hart. He'd been some time answering her cry for help. Before she could get up and out of bed the door opened, and Bob stood in the doorway. Douglas Hart pushed by him as Bob said, 'It's Doug, Daisy. He's just arrived. I told him I had no idea what was wrong. I got home almost an hour ago. You were asleep.'

Douglas was at her side, sitting on the bed,

reaching for her hand. Bob hovered in the door-way.

She said, 'I panicked, Douglas, I'm sorry. I seem to have stopped now. I'm sorry.'

'No, no my dear. The apologies are all mine. We have a new girl at the surgery. Just while Samantha is on vacation. She is, unfortunately, over-zealous about protecting me from unnecessary visits.'

He took her pulse, then checked her blood pressure. Bob said from the doorway, 'Do you want me to stay?'

Daisy said, 'Please Bob.'

'Has she lost it?' Bob inched into the room. Mary had come up behind him, pulling at his sweater.

Douglas Hart looked at him. 'No, she hasn't. This little tyke is determined to be born.' He patted Daisy on the arm.

'Thank God. Oh dear God, thank you!' Daisy felt the tears again. She was shaking all over, holding on to the doctor's sleeve, putting her other arm out towards her husband, fingers pleading, willing him to come to her. Bob didn't move. Didn't speak. 'What must I do, Douglas? Why did it happen? Will it happen again? I'm afraid.'

'The answer to all those questions is a little in the Lord's hands and quite a bit in yours.'

'Tell me. I'll do anything.' She had stopped the silent pleading with her husband. His face in the shadows of the room was unreadable. At one stage he shook off his mother's hand when she tried to get his attention. Daisy heard her shuffle away, muttering to herself.

'I suggest you stay in bed until I or my partner tell you otherwise.' Douglas smiled, and patted her hand.

'Stay in bed all the time?' she asked.

'Yes, Daisy. That's what I said!' laughed Douglas. 'Plenty of women have to, you know, if there's a difficulty with holding onto the child. You've been on your feet too much. Bob here must wait on you a little more.' The doctor turned his face to the man at the bottom of the bed. 'Sorry about that, old pal. Your work's going to be cut out for a while I'm afraid. Young Robert's going to have to be at that gas station for longer hours. What about Sharon? Can she come after work?'

'We don't see much of her these days,' Daisy said glumly. How on earth was she going to manage? Then, 'Dorrie will help, I'm sure. I'll have to make out a roster. Will they have to bath me? Everything?'

'Good girl. Perhaps Bob here can make you some hot soup or something. I want you rested and peaceful, over the next few days at the very least. I'll keep an eye on you, and if you behave yourself I'll allow you the odd journey to the bathroom!'

Daisy smiled. Turned her face towards her husband, who walked now round to the other side of her, facing the doctor, talking to Douglas across the bed. His voice was harsh. He'd been drinking, but then only Daisy would have known. She shrank back against the pillows, her face pushed into the shadows of the bedside light as it fell mainly on the bedcover.

Bob said, 'Isn't this stupid Doug? If she remained on her feet she might lose it. Wouldn't that be better all round?'

Douglas Hart looked surprised. Daisy put one hand across her mouth, as if to stop the fury that was building up in her from spilling out to mingle its acid with the bloodstains she lay on.

The doctor said at last, 'I'd no idea this would be your reaction Bob. I thought you and Daisy had talked all this through when there was still time for a termination.'

'*She* thought it through, Doug. I want to make that clear for you. I don't want this child. Nor does anyone else in the family. For Christ's sake, the woman's fifty! What the hell will she do with it? She's gone mad. The whole darn town's talking about it. Wondering whether she's been taking some sort of drug – you know – Christ, I don't know what's going on any more than anyone else does! She needs some sort of treatment, that's for sure. Maybe she needs one of those brain doctors they all go on about in California. I've never heard of anything like this round these parts. Nor's anyone.'

His face was red with anger, and Daisy knew the outburst was being helped and encouraged by the beer inside him. She would have liked to stop him, held his hand, called him darling, hated him, anything to stop the torrents of pain, anger and ignorance that came from his mouth. But she was afraid. Afraid to bring it all out in the open, all the resentment, all the misunderstanding, but afraid primarily in case she started to bleed again. The sight of Bob's red face and his arms flailing as he tried to find words that would be effective as well as truthful, considering his obvious confusion, made her want to cry and laugh at the same time. Why did everything have to turn so noisy in this family? Did no-one ever see how ridiculous they looked as they tried to make a point when the truth had been hidden or lost so long ago. Real emotions were sat on, squashed with embarrassment. If she hadn't wanted this child, if they had all had their way, Daisy doubted if the abortion would have ever been mentioned again in her lifetime. How does one master that subterfuge? How does one sweep things under the carpet, bury them in the sand of one's mind, then turn away and carry on the life that had been mapped out for them, generation after generation? 'Just a little hiccup, Mr Francken. Your wife has got herself pregnant at fifty. Never heard of such a thing. Doesn't happen round these parts, dispose of it quickly. Then you can get on with leading the life, the existence, that suited our grandfathers: handing down the family business, retiring early to let the youngsters have a go. Traditions and values must remain. Big city life can race into its own destruction. But we've always done it like this, and I'm damned if we'll change it now. That's not the ways of the Midwest. This is the real America. Women have children when they're young, stay home to be mothers, grow old as grandparents.'

'Your wife is simply having a baby, Bob. Nothing else. Babies have a way of appearing, even when it's not convenient. Daisy must just take extra care, and all of you will have to work something out to accommodate that.'

Douglas Hart was a patient man: a temple-going man, a Mormon, which could make Bob Francken see red at times. 'Don't give me all that crap about "souls coming from heaven at the right time, so there's probably something real special about this one!" ' Bob said over-loudly. 'Suppose my wife dies because you didn't give her better advice? You should have insisted on the termination from the very beginning. She would have listened to you. She's sure as shit not going to listen to me!'

Daisy winced. Bob usually kept bad language for his pals. Douglas Hart, good Mormon as he was, and had been from the time he was born, ignored the abuse and remained calm. 'Show by example' whirled round his head, and he sadly wished once again that he had settled in Salt Lake City and gone against his German wife's wishes to settle near her folk. Catholic folk should have like-minded doctors.

Daisy said quietly, 'You're being abusive, Bob. Douglas knows I want this baby. It's too late for what the rest of you want. You are going to have to adjust.'

Bob leaned towards her. 'What if this is a sign,

honey? Maybe you should do nothing, maybe it's not supposed to be born, maybe it's not right to hang on to it.'

'Now you're being ridiculous.'

He straightened up, dropping for a moment the bedside manner. 'And you sound like your mother with that voice. Why are the English so frigging sure they're always right?' And as it was a rhetorical question, he turned immediately and walked out. All Daisy could think at that moment was how silly he looked, and from the back he seemed for an instant just like Gary as a two-year-old, when he couldn't get what he wanted.

Douglas stayed with her for some time. He looked worried, but said it was nothing to do with the progress of the baby, which he felt had more than a good chance, considering the tenacity both mother and child seemed to be showing. No, it wasn't that. He was worried about Bob's attitude to everything, his lack of acceptance, his anger, and his obvious choice to be as unhelpful as possible.

'I'll call my mother,' Daisy said. 'Maybe she'll come over, even for a couple of weeks. She's young and strong for a woman in her seventies, and since Dad retired, they seem to have little to do except play bridge.'

'Don't think there's much of that in this town!' But Douglas seemed relieved on at least that matter. 'And I'll try and have another talk with Bob. Maybe it's time Mary went into some sort of care unit. Trouble is, she still has such lucid days. It's the incontinent business I'm concerned about. It's too much for you.'

Once he'd gone, Daisy called Dorrie. 'Can you come and help out this evening?' she asked, after explaining as much as she could about the events of the day.

'That husband of yours is real dumb,' Dorrie said. 'What's he trying to say? Is he going to kid us the child isn't his?'

Daisy laughed, but remembered her mother-in-law's words. Bob wasn't senile, even if he *was* acting like a child lately, so how could he ever contemplate such a thing? She shook her head, and dismissed the idea.

'Don't lie to yourself, honey,' Dorrie said later as she washed her friend and changed the bed-covers, 'Bob Francken has never grown past twelve. Mention a man who has and you'll have a faggot!'

'That's an interesting point of view.' Daisy was loath to delve any deeper into the remark, thinking as she was of Gary, and his revelations at the holiday. When she did remember it later, she realized her youngest son did seem to have grown up a little. Maybe maturity really was, after every high school kid in the world being told time and time again, simply knowing what was right for you and sticking to it.

Then Dorrie prepared to leave, telling Mary that she would pick up some incontinence panties for her the next day, because it would help everyone out and maybe make *her* more comfortable at the same time. Mary was furious. And in front of her son as well. It was too cruel.

'Happens when you're old,' whispered Dorrie to Daisy as she stood to say goodbye. 'The poor old thing has completely reverted to childhood. Although I do wonder at times if she was as unattractively contrary from the day she was born. Imagine. Anyway, honey, I've cleaned and watered everyone – fed them as well! Your fella's off to the local bar, to commiserate with the rest of the guys I expect, the old gal's tucked up with a hot water bottle, and you look sleepy already.'

'It's been a long day. I don't know what we would have done without you.'

'Stop worrying. I think I'll have a few words with that daughter-in-law of yours tomorrow as well. 'Bout time she helped out. And I'll bring those panties in for the old gal. That'll set her off again!'

And she was gone. Daisy knew it would be well-nigh impossible for Dorrie not to spread the entire evening's events at the Franckens' house round the town the following day, but there was nothing she could do. Dorrie had a good heart, even if her mouth was a good size as well. Daisy, having always been so private, was horrified that everyone would soon know even the most intimate details of her life. Oh well.

She would telephone England in the morning, and talk to her mother. Her eyes closed with fatigue, and she felt the child within her stir slightly. It was just the two of them. It might have to be enough. The road ahead seemed rockier than she'd hoped for, but things could still change. For the better as well. After all, Bob had loved babies once. And so he would this one.

She stirred in the night, maybe early morning, her eyes were scarcely aware she was waking, and she seemed to remember she heard the front door open and then close again. She expected to see Bob creeping through into the bedroom and lifting the bedcovers too high so that he could fall in beside her, hoping she wouldn't stir and complain about the beer on his breath. But he didn't appear. And then she was asleep again before she heard his footsteps and the stumbling of his unsteady walk as he made his way to the small spare bedroom at the bottom of the upstairs corridor, the room that Gary had used before he went off to college. The bed was not made up, but Bob crashed out on the bare mattress, still wearing his coat and his cowboy boots. It was the kind of thing a man could do when he didn't have a woman breathing down his neck.

Chapter Five

In the morning, Daisy opened her eyes as the door of the bedroom was closing. A glass of orange juice had been placed on the bedside table.

'Bob, is that you?'

He stood sheepishly in the open doorway. Silent.

'Do you have time to talk?' she said, one arm came from beneath the bedcover and reached out to him. She felt the coldness of the room, her breath on the air. Then, 'My God, it's freezing in here. It's like being back in England. Remember?'

He laughed, relieved at her good humour. 'I'll bring an extra heater in. Will you be getting up later?'

'You heard what Doug said, honey. It wouldn't be wise. Not if we want to keep the baby.'

He frowned. 'I don't Daisy. I won't change my mind. The only reason I'm going with it for now is that I don't want to lose *you*.'

She patted the bed beside her. Bob inched towards the bed, but remained standing. 'Sit with me,' she pleaded, 'talk to me. I can't do this on my own. I need you, darling. Hear me. Listen to me.' She edited herself from adding 'just this once'. Treading carefully was her greatest skill.

But even the 'darling' fell on deaf ears and out of fond memories.

Bob shifted his feet. 'I'm terrified to come near you, darn it! All that blood. I brought the juice in to you this morning because I realized it wasn't the time for you to do anything for yourself. I'll stay home today. But then hopefully Sharon will take over. She's sat on her butt long enough over all this. Sulking does nothing for her. And Robert's face gets longer as each day passes. It's all pissing me off, I can tell you!'

'What about her work?'

'They'll give her a week.'

'Then?'

'Jesus Christ girl, I don't know! What about your mom? I spoke to Marje last night. She's no help. Mentioned something about John coming over. Can't think what that could do, he can't manage his own wife, let alone mine. To say nothing of the old girl.' He took a step forward. 'Why girl? Why are you being so stubborn? Why are you hanging on like this? Holy shit! Who on God's earth would want a child hanging round her knees at your age? You weren't even that pleased when the boys came so close together. Why now? Just explain it to me.'

Daisy pulled herself up in the bed, head pushing up the pillows to support her. The child inside her stirred at that moment, as if even that slight and gentle movement had wakened her. Daisy smiled and placed a hand defensively across her stomach.

'There you go again!' Bob said, an exasperated

look on his face, his arms flailing with exasperation. 'It's that look that comes over your face all the time. As if you're the Holy Virgin, for Christ's sake!'

Daisy was cross then. Palpitations rose in her throat. She mustn't get angry. It was silly to take this man of hers seriously. 'Don't be stupid Bob. It's just that she moved, and I like to feel that. Here, put your hand on me. It's your girl too, you know. She'll need a father. You always said you wanted another girl before Gary was born.'

'Serves me right, then. Something odd about him.' He didn't, or maybe couldn't, pursue the subject of his youngest son. It was too dark, this feeling he had, too dark to see the light of day. The Franckens were a proud lot.

Daisy sighed. 'I want this baby, Bob. I want her so badly, if I have to stay in bed for the next four months, then so be it. This one feels like mine more than any of the others did. No other person will take her and mould her into something else, something disconnected from me. It happened with the others. You must see that, after all these years. I'm not even sure any more that I was a very good mother. We were all so distant. So much pretence. Not this time. This feels like a miracle.'

'Holy shit, woman! I swear you're going crazy! You talk like you are. The old girl says you're pissed off with her all the time, that you've changed, got mouthy, I don't know. You're not the girl I married, I can tell you that. Never thought the word stubborn would come out of my mouth when I was describing you.'

'Well I guess you're right, Bob Francken. Maybe I am different from that young girl you were obliged to drag to good ol' Idaho with you all those years ago. Maybe I'd had no chance to know what I was before we met, and afterwards, away from home and family, I just slipped into trying to be like all of you, and maybe, just maybe, it never really worked. It's mighty late at my age to decide who and what you are. Hard for other people, that is. Especially if they'd believed you were happy that way all those years.'

'You never said you weren't! How's a guy supposed to guess?'

Both their voices were raised in growing anger by now. Daisy could have sworn she heard old Mary shuffle her way to the other side of the bedroom door so she could eavesdrop.

'You can listen too, Ma-in-law!' Daisy said loudly. 'Do you good to hear a few home truths for once!' She turned again to Bob. 'Your mother,' she said, 'has made my life uncomfortable since the day I arrived in this country. And if you could never see that, Bob Francken, what you've felt for me all our married life is beyond me. You never once said anything directly to her, never once spoke up for me! The only good years for me were when we were on our own in the rented house. That was all, goddam it. Maybe I'm like this now because I'm at the end of my tether. Maybe it's the baby. Yes, it *is* the baby! I knew you wouldn't want it. I knew you'd sulk at the beginning, as if it had all been my own idea. Maybe, even, you'd come to believe your mother after all and picked up on the idea I'd trapped you into marriage in the first place, just so I could become American! Well I'll tell you now Bob, I didn't trap you, and I have never wanted so much to come to the States that it would make me do such a thing. I was too young. And despite what your mother says, too darned innocent. *You* were the one who should have known better. And anyway,' tired now, Daisy sank back once more against the pillows, her hand to her chest, wanting the palpitations to cease, 'anyway, I loved you Bob. I'd never been in love like that before. I'd have gone anywhere you took me. I wanted *you*. The baby just came with the deal. Maybe that's why Marjorie has always disliked me. I don't know; I no longer even care. This one, this child, this baby growing inside me now, is all mine. If you want to come along for the ride you're more than welcome. If not, then I'll go it alone. *We'll* go it alone, I should say!'

Exhausted, she said no more, but picked up the orange juice that Bob had brought and drank it. Not used to making such long speeches, she felt as if all the stuffing had been knocked out of her, but exhilarated at the same time. Bob, surprised, went to the door and said quickly without looking at her, 'I'll make some tea.' Which made Daisy laugh.

Still, the fight had been coming, but it left neither of them with a solution to the dilemma.

She would telephone her mother, ask her if she could come and stay for a while. That might solve the immediate problem. In fact, her mother-in-law might quite enjoy it. They'd always got on well, especially as Daisy's mum had always been mightily impressed with America, and believed her daughter highly lucky to have made a catch like Bob, and told Mary so often.

It was her mother who picked up the phone after only one ring. 'Sheppy here,' she said, with the very best of her telephone voices, which had always made Daisy squirm as a teenager. They had been the only ones in the street who owned a telephone in the forties. Sheppy was very proud of the fact, and believed she had to find a voice that would establish their rise up the social ladder. It was early evening in England. Even after all these years Sheppy always started the conversation by saying, 'Where are you calling from? You sound like you're just down the road!'

Daisy laughed. 'I'm still here, Mum. In America, I mean. Where else would I be?'

'Amazing! The things they can do. Over there, I mean, not here of course. Nothing gets done here. Except all these louts going on strike for more money. They'll ruin the country.'

'Are you keeping well, Mum? How's Dad?'

'Not too good, Daisy. The damp got into his bones badly this last winter. I told him, we should come and stay with you as soon as December starts, maybe sooner!'

Sheppy believed everywhere other than England

had sunshine all the year round. When she'd visited Idaho, the sun had always shone, but then she and her husband, Graham, had always taken their holiday in August. It would never occur to them to change it. Eccentric, the English.

'Mum darling, our winters are worse than yours, believe me!'

'How funny. That couple next door, you remember, that came into money and moved to Kingston, well I see her in the town sometimes, and she tells me they pop over to Spain for the winter months these days and it's really very nice, that is if you can get over the language difficulty!'

Daisy laughed even louder. 'Idaho is miles from Majorca, Mum. And believe me, nothing like it!'

'Oh well, you live and learn I guess.'

'I need to ask you something, Mum. I feel awful about it, but there seems to be no-one here I can turn to. I know you're not getting any younger, and what with Dad feeling badly.'

'Is it the baby? Have you lost the baby? It would be a blessing Daisy. Oh, I hope so. All this nonsense at your age, so unnatural, nothing like it in my day, we got the babies over when we were young so we could have a bit of peace in our old age! Have you lost it? I've prayed you would.'

Daisy spoke quickly, interrupting her, desperate to shut her up. 'For goodness sake, Mum. I knew you weren't pleased when I first told you the news. I never realized you felt that vehemently about it. You sound like Bob.'

'You can't blame your husband, Daisy. He

wants to retire. Is Mary in a home yet? She should be, you know. I said to your dad, "When my time comes, Graham, just turn me into one of those old people's homes. Don't take the burden on yourself." Not that I think I'll go before he does, mind you. Women always last longer than men.'

'Oh Mum! Don't say that. Don't wish it on yourself. You know you'll miss him.'

'Happens to us all. I'm not frightened of dying, my girl. And it's a better place we go to. I won't struggle, I can tell you!'

Daisy shifted uneasily. Her mother inevitably fell into this sort of conversation, however the telephone call started.

'So you've still got the baby then? Well, on your own head be it. Whatever I say will have no effect on you, I can tell that. You always had your own way. Even as a girl!'

What was she talking about? Daisy knew she had never had her own way, for God's sake. Her mother spoke fabricated clichés that over the years she'd come to believe. 'Well, give my love to Dad,' Daisy said.

'All right dear. I won't wake him now. He's nodded off while the religious programmes are on. He likes the variety shows best. We always have the variety shows on Sundays.'

Daisy thought, nothing ever changes in England. Part of the old adage occurred to her: 'We've always done it that way, so it must be right'. Her mother paused, as if thinking of something else.

'I've forgotten now, Daisy. You wanted to ask me a favour. What was it?'

'Nothing really, Mum. Look after yourselves. Big hug for Dad. I'll call again soon.'

And the telephone was replaced in haste. Daisy was too tired and exasperated to even cry. And she wanted to, quite badly. Thinking of that, she dozed off to sleep again, which was her answer to everything these days, and when she awoke later in the afternoon, the house was full of cooking smells and she could hear Dorrie's voice from the family room.

It was dark outside, and Daisy could see through the nets at the bedroom window that it was raining again. Next door, in the other room, was company, a fire, and good smells that came from someone else's cooking – always more enticing than one's own. She got up from her bed and drew the curtains across the window. Shivering, she leaned forward to turn on the fire, and stumbled badly, stubbing her big toe against the iron siding of the bed.

'Ouch! Bloody thing!'

From the open door, Dorrie said, 'What are you out of bed for, may I ask? Do you know something that Douglas Hart has overlooked? Or have you found something to be stubborn about after all these years?' She strode across the floor and took Daisy's arm in a death-like grip.

'That hurts,' Daisy muttered. And then, once back in bed, the lamp on at her side, Dorrie's smile big enough to dent the winter chill of the room, she asked 'What's going on out there? You're making Mary laugh. I thought I must be dreaming. And what's that lovely smell?'

'In order of questions I'll tell you. That is, if you promise to stay in bed.'

Daisy nodded. Snuggling down beneath the quilt, she felt like a small child again. Those too few years of early childhood, when you know you are completely safe in this enormous world, able to trust every living soul who smiles at you. Those years before you're warned about strangers, and the opposite sex, and people whose eyebrows meet above the middle of their eyes.

Dorrie said, 'I've spent the last hour trying to convince that poor old confused woman that incontinence panties are quite the rage these days, and if she got off her butt once in a while I'd take her down to the seniors' social club at the church twice a week, and she could ask the other folk there what colours they could be purchased in. The panties, I mean, not the old folk. Now there's a thought! And when I told her the names of certain members of the church who now enjoy the social club, she got quite excited, and almost hysterical at the thought of them all discussing the colour of their new-fangled underwear. Especially old Mrs Steiner, who she seems to loathe with a fury that makes her almost delirious, for God knows what good reason. Mary says she's Jewish, the Steiner woman, I mean, and has been hiding it all these years. Though why she should is beyond me. Personally I would think it something to be proud of, what with all the shit the Jews have put up with for centuries. "Always thought she was too good for everyone in the town, ever since she came to live with her daughter after being in New York all those years." Your mother-in-law is still talking about the Steiner woman at this point, and is whispering all this deluded rubbish into my ear, believing somehow I might think the same way! Said that "She," Mrs Steiner that is, "never bought bacon from the market, or pork come to that, which was just unheard of in any good German family. Serves her right. Bet *she* didn't expect to wet her pants when she reached whatever age she pretends to be!" Now why on earth does she hate the woman like that? Did old Father Francken have his eye on her at one time? He always had an eye for the broads, that one. Finally, Mary chuckled with malicious glee and said joyfully, "can't be so snotty when you're sitting in your own pee, can you?" Completely forgetting for the moment that she'd been sitting in hers all morning! Shocked me, she did. Using the word pee, I mean. Oh how the mighty have fallen. Never thought your mother-in-law would get past the word "urinate". I mean, she still says *manure* for God's sake. Then she went off into screams of cackling, the like of which I've never heard. Well, not since that dreadful high school production of Macbeth your Marje did all those years ago. D'you remember? Had to cover our ears, the witches were having such a great time. "Bubble, bubble, toil and trouble." All with great grins on their faces, all for that cute kid that was playing Macbeth. Still, it was the only time I've understood what the play was about! And seeing your Marje petting with, what was his name? The boy with the acne who played Macduff – Rocky something or other. Remember? When one of the cardboard trees fell down, and there they were? Best bit of the evening. Marje didn't speak to anyone for weeks after. Said someone did it on purpose. God, what days they were.'

Dorrie was laughing herself by then, and so was Daisy, tears of mirth streaming down her face. Dorrie hadn't let go with one of her memories like that for ages. Or maybe these last few months Daisy had not found much time for anything except the future.

'Dorrie, for goodness sake, how do you know poor old Mrs Steiner wears incontinence pants? Do you know everything that goes on in this town? Is nothing sacred with you?'

'I don't know, honey. About the panties I mean. Don't click your English tongue of disapproval at me, either. I just wanted your mother-in-law in a good mood before supper tonight. And that's the answer to your next question, Princess Grace. I've brought a pot roast over from the diner. Should put everyone in a good mood. Then I, or even you, depending on what events take place during the course of the evening, can tell the Franckens quite frankly,' she paused and thought, then went on, 'that sounds odd, "frankly the Franckens". Oh, well, never mind. Anyway, one of us can tell this lot what you intend to do for the next four months, and what is expected from them.'

Daisy pulled a face. Then, 'OK – you're right. And thank you. You are always more entertaining than anyone else I know.' And she giggled.

Dorrie smiled. 'What? What you thinking?'

'About Mrs Steiner. Suppose she doesn't wear those kind of panties?'

'She doesn't. It was her daughter-in-law I asked about them first. She was in the drugstore early on. She told me, in that very snotty way of hers, "*My* husband's mother," – her exact words, I promise – "is still dry, thank the good Lord, and that would be the final straw if it happened." Meaning, I suppose, it would be off to the retirement home for the poor old dame. Which she would hate, I believe, because apparently, so her daughter-in-law confided, she can't chew her meat any more, and refuses to eat it in any other form, mashed or something like, which makes her very difficult to cater for because she's virtually a vegetarian. Can't be many of those round these parts. Old Mrs Steiner, I mean. The vegetarian. Which throws old Mary's theory right out of the window anyway – about the pork, I mean. Was that any clearer to you than it was to me?'

By this time Daisy was crying with so much laughter that she could only hug Dorrie wordlessly by way of telling her how glad she was that she was here, sitting on the side of the bed, waving her arms as the story unravelled, like she'd always done, and making the mattress squeak against the iron frame as she bounced up and down to make a point, or seal a joke in the narrative.

When Dorrie stood up to go, the telephone rang. 'You rest,' she ordered Daisy, 'I'll get it. Probably that Sharon of yours asking if she can bring the dessert for tonight. She's good at all that. Skinny as well. Neurotic.'

But it wasn't Sharon. It was Marjorie's husband, John.

'Hi John.'

Daisy looked up at Dorrie as she was standing over her, holding the telephone in her hand. 'John?' she whispered, surprised. She hadn't seen Marjorie for weeks.

'How y'doing? Good. Hold on, honey, I'll see if she's awake.' Dorrie put one hand over the mouthpiece and winked at Daisy. 'It's our son-in-law, girlfriend. Are you awake?'

Daisy nodded. Puzzled, not wanting much to talk to her daughter, who would only spoil the warm and comfortable feeling that Dorrie had created so easily about her, she spoke tentatively into the telephone. 'John? How nice of you. Everything all right? Is Marjorie there?'

Dorrie started to leave the room, but Daisy motioned for her to stay, and she sat down heavily on the bed again, bending forward so she could hear both sides of the conversation.

John was worried. 'No, Daisy. She's in court today. Bob called from the garage and said you'd had the doctor in, and you've been told to stay in bed. Is there anything I can do? I feel bad that we haven't seen you in such a long time. Marjorie has been busy, and I've been editing the book. It's gone for publication at last. I'm truly sorry we've neglected you. Days seem to just fly past.'

Daisy thought how tentative he was over using the word 'we'. She could imagine Marjorie filling her busy life with even more to do, merely in order to escape the sight of her middle-aged mother growing more pregnant every day. But the same thought had never crossed her mind about her son-in-law. He'd even called from Aspen that Christmas, enquiring about her health, and Daisy had felt pretty sure it was a phone call delivered without the approval of his wife. How strange it was that, like Marjorie, he hated the idea of children in their marriage. A gentle man. An easy man. One in touch with his female side. Daisy had read that recently in a magazine. She'd laughed about it with Dorrie. In more affable times, she would have shown it to Bob.

'It's OK John, dear. I understand. Did Bob tell you that I was to stay in bed for the rest of the time?'

'Yes. How will you manage?' He paused, and then, obviously with some embarrassment, said, 'He suggested that Marjorie took some time off and came to stay with you. It seems it's impossible for her right now.'

There was so much unsaid in his voice, Daisy could feel his loneliness. She would never understand her daughter, who didn't seem to appreciate when she'd got a prize like John. 'Still,' she thought, 'none of us know what goes on under someone else's bedcovers.' And for a moment she was thrown into brief confusion at the shudder that went through her body at the thought of John in bed, and in love, with Marjorie. Most peculiar.

But she said at once into the telephone, 'I understand, John. You mustn't worry about me. Dorrie's here now. We'll all manage, I'm sure.'

'I could come over and stay, you know. I'd like the change. And I'm sure Marjorie wouldn't mind having me out from under her feet for a while.' He laughed, trying to make light of something that he hadn't mentioned, almost as if the fight he'd had with his wife and couldn't tell Daisy about – after all, it was their business – had been the instigation for the telephone call. Or so it seemed to an intuitive Daisy. She longed to say something comforting to him, to interfere, to tell her daughter how unloved she made her husband feel, how he stumbled to find words, how the poor man sounded more left out of life than even Daisy. She put her hand across her stomach as she felt the child inside her stirring. She had this. Her future. Her chance to make a better job of motherhood the second time around. And sitting there in her bed, the rain outside turning to hail, the baby in her womb kicking so hard she could see the ripples in her stomach, longing to communicate with this man at the other end of the telephone, she said at last, 'Thank you John. I couldn't ask you to put yourself out like that for me. Give Marjorie my love, and say her dad will probably call her again in a day or two. Dorrie's telling me that supper's ready. It was so nice of you to call. You are so kind. Always.' And she put down the telephone and burst into tears, because as soon as she replaced the receiver she wanted to go on talking to him.

'You're hungry,' Dorrie said, patting her none too gently on the shoulder, 'it's that baby in there. Telling Mom she wants some food. Pregnancy always makes you cry a lot.'

'I expect so. Sorry about this. Can you pass me those tissues? I'd better pull myself together before the others arrive. Don't want Bob to see me like this. It'll only upset him.'

It was a very little white lie, and it made her feel better, but it didn't fool Dorrie. As she straightened the bedclothes round her friend, Dorrie said, 'He's always been a bit soft on you, that son-in-law of yours.'

Daisy looked up at her with surprise. 'Goodness Dorrie, whatever makes you think that?'

'Used to watch him when your Marje first met him and brought him home. He used to stare at you all the time. I reckon he married your girl because he believed that old cliché that all daughters turn out like their mothers. Wanted a nice quiet girl. One that never made much noise in the house. Went round like some lost soul, just producing food or clean socks, or hot water bottles whenever someone yelled for it. Must have had quite a shock when Marje turned out more like her dad. Shut him up fast, I bet. Like to be a fly in their bed when they're doing the deed, I can tell you. Bet I know who climbs on top pretty quick just to make sure he knows who's boss!'

Daisy couldn't help laughing. 'You really are quite dreadful Dorrie! But seriously, d'you really think they're unhappy?'

'You must be blind, honey. Look up from the floor sometimes. See the look of emptiness in his eyes, and the look of fear in hers.'

'Fear? Why fear? Does he hit her, do you think? I'd say something if he did. But he's so quiet, so gentle.'

'If there's any pushing around going on in that union honey, it's not him. No. She's scared of losing him, I reckon. Who else'd have her? Men round here like their women quiet. They can go on doing all those bachelor things, then. All that arm wrestling, and seeing who can pee the longest distance, and drinking with their buddies until they throw up. You know, all those sort of manly things! Your Marje wouldn't stand for that. Like me in that way. Mind you, I'm not for all this liberation stuff, or going without a bra,' she cupped her two large breasts in her hands. 'I'd fall straight over with the weight of these things, I can tell you! But I reckon they got me my old guy. They were pretty pert when I was young, and I think he thought they'd stay like that for ever. I told him once, if he hadn't messed around with them so much since I was fourteen, they might not have dropped so far! I've got him believing that's his fault as well as every other darned thing

117

that goes wrong! I blame him when it snows. But you know what they're like, honey. Men love tits. Always have and always will. And I hate to say it, but that's the only way your girl takes after you. Neither of you have got any sort of breasts worth mentioning. So there you are. I think she's scared she's going to lose him.'

'Poor Marjorie. I've not been much of a mother have I? Too late now, I guess.'

Dorrie went to the door, stopped and turned. Daisy smiled, waiting for the exit line.

'Anyone who sat through those school plays year after year couldn't have been that bad a mother!' And out she went, calling to ask Mary whether she'd managed to put those panties on yet, and did she want to pee before dinner. Might as well keep them dry as long as possible.

The telephone rang again, almost immediately, before she could think about John's telephone call or Dorrie's extraordinary observations. This time it was Gary.

'Hi Mom. What's up? How're you doing?'

Hearing his voice filled her heart. 'Gary, darling. You sound so near.' (Good grief, she was beginning to sound like her own mother.) 'How are you, son? Plenty of work?'

'That's why I'm calling, Mom. My great news will brighten the gloom of that Idaho winter for you. It's ninety degrees here! Not that I want to rub your nose in it!'

'Is that the news? Did you call me just to give me the weather forecast, Gary Francken?'

He laughed, and Daisy felt proud, as she always did when she amused any one of her children. 'I've actually had an offer on one of my scripts. A small movie. No budget really.'

'None? How will they pay you? What will you live on?'

'No, no! It's just an expression. No budget really means a very low one. Independent film. You know.'

'I see.' She didn't of course. She could still hear Bob's voice a few years back: 'He wants to be a writer? Well he's got to get something in print before I believe that. He needs work, man's work. Something with a future. Waiting on tables is a woman's job!'

'Your dad will be so pleased when he hears the news, darling. I'll tell him as soon as he gets in,' she said.

Gary talked about Jason then, telling her to watch out for him because he'd just done a nation-wide commercial for some make of jeans. She said she would look forward to that, but didn't have the heart to tell him about her narrow escape with a miscarriage, or relay the news she would have to spend the next few months in bed. Bob had never got round to getting a television for their own bedroom. Mary had one in hers. But then there was no better way to hold her attention and keep her quiet. 'Puts her to sleep as well,' he'd said at the time. Marjorie called it 'moving wallpaper that passed for entertainment'. Daisy didn't tell her daughter how much she and Bob enjoyed television, and she missed it with all these weeks of lying in bed ahead of her. She could be really snooty, could Marje.

'I'm well darling,' she answered his query regarding her health. How could she worry him on this special day when he'd sold his first script? 'What's it about, son? The script you've written. Will we see it here? On the television I mean?'

He laughed. 'Don't think it'll go that well in the Midwest, Mom. Small art houses, and with some luck, Europe. It's the story of a gay man who kills his lover because he finds out he's been sleeping with a woman.'

'Oh.'

'Might be a good idea to leave the story bit out when you tell Dad,' Gary said, trying to keep the sarcasm out of his voice.

Daisy couldn't help laughing. 'I won't tell your dad,' she said. 'Just the good news. And I'll exaggerate the salary. OK?'

'They'll give me a fee. And maybe some points if I'm lucky. But it'll lead to more if the gods are on my side. A foot in the door is all I need right now. One day, it will not only be screenplay by Gary Francken, but produced and directed by as well! OK? Love you, Mom. I'll give you a bell soon.'

And he was gone. Back to his world. To his other 'loved one'. And she sighed when she realized how little she understood that other life of his, going on so energetically in what seemed to her almost like a foreign land. For goodness sake, she didn't even know what an 'art house' was. Or 'getting points'. And she hadn't the courage to ask him. She wondered for the umpteenth time if she was a little afraid of her own children. She seemed to crave their approval far more than they craved hers or Bob's.

Chapter Six

Stamping the mud off his boots in the hall, and then leaving them there to dry out, along with his socks, Bob came in to see her in his bare feet, still gruff in his manner as he bent to kiss her cheek, and ask her how she'd been all day.

'Well husband, I hate disappointing you, especially after how well you expressed your feelings this morning, but I'm just fine. Your daughter here,' she patted her stomach, 'is moving about quite nicely and obviously intends to wait and be with us at the right time after all. That is, if her parents decide to behave themselves. Where have you been all day? I thought you were going to stay in.'

Bob shifted awkwardly and looked away from her out of the window. Daisy knew the stance. So, it was someone other than his drinking pals who was offering a sympathetic ear and a shoulder to cry on? She should have guessed. To think once that she thought he would grow out of his longing for pastures new when his life wasn't going smoothly. A fool she'd been. Bit late now. She felt too bored with all his infantile carry-ons to even listen to the story he would weave. Realizing she no longer cared about his 'peccadillo', she pushed herself down under the bedclothes and shut her eyes. 'It doesn't matter anyway,' she said. 'Dorrie was here. Mary seemed happy, and I've been sleeping all day.'

'I'd called her. Dorrie, I mean. I wouldn't just go off – you know that darn well! She got someone else in at the restaurant. Said she'd fill in here until Sharon could take that week off.'

Daisy opened her eyes and stared straight at him. He'd obviously spent a while alone with his mother that morning, realized he was more than likely going to have to put up with her all day, something he'd never done before, and if he couldn't get out of the house he'd be stark raving mad by sundown. So, once Daisy was asleep, he'd called Dorrie. His 'friend', whoever she was, was waiting for him.

'God, you're pathetic!' When the words fell so easily and snappily from her lips she surprised herself as much as she did her husband, whose eyes narrowed enough for her to see, and be pleased, at his discomposure. For years she'd wanted to say something similar and never had. Now there they were, those scathing words, hanging between them, large with sweat and tears, having been locked inside her all those times he'd found someone else's bed to crawl into. The arnica for bruised egos. She'd never realized before how angry she'd been with him, those times it had happened. How she'd pushed it away, waited for him to get over it, convincing herself she'd done what was best by letting him believe she'd never known. It happened to several of her friends' marriages, and only one of those women, as far as she knew, had had the courage to walk out. Sex had never been high on her own list of priorities, so it would be foolish to break up a marriage because of it, but when she'd been very young, and still new to being a wife, she'd felt hurt, and wondered often how a man could say 'I love you' on the telephone when he called from the office to tell you he was staying in town that night, and then say it again to some other girl a few lustful hours later. She'd always been so glad to see him when he came back for the weekends, and held her again, and she could tell herself she'd imagined it all. She'd never refused him of course. Sex, that is. Even when she'd felt betrayed and a bit of a fool. 'That's something you don't do', her mother had once said to her, which was strange advice coming from Sheppy, who'd always had a twinkle in her eye after a late morning in bed with Daisy's dad. Daisy had grown up believing her parents had rather a healthy and busy sex life, one in which it had never crossed her mother's mind to refuse him anything, not if the laughter and various other noises coming from the bedroom were anything to go by.

She said now, 'Is Robert or Sharon here? We have pot roast apparently.'

'Shall I go and help?' Bob had already moved to the door. 'Or am I too – what was the word you used?'

'Pathetic.'

'Hell only knows what you've been blabbing on about, Daisy. I had a job to do today, and Dorrie was good enough to help us out. It didn't bother Mom. Besides, changing an old woman's underwear is woman's work for Christ's sake!'

Daisy smiled bleakly at him. 'That wasn't what I was blabbing on about, Bob Francken. Though it does seem that these days most things that come out of your mouth are pretty pathetic. It was the reason behind your departure. I just wanted to let you know that I know what's been going on all these years. The little adventures you take on occasionally. I wanted you to know that you've never fooled me, however much I've pretended to be fooled.'

Bob opened the door. 'You must be delirious, Daisy Francken. Better have a word with Doug when he gets here. He said he'll be up after surgery. I met him in Sam's on my way home. You must tell him your mind's wandering.'

It was her turn to narrow her eyes. But the bedroom door had already closed behind him, so she laughed instead.

Douglas Hart was just leaving as Robert and Sharon arrived, and through the open bedroom door, Daisy could hear them all talking in the other room.

'Your mother's fine, Robert,' Douglas was saying, 'she's being sensible, and I have no doubts we'll be bringing a healthy sister into the world for you when the time is right.'

Robert muttered something which Daisy couldn't catch, and she heard nothing from Sharon. Then Mary was complaining loudly from what was obviously her seat at the table. 'I've been sitting here waiting for you. If I eat this late I won't be able to sleep. No consideration from anybody. Come and sit down. Your mother's only having a baby, for Lord's sake. If it's true of course. It's probably gas. I read a story like that in the *Enquirer*. Come and sit down. Come and sit down. I'll be past hunger by the time you lot want to eat!'

She heard Douglas laugh, and Bob say grimly, 'Keep your mouth shut, Mom. We don't want the neighbours to hear all our business.'

'Too late for that, son. Too late for that, I can tell you. Sharon here can tell you all the gossip! You ask her. Under the hairdryers, that's where it all goes on. Silly women with nothing better to do.'

Somebody shushed her. Probably Sharon. Daisy heard her daughter-in-law's stiletto heels clicking across the hardwood floor on her way to the table.

Douglas laughed again, and then Daisy felt the wind whip down the hall as the front door opened, then closed again, to let him out. She heard him call out, 'Filthy night! Keep her well wrapped up. Mary *and* the mother-to-be. I'll look in again in a couple of days. Filthy night!'

Then Robert put his head round the bedroom door. 'All right, Mom? I'll come in and see you when Gran's having her hair done. If we get that far.'

'Go and have your food first, son. And Robert?'

He had turned to go. 'What is it, Mom?'

'Don't I get a kiss?'

He moved towards her and bent down to kiss her cheek. In her haste to reach up to him, they missed each other somehow, and his lips landed rather limply on her ear. She searched his face. And for a moment she saw misery in his eyes, and her heart felt heavy. 'I love you, son,' she whispered, 'you know that don't you? Is everything all right?'

Like Bob then, he couldn't catch her eye. 'I'm all right. Bad time all round, really.'

Sharon called to him, and he smiled weakly, shrugged his shoulders, and left his mother abruptly, pulling away from the aborted kiss as if he were ashamed to be seen, ready to sit round the family table and eat Dorrie's pot roast and maybe have a beer with his dad. It saddened Daisy to believe Sharon ruled him. She'd rather liked her daughter-in-law up until recently. These last few months Sharon's guard had been down, she seemed irritable and pent-up about something she seemed to be holding in, some secret between her and Robert. Daisy had never seen him so unhappy. Had she really been so blind? Had there always been difficulties within his marriage? She sighed again, and was glad when Dorrie decided to sit with her in the bedroom to eat supper, and gossip to her, while Daisy swallowed as much of the tender beef and vegetables as her own melancholy would allow.

Dorrie went home soon after nine. She was to open the diner for the early breakfast next morning.

'Folks round here rise early,' Mary muttered to no-one in particular. 'What am I going to do when I need my coffee first thing, and that wife of yours is still in bed ill? Your dad got his eggs and sausage every morning sharp at six, however much the baby had cried all night.' Then, irrationally, 'I'll do the same with the next one, you'll see.' Satisfied, she sat back while Sharon pulled at her hair, speechless and sullen, muttering something to Robert, who'd burst into laughter at his grandmother's words.

'Don't be stupid, Ma. Think what you're saying, for Christ's sake!' Bob said, exasperation in his voice. He looked so irritated that Mary shut her mouth at once and closed her eyes, while Sharon started back-combing the old woman's hair.

Bob cleared his throat and looked nervously up at his daughter-in-law. Sharon had always been so easy to ask things of. He wondered about this time. And he couldn't catch Robert's eye as his son stared blankly at the television. The atmosphere in the room cooled considerably as soon as Dorrie had loaded the dishwasher and gone home. Bob longed for the comfort of Daisy as she bustled around preparing for bed, making cocoa, and bringing him a beer. God, he hoped this baby was never born. Their lives now were completely shattered: if Daisy had the child, it would only get worse. He sighed very gruffly, hoping against hope that someone would ask him gently what was wrong, and could they do anything? There was only the television, loud and intrusive.

'Turn that noise off, son. We all need to talk.'

It was Sharon's turn to sigh. Robert shot her a look, then pressed the remote control, and watched the screen dismally, as if the solution to all this would flash up on it like a message from above. No such luck.

His father said, 'Have you done with Gran, Sharon honey?'

'Yep. Shall I take her to bed? She's asleep already.'

'Let her be for a while. Come and sit over here. I need to ask you a favour.'

Sharon sat next to Robert on the sofa and glared at her father-in-law. Bob remembered when she used to flirt with him. He'd rather liked it, daughter-in-law or not. Pretty girl, domesticated and motherly, like his Daisy. Though Sharon did seem to speak up for herself rather more than Daisy. You never quite knew which way she was going to jump. Bob had always preferred his women quiet and docile. Not afraid of him, mind you. Good God, no. He'd never raised a hand to the opposite sex. Never would, either. His mother had raised him to be respectful of the 'weaker sex'. Bob had often looked askance at her when she said that. Weak had never been a word to describe his own mother. It's just that he liked to be boss in his own house, like any man did – any real man, anyway. He sighed again. His mind was wandering on a course of its own. Things in this family had to be put on an even keel again.

'Go on, Dad,' Robert said, trying to keep the irritation out of his voice, 'what's on your mind? Not that we can't guess. Hard to think of anything else these last months.'

'It's really Sharon I'm asking, son. This is woman's work. Though I had been thinking it might be a good idea if both of you could move into the house for the next few months. You can use the old attic room. Plenty of space. And it might sort our little problem out.'

There was a moment's silence before anyone spoke. Only Mary's snores cut across the silence in the room. Even the wind outside seemed to have run its course.

'No.'

Bob looked at his daughter-in-law in surprise. 'No need to be so hasty, girl. You could always think about it a little. What's so difficult?'

'If you knew that Dad, you wouldn't be asking *me* to do *your* job!' Sharon was furious. The tone in her voice almost made Bob shudder. He noted quickly that his son did. He probably knew from experience where such a tone could lead.

'Sharon, honey, I have to work! You know how it is.'

'So do I, Father-in-law. I work too.'

'Cherilee would understand. I'll go and have a word with her. She'd bring another hairdresser in while you were on a leave of absence. I work all the strange hours under the sun, you know that. You could go back when the baby was born. And let's face it, honey,' he lowered his voice and glanced towards his wife's still closed bedroom door, 'you know, as we all do, for Christ's sake, the girl may well not be born at all if Daisy's not careful.'

'Perhaps that would be better all round,' she said unemotionally.

'For God's sake Sharon!' Robert's voice, loud enough to make Mary start up in her sleep, then settle again, muttering to herself in an irritated way.

'What?' Sharon dug him in the ribs sharply. 'What is it, mother's boy? Frightened to speak up to your own father? You've been agreeing with me about all this for the last twenty-four hours. Ever since we heard about this last drama. You are such a wimp, Robert Francken! Can't you even stick up for your own wife?'

Robert sank further into the sofa. It was useless to say anything. Sharon's tirade had a long way to go. He knew the signs. And he had no idea where it would lead this time. She'd never been like this in front of his dad. Things would get worse, or it would all end in tears. Those he could cope with.

Bob spoke again, surprised as he was at her vehemence. 'All right, all right. But it would be easier if you stayed here and stopped working for a while. I thought you'd like the rest from hairdressing.'

Sharon laughed derisively. 'Don't do me any favours, Dad.'

'So stay at your place. Come over first thing to get the day started. Go to work, then come back here in the evening. Perhaps I could get somebody in to sit with Mom, and keep an eye on Daisy. Cost a bit, but what else can I do?' Then, turning to Robert, 'It's not man's work, I realize that son, but it's different when she's your mother. What about working it out between you and Sharon? I'd pay your wages, but instead of the garage, you'd be here most days.'

'Daisy's also Marjorie's mother,' Sharon snapped, 'in case you'd forgotten! I don't hear any cries of help to that part of the family.'

'Come on, be fair, girl, Marje's job can't give her that amount of time off. The girl's got a career, not just work!'

Sharon reddened with fury. Robert didn't look at her. She said loudly, 'And mine isn't? My boss Cherilee would tell you different. I'm a stylist, for God's sake. I don't just wash hair any more. I want my own place one day. I can't just stay at home 'cos your wife decides to have a baby at her time of life! It's *your* problem! Yours and Daisy's. We don't tell you ours, let alone ask you to get involved in them. She shouldn't be having this baby. You all know that. But you've all just sat there and let her get away with it! She could have had an abortion for Christ's sake.' She started to cry at this point, and Mary began to wake up. 'I don't agree with them either,' Sharon went on, 'but when the mother isn't suitable, it should be compulsory. Why didn't you just insist on it from the beginning, Dad? Too embarrassed to talk about it? Even to the doctor? Everyone knowing what you'd been doing at your ripe old age? Wondering what your girlfriends would say?'

'I've had enough of this,' Bob rose to his feet. 'I'm not putting up with this in my own house. Keep your wife in order son. And when you've done that, put your grandmother to bed. I'm going in to see if you've woken your mother. I'll speak to you both when I've seen to your ma.'

Daisy was lying with her eyes open when Bob came in. 'Do you want a hot bottle, Daisy? Mom's just going to bed. I'm sorting something out about tomorrow.' Bob picked up her dinner plate that she'd pushed to one side after eating only a little. 'Not hungry?' he said. 'Thought Dorrie would have insisted, seeing that she made the darn pot roast.'

'I told her I'd finish it later. When she'd gone. She believed me, I guess.'

'Want a quick word with Robert and Sharon before they go?'

'Is it worth it?'

Bob paused and looked at her for a long moment. He put the dinner plate down and went to sit beside her on the bed. 'Look, honey, everyone's a bit crazy at the moment—'

'I know. I heard.'

He moved as if to take her hand, or bend to kiss her, but Daisy turned her head from him, terrified she'd cry, and he'd be unable to cope. Weeping in women had always scared him. He had always been afraid they might ask something of him, some emotion he couldn't muster. This time it was Daisy's turn to withdraw. And Bob knew it, and pulled away immediately, rising from the bed, afraid that her vulnerability would shame him too much.

'We must get a television in here for you,' he said out of the blue.

And Daisy smiled. It was always so much easier when they didn't bare their souls.

Daisy sat up in bed after he'd gone back to the family room, and stretched across to Bob's side of the bed to put the radio on. Funny how she always stayed on her side of the bed, even when he wasn't there. If he remained in the spare room she would be able to move to the middle if she felt like it. She smiled to herself, stretched her legs, and felt the cold of the sheets where Bob had always been. They'd never slept apart in all the years of their marriage. It had been uncomfortable sometimes, when she was pregnant with the other three, and the excessive heat of his body had all but pushed her out of the bed. But Bob believed in a double bed, said it was essential for a happy marriage, trotted out all that old stuff about 'if a marriage gets rocky, the rocks are in the bed'. And however much Daisy had longed for cool sheets and solitude, she'd said nothing. Until now. And this time she'd have to tell him. About staying where he was until after the baby came, until it was safe.

She heard Sharon take Mary to the bathroom and then put her to bed, hot water bottle as well. It was time for the others to help. In recent years, Daisy had felt sometimes as if she was in unpaid service, what with all the demands her mother-in-law laid on her from day to day. It was different when it was your own. And Mary had never felt like that to her. With your own, you could serve with a passion. In that respect she felt sorry for Sharon. Why was it *her* turn to pick up the burden of her father-in-law's mother? Robert would just sit there: inert. He'd learned from his father: this was woman's work. Besides, women were better at it, at caring that is. She'd heard Bob say that so often. As if he was handing out compliments. And the women in the room would smile back at him, and get up to replenish the men's glasses, believing themselves, more often than not, especially blessed. Even her own father had been 'served' and cared for by her mother. Daisy herself had never thought about it. Her own mother had always been there when she was growing up, after school, when she had measles or 'flu, and when she needed help with her homework. Still, times were changing. Women had careers. Kids got their own tea after school, until Mom got home. And Dad did the dishes as well as the car. Well, some of them, anyway. And thinking of herself, and always being there for the children, she thought of Marjorie, and wondered if she remembered those days, and how she thought of them now, and from Marjorie, Daisy's mind switched, for no apparent reason that she could think of, to John, her son-in-law. She smiled. He seemed to be like no other man her generation had met when they were seeking soul-mates. He was indeed what people were calling a 'house' husband. And as much as Bob could see no stamina in such a man, Daisy had liked him from the moment Marjorie brought him home, and announced to her parents that this was the man she intended to marry. Daisy remembered thinking at the time, 'Can't say I blame her.' He and Marjorie had lived together in Boise for a year before they married, and even that ceremony had puzzled Daisy. She knew they both wanted a child-free union, Marjorie had said as much. Daisy wanted to ask, 'Why get married then?' But of course she hadn't. And people lived together all the time these days. 'Living in sin' their own Father Harris had called it. Years ago, people kept things like that quiet.

It had been so nice of John to offer to help. She felt she might have liked that, the idea of John being there every day. Then she laughed to herself at the image of Bob sitting in the evenings with his son-in-law and having a conversation about absolutely anything. The two men had nothing in common.

Raised voices from the other room broke her reverie. On the radio they were playing songs from the war years. They reminded Daisy of the time she and Bob had first married and she was carrying Marjorie. They'd been waiting for Bob to be sent home to the States, and she knew it would mean a long time apart. He was her life then. She'd relinquished hers already. It had slipped through her hands so easily, so willingly, given to him on a plate. And he'd taken it as his right. She couldn't even remember these thirty years or so later what her young life had been, where it had been going, or even what she had wanted.

She heard Robert come noisily into the hall and pick up the telephone, Sharon behind him. Daisy could hear the stiletto heels on the hardwood floor between the rugs. Who could he be calling at this hour? She squinted at her watch that was lying by the bed. It was almost midnight. Amazing that he and Sharon could still be here. And he sounded angry – unlike Robert. Bob had obviously stayed in the living-room, because she heard the television in there go on very loudly, as if to drown out every other sound in the house. Bob was being an ostrich again. But Daisy could hear her son. He almost shouted down the telephone, ignoring Sharon's plea to keep his voice down, that he'd wake Mary and then things would get completely out of control. Daisy wondered for a moment if her daughter-in-law was talking about her.

It seemed that Robert was ignoring his wife at that moment, which meant his intent was far more important than his wife's anger. Daisy listened to his side of the conversation.

'Gary? You still awake? Well we need to talk. What d'you mean at this time of night? It's about Mom, of course. What else is screwing things up just now? But then you're not here are you? We're putting up with all this shit going on while you're sunning yourself by some frou-frou swimming pool! You're needed at home, man! Mom needs someone here all the time and the rest of us have jobs to go to.'

Daisy could bear it no longer, and picked up the telephone by the bed. Quietly, so the boys wouldn't hear. It was Gary's voice she heard first.

'I'm in the middle of doing a deal, man. No way can I leave right now. Can't you guys work it out for yourselves? Christ, there's the three of you living on top of each other! That's what you get for staying home all these years, man. I warned you!' He laughed.

'Not funny, man. Not now. She can't get out of bed. Doctor's orders.'

'She didn't tell me. Let me talk to her.'

'Did she tell you that Gran's impossible right now? Peeing herself and God knows what else?'

'She's an old woman. Tell Dad she should go in a home. Mom's been bearing the brunt of all that for years. What about Dad, anyway? Time he got off his butt, looked after her, learnt to scramble an egg or two. For fuck's sake, my life's here! Dad and I couldn't spend one day in the same house. You know that. It would be worse for Mom. Sharon's the one who thinks Dad's dandy. Let her live with him, and give you a break from all that neurosis as well. Kill two birds with one stone. Know what I mean brother?'

Sharon had grabbed the telephone in time to

hear the last words. She was furious. 'It's not funny Gary. We all do jobs we can't leave. You've *got* to come. She's your mom, not mine. What are you actually doing right now anyway?'

'Right now, sister-in-law? You wouldn't want to know. It would scar your puerile little mind for ever.'

Sharon flung the telephone back at Robert, or that's what Daisy assumed anyway. In the commotion outside her door, while Robert was reclaiming the telephone from the floor where it had missed him and landed, *and* trying to calm his wife down enough to continue the conversation with his brother, Daisy replaced her own receiver quietly, got out of bed, found her slippers and robe, and made her way to the door. This had to be stopped. Someone would say something they'd regret. Too many cats would be out of the bag. Bob was obviously going to sit tight in the living-room. It was up to her.

She opened her door, and stood there, listening to her middle child screaming down the telephone again.

'That's my wife you're giving all that crap to! Watch your mouth! We need you here now, man. Pack up that typewriter of yours and get your butt down here by tomorrow! Dad is incapable of looking after himself and well you know it. Mom's done everything for years. If she goes on she'll be ill! She's ill now!'

Nobody turned to see Daisy standing there. But Daisy saw Bob in the living-room get up and

139

turn the television down. Watched as he came towards the open door of the living-room, and stood there quietly, listening to his sons ranting at each other, saw how he kept his eyes down, as if figuring out the pattern on the rug, realized that he too had no idea Daisy stood across the hall from him, back in the shadows, listening and watching.

Robert was red in the face. Sharon was crying in the corner by the front door, and occasionally stamping her foot as if she couldn't make up her mind between anger and tears. Then Robert said, 'It's up to you, fairy! Time to leave all your little friends for a while and come home. You won't be missed, brother. They tell me Hollywood is full of shit like you. Seems to me that home'd do you good after all the prancing that goes on there. Don't tell me all you faggots don't cook and keep house for each other. Sounds like the right job for you. Time Dad and Mom found out anyway.'

You could have heard a pin drop in the hall. Daisy leaned back against the door and held her breath, waiting for the explosion. She was almost too angry to cry. And worse than that, it was the last thing that Bob needed to hear. Her husband came into the hall and took the telephone from Robert. He spoke quietly into the receiver, shaking now, Daisy could see that from where she stood. She edged out in the hall. Sharon stood with one hand across her open mouth, eyes large, tears drying quickly on her cheeks. Robert stared mutely at his mother, the anger gone from his face, then he turned to watch his father.

'Don't need you here,' Bob's voice coldly into the telephone, Gary silent at the other end. 'Don't want you here. Me or your mother. Get out of our lives. Decent is what we are. I'd be ashamed. Ashamed of my own son. Don't want you here. We can manage.'

And then the telephone went down without, it seemed, another word from Gary. Daisy went immediately to her husband, and as she put out her hand to touch his arm, he turned his face towards her. The coldness in his gaze took her breath away. She felt herself gasp, shrink back, her hand dropping once more to her side.

'I knew it,' Bob said, 'I've known it for frigging years! Just put it out of my mind. Something peculiar about him from the beginning. Him and his nancy, fancy ways! Jesus Christ!' His voice got louder, the coldness in his eyes turning to fury, pain, humiliation. He reached out towards his wife, his hands hard on her shoulders, as if to push her down. 'He told you didn't he? Told you years ago. You let him poison this family for years without kicking him out! I can tell by that look on your face. Why wasn't I told? Don't I have the right to know my own son's a faggot?'

'Don't say that, Bob. Don't use that word.'

He sneered at her now. 'What do you suggest then? What is it now, if it isn't "fairy", or "faggot"? What damn word is there for them these days? Are we coming right out with it these days, and calling a spade a spade? Is it "pervert"? Is that my son? Hello neighbour, I'd like you to meet my son, the pervert! But then perhaps the whole frigging town have known for years as well! Jesus Christ woman, what's happening here?' He swung round to face Robert. 'Did he tell you? Or did your mom drop it into everyday conversation one day? Oh by the way son, your kid brother's a faggot. Don't tell your dad, it might upset him!'

'I guessed, Dad, for Christ's sake, Sharon and I just guessed. I suspect even Marje knows, and John. We thought you knew.'

'Sweet Jesus.'

Daisy said, 'He told me at Thanksgiving. I didn't tell you because I knew how you'd react. And you needn't worry about him coming home any more. He'd made up his own mind then. God knows when we'll see our son again after tonight. How could you, Robert? Just blurt it out like that.'

'Not my son,' Bob was muttering, pulling his overcoat from the hall rack, throwing it round his shoulders. 'Your son, Daisy. Not mine. You deal with it. I should have faced it. It was all there, staring me in the eye, I could have done something about it years ago. Could have knocked it out of him. You've made a fool of me, woman!'

Daisy, angry now, shaking, clutching her robe round her as Bob stood now at the open front door, the wind cold, filling the hallway with a chill that settled on all their hearts. Cold winds and unloving thoughts.

'Like what?' Daisy said, pulling at Bob's sleeve.

'What would you have done? Locked him in a cupboard to shame him? Beat him, like you did Robert? Send him to doctors? Like old Reverend Brown did to his eldest boy? Remember the Reverend in the next town? Back in the fifties. Why d'you think that boy killed himself at sixteen? Is that what you'd have done to our Gary? And then find him hanging on his sixteenth birthday? Hanging from one of the beams in their garage. Would that be better for you?'

'Leave me alone woman! Let go my arm!'

'Where are you going, for God's sake? Don't walk away from this, Bob Francken. He's your son whether you like it or not. And he's welcome in this house when and if he ever wants to come. I'll see to that.'

'Then you'll do it alone. I'm going for a drive. I need my own company, woman. Too many females in this family. Let me go. I'm sick to my stomach.'

Chapter Seven

Daisy watched him into the car. The wind was sharp against her face. Her lips numb. Her anger, her search for pity towards a husband who had shaken her soul too much in the last few days, settling within her heart and turning what was left of her sweetness to bitterness. She closed the door, the very gesture taking on a meaning she was finally beginning to embrace. Tiredness drained her, releasing her from any other emotion. Robert was helping Sharon into her coat. Daisy couldn't see her daughter-in-law's face as she turned away from her to button her coat. At least she'd stopped crying.

Robert said at last, 'I'm sorry, Mom. I didn't think Dad was listening. And I was pissed off at Gary.'

'It's all right son. It's not your fault. I should have said something before. I was waiting for your dad to get used to the idea of the baby first. Bad timing.' She closed her eyes for a moment. 'I never thought things would get so bad as this. Foolish of me. I've known your dad long enough to realize he always expects things to go his way.'

Robert moved towards her. 'I'll help you to bed, Mom. We'll sort something out in the morning.'

And as he started back to the bedroom, holding her arm, she reached up and patted his cheek. 'Don't worry, son. I'll talk to Dorrie in the morning. We'll sort something out between us. And I'm sure it'll be safe for me to get up again in a few days. As long as I'm careful. Gran'll just have to get used to Chinese or pizza for the next few months. And learn to change her own nappy I guess!' They smiled at each other ruefully, gently, quietly, both wondering if they could ever find their way back to each other.

But Sharon took care of that. 'I don't blame your dad, Robert. I feel real sorry for him, a man like him. A *real* man, like him. Must be rough having two sons that can't find it in themselves to be a man.'

Robert glared at her. 'Can it, Sharon. I'll get Mom to bed, and we'll get home. She's tired. Look at her, almost asleep on her feet.'

'Very solicitous of her all of a sudden, aren't you? After all these years? After the damage she's done to you?'

Daisy stared at her. Robert said fiercely, 'I said leave it, Sharon. We can finish this at home.'

But there was no stopping her. 'Why not here? Get it all over in one night. One big shock instead of lots of little ones, eh? Spew it all out. Like you did to me when you were ready to leave this house, desperate to get married.'

'What are you talking about, Sharon? What's going on here?' Daisy didn't want to hear any more, wanted to shut her ears to their domestic troubles. It was time to move on from a child's problems, even if that child was yours. But it was too late. Her daughter-in-law had already said too much.

There was a long pause, as if Sharon was making up her mind about something. Robert had sunk into the chair beside the telephone. Daisy wrapped her robe round her even more firmly, as if by keeping every bit of the cold out, she could stand firmly and control her shivers. She reached out and put one hand on the wall behind her, just in case. 'Well?' she said impatiently to the girl standing petulantly in front of her. Because that really was the look on Sharon's face: petulant. Perhaps those without passion could only muster that look when they were angry. No white hot fury, no veins protruding from faces reddened with high irritation. Just petulance. It was as if someone had taken away her favourite doll. No, less than that – as if someone had cancelled her hair appointment the night she was giving a Tupperware party. Daisy steeled herself for more dramatics. 'Go on, for God's sake, Sharon. I'm not standing here all night. Tell me your slant on all this. You've kept quiet for long enough. Let's hear your opinion on how I'm treating my husband, and how I've brought up my children.'

'Robert told me how you used to push him away when Gary was born. How you fussed over the baby and ignored him. How it made him sick to watch you breastfeeding him, sometimes even in public. Even Marje said she hated it. The

146

way you'd just get your breast out to stop Gary yelling.'

'Gary was always yelling. He was a hungry child. You care little for propriety when your child is crying. I shouldn't have to defend myself for that. If Robert was upset, if he felt pushed aside, I'm truly sorry. As for Marjorie, I can't really believe she'd say something like that to you. She has her faults, but she's more discreet than that.'

'She didn't tell me. She told Robert. When she had to look after him because you were drooling over your favourite child.'

Daisy said nothing. Gary had been her favourite. She'd hoped the others hadn't noticed. She had felt ashamed then, and in reminding her, Sharon had brought back that feeling. 'I loved all my children the same,' she said unconvincingly, 'and Robert has always wanted to be with his dad. Bob took him everywhere. The first son.'

Robert looked up at her. 'I never wanted to be with Dad. I hated the fishing and learning about guns, and being thrown on that horse when I'd scarcely grown. Anything to make a man of me, Dad would say. I'd throw up when I knew I had to ride with him. I wanted to stay home with you. Sit on your lap again. Listen to you reading from all those books you brought from England. But you were too busy. And Gary yelled all the time. He seemed to yell for the first seven years of his life, and you had no time for anything else. All I can remember was you being tired. And it was you I wanted.'

147

Daisy stared at him. 'I had no idea, son,' she said softly. 'I really had no idea. What can I say?'

'Nothing now. I'm grown. I wanted my own family. That's why I got out. I'd had enough of Dad's heavy hand. He was using his belt on me when I was seventeen, for Christ's sake! Still trying to make a man of me, I guess. It was pretty damned humiliating, I can tell you.'

His head went down again, and Daisy shut her eyes against memories she never should have allowed to happen. She remembered the raised voices, the locked bedroom doors, the night Bob broke that same door down to get at his sons, though Gary had disappeared by then, the way he always did when there was trouble, staying at a friend's house until his father's rage had died a little. It was always Robert who got it. If she tried to protest, Bob would brush her aside. 'A good thrashing never did me any harm,' he would say, taking down that belt of his from where it always hung, where the kids could always see it, behind the kitchen door. Daisy had wanted so much to retort, 'That's not true. It's not true. Look at you, a man full of leftover demons.'

She had never been smacked as a child growing up in England, let alone beaten. Her family had never believed physical punishment an answer to a child's misdemeanours. Not so with the Franckens. Or some of their neighbours in those days. It was a part of a boy's learning process, it seemed. Even Marjorie had got it once. Caught smoking at school, or something equally as innocuous. It had never happened again to her. Not that she did everything she was told from then on, she merely made sure she was never caught by becoming the 'best goddam liar on the block'. The boys were never so devious, especially not Robert. But there it was, her new life, and the way Bob wanted to rear their children became the only way. Like in so many other things. And she'd looked the other way. What else to do when you're miles from everything you know, and afraid of your own shadow, your mother-in-law, and even your young husband when he got that certain look on his face. Daisy had hoped he'd mellow over the years, and, of course, like most people, he did. When he had grandchildren, Daisy would ponder, he'd be much gentler, not so strict. Which brought her to the case at point: Robert wanting a family of his own.

Before she could open her mouth to speak, Sharon said, 'We can't have children. We might never have children. So what do we do about it?' And she burst into tears once again.

Daisy turned to her son. 'What's she saying? Is there something wrong? Can't she have children, is that it? Is this the problem you've both been so unhappy about? You should have told me.'

'Your news kinda took us by surprise, I guess. Anyway, we're not really into all that baring one's problems as a family, are we?' It seemed to Daisy that Robert was looking everywhere but squarely into his mother's eyes.

'And poor Sharon felt even more unhappy, I

suppose? When she heard my news, I mean. I'm so sorry. I should have trodden more carefully. Being "hungry" for a child that is long in coming is very painful. Forgive me dear.' She moved towards her daughter-in-law and put an arm out to hold her, stop her tears, but Sharon brushed her aside, her voice ugly. 'It's not me, it's him,' flinging one finger in Robert's direction, 'he's the one who can't get me pregnant! Five years we've been married. Five years! And I think I must be still a virgin, for goodness sake.'

Daisy looked from one to the other, bewildered. 'What do you mean? You're making no sense girl. Still a virgin? Are you trying to tell me that you and Robert have never made love? I don't understand. I thought you'd spent nights together even before you were married. Didn't that mean anything?'

'I didn't want to do it then. I wanted to be different. I wanted to walk down that aisle a virgin. And I did. And Robert never pushed me, like other boys had. I thought he was a real gentleman. Not many of them round these parts. I had four brothers when I was growing up. That's not easy for a girl I can tell you. All sorts of things go on in families.'

'And then,' Daisy said, 'when you did marry, what then?'

'We just played around, you know – that's all. Your precious son doesn't like it or something. He's never done it, he says. That it isn't me. He just doesn't like it.'

'I still don't understand,' Daisy said, looking

from one to the other, desperate to be in bed, desiring sleep, seeing the bizarre nature of this entire conversation at the end of such a traumatic day.

Robert, at last, took his hands from his face and said quickly and desperately, 'I can't do it, Mom. That's what Sharon's trying to tell you. I can't make love, have sex – oh shit, I don't know. All that talk with the guys when I was younger? Load of crap! Now you know.'

Daisy stared at him. She felt she ought to go to him, comfort him. But she had no idea what to say. And just standing there, confused, bewildered, she was at a complete loss. Once more she realized she was letting him down yet again, and that perhaps we don't all come naturally equipped with motherly wisdom from the beginning after all.

'Couldn't you have done something, Robert? Talked to someone?'

His voice was almost inaudible, she all but bent to him so she could hear. 'Like a "shrink" you mean? Then Dad would find out, and I'd never hear the end of it. Besides, I thought it would work out eventually. We both did. Then when you got pregnant, something seemed to snap in Sharon. It's my fault. It's all my fault.'

There were tears in his eyes, and Daisy couldn't bear to see them. 'It's nobody's fault Robert. You must get help.'

'Well, someone made a mess of it,' Sharon muttered. 'Seems funny to me that there's two of them in the family with the same problem.'

Daisy faced her daughter-in-law. 'If you mean Gary, then say it. But I don't believe that Robert is homosexual. Gary is, and it isn't a problem with him, I can assure you.' She shifted her eyes back to her son. 'We'll find someone you can talk to, son. I'll ask Dr Hart.'

'No!' Sharon screeched. And Robert shook his head vehemently. 'Don't do that, Mom.'

'Why not? You can't just do nothing. Maybe it won't right itself, and then where will you be? Marriages can't work like this. Douglas will know what to do.' She didn't know whether Robert could be helped. She'd never come across any-thing like it before. But then, maybe there were a lot of people, men and women, who hated the idea of sexual intimacy, yet remained married and together quite happily. It had never crossed her mind. Now it was her own son, and there was nothing she could say to him.

'I've talked to him already,' Sharon said. 'He asked me why I wasn't pregnant yet, after all those years at school going on about being a mom one day. So I lied. Told him we were trying and it just hadn't happened. He wanted to carry out all these tests to find out if there was anything wrong with me or Robert. But I started to cry. I didn't want to be mucked about with. Our family have never had any trouble having babies. He'd start talking to Robert. And then it might all come out. Then what would it be like? Have Douglas Hart think I've found me a husband who won't even make out with me? No, thank you! I was at school with Dr Hart's daughter. I'd be a laughing stock.' Sharon's tears were pouring down her cheeks, anger and sadness and confusion alive in her eyes. 'We thought it was time you knew, that's all. Specially now. You're going to have a baby and I'm not!'

Robert said bitterly, 'It's you who wanted to tell Mom. For Christ's sake, I had to work real darn hard to stop you blurting it out to Dad in there. What would he do if he had two "frou-frous" for sons? It would kill him. Tell her, Mom.'

'Neither of you are "frou-frous", son. I hate that word. Don't be silly. And your father isn't always right. Time you learnt that and sorted your own life out the way you want it, not his way.' Daisy staggered a little, suddenly with tiredness.

Robert stood up and took her arm. 'Get to bed. Dr Hart'd freak out if he saw you now.'

'You need help. You can't just leave it like this,' she said as he propelled her into the bedroom and helped her into bed. Robert bent to tuck her in. 'I'm sorry, darling,' Daisy said. 'Forgive me for pushing you aside all those years ago. I didn't realize, and I should have. I'll make it up to you somehow.'

Before she drifted so quickly into sleep she heard him say, 'Don't tell Dad, Mom.'

And then she was gone, dreaming of babies, and stillborns, and Sharon as the midwife trying to take her child from her. She didn't hear them go, Sharon and Robert, didn't realize that night that Bob didn't come home, and slept right through her mother-in-law waking up about four in the morning and yelling for someone to take her to the bathroom.

It was Dorrie who came to the rescue, of course. She ran between her own house and the diner and the Franckens': doing the chores, shouting at Mary, and keeping Daisy well fed with gossip. Daisy was curious how the town was dealing with the news of the pregnancy.

'Are they supportive or otherwise? Or is it best I don't know?' she said to Dorrie one afternoon, when her friend had come straight from the diner after the morning rush.

'Some can't talk of anything else. Very fed up that your Sharon won't give them any titbits to mull over under the dryer. What else do they go to the beauty parlour for? Some of the guys feel sorry for Bob, isn't that typical? Like *he* was giving birth! The young 'uns ignore the whole thing, most of them anyway, while the rest think it's neat. The usual mindless prattling – you know – She's too old; she's a strong healthy woman; she's crazy; who does she think she is?; poor old Bob; serves him right at his age; he'd better be there when it happens, so he can make sure it looks like him and not old Sam in the hardware! He's always been a bit hot for Daisy!'

Both women laughed. Daisy said, 'I hope Bob doesn't start to believe them. We've slept apart for weeks now. Poor old Sam better watch out!'

'They believe anything in this town if you say it sure enough. I remember crazy Dan, who used to work for Bob's dad, getting one of the high school kids pregnant, and marrying her with a shotgun at his back. Literally! Years ago now, before you came. He said he had no idea how she got that way, and he meant it, though the poor girl was a simple little thing and insisted it was his. Couldn't be mistaken when she had twins nine months later, though – twins! Would you believe, they were as like her cousin Eric as peas in a pod. Girls, too, poor babes. They had Eric's ginger hair, and his long, runny nose. Constantly sniffing as they grew up, the three of them, and all of them wiping their noses on the sleeves of their sweaters! Enough to turn your stomach. No-one had the heart to tell poor Dan. He was as proud as a peacock with them. And Eric left town. How did I start this conversation? Oh yes. While the girl, the mother I mean, was hugely pregnant with these offspring, she was constantly throwing up. You know what it's like, I remember you with your Gary. I think it must be the difficult ones who make you sick. Anyway, she was spewing her guts up so much that crazy Dan went to the old doctor we had in town in those days and asked him if it was dangerous, and was there any chance of her puking up the baby as well as her guts!'

Daisy threw back her head and laughed more than she'd done for months. 'You're making it up,' she said, 'you must be. No-one can be that stupid!'

'Crazy Dan was. Never went to school unless they made him.'

'I can see where he got his nickname, anyway.'

Daisy saw more of Dorrie those days than the rest of the family. She'd tried to talk to Robert again, but it seemed to her that when he and Sharon popped in to see them after the last drama, she was never left alone with her son long enough to bring the subject up. They seemed to be battling on, the two of them, in their confused alliance, but even Daisy, in her innocence, couldn't see where and when it was all going to explode. Sharon's face got more and more drawn. Robert looked more and more haunted. Neither of them ever brought it up again.

Marjorie telephoned her mother every week, on Sunday mornings, and asked her if she or Dad needed anything. Hating the telephone, Daisy was always brisk with her. 'We're fine. We know you're busy. Give our love to John.'

And all the time, Bob and Daisy pulled further and further apart, he staying out late and drinking too much, Daisy resigned, patient, waiting for the weeks to go by, feeling stronger as they did, bored with so little to do, but never losing that stubbornness of will that finally held her back from putting a hand out to her husband and telling him she loved him, or needed him, or indeed, anything that would stop that wall of glass coming down between them for ever. But it was useless. The Francken family were doing their usual dances around complete confrontation, and this time it could only end in disaster.

'I don't love him any more,' Daisy blurted out one day to Dorrie.

'So what, honey? Marriages go on. Who needs all that stuff when the most exciting part of a day is taking your shoes off when you get home. I'd take that and a hot shower over all that carrying on any day.'

'It's not just the carrying on, though, is it?'

Dorrie didn't answer. She took Mary to the day centre every morning, where she got her lunch, 'and some interesting conversation, for once.' She'd sniffed that remark to Daisy more than once when she was brought home at the end of the outing, looking brighter than she'd done for years, albeit more confused every day as to where she actually lived.

Dorrie whispered, 'Don't you believe it, honey. They're all asleep when I get there to collect her! And most of them stay like that all day. Interesting conversation my butt!'

Daisy would go and sit by the unlit stove in the sitting-room when she was alone. Douglas would pop in some days and stay for a coffee and a chat, and complain half-heartedly about her not staying in bed. 'At least you're resting,' he conceded. He showed her the column in one of his medical journals where Daisy's case was mentioned, and the statistics of a safe birth with women over fifty. 'You're past the five months,' he said. 'As long as you avoid stress you'll be fine. And Bob'll come round. I'd bet my bonnet on it, to quote one of your favourite expressions.'

Daisy smiled. She'd stopped thinking about it. Bob never mentioned the baby. Scarcely mentioned a word to her in the evenings when he did stay in. Didn't ask to come back to her bed. Had done so once, home drunk one evening, and feeling cold and unloved, wanting his old life back in that maudlin fashion that pervades a person when too much beer has gone down.

'Better not,' Daisy had said to him, trying to keep her voice light, and stop the sudden palpitations that invaded her at the thought of Bob's body next to her once again, his breath distasteful with the smell of beer, his hair smelling of cigarettes from the atmosphere in the local bar. And then, just in case her voice had sounded too pleasant and regretful as she let him down lightly, and he found the courage to persist, she said gruffly, 'You stink of beer and cigarettes! I would be sick as a parrot.'

'You sound like your ma. It's that prissy English voice again. Why do you lot always think you know everything?'

'Because we do,' Daisy had snapped back. 'It happens that way when you've been around as long as we "lot" have.' Her bitchiness to him still took her by surprise. And she knew she was in the wrong most of the time. But she couldn't stop. All those years of 'yes sir, no sir', had found their place of vengeance in her acid tongue and her now unloving heart, which was too full of dreams for the child growing inside her.

One morning, sitting alone at the kitchen table,

her feet up on a stool, reading the newspaper, she heard a quick tap on the back door. She called out, 'It's open. Is it you, Dorrie? Did you get the doughnuts? I have such a craving for them.' But when she looked over her reading glasses as the door swung open, it wasn't her friend.

'No doughnuts, Daisy. And I'm a bit cold to dunk in your coffee.'

Her face lit up. 'John! What a lovely surprise! Is Marjorie with you?'

Her son-in-law stamped the snow off his shoes – the winter seemed to be going on for ever that year – and shut the door quickly to keep the cold out. He came and kissed her on the cheek. His eyes were twinkling. 'Was it OK to disturb you? Have I messed up your routine?'

She held on to his hand and smiled up at him. 'Not at all. I am *so* glad to see you. I can't believe it. Here I was, telling myself how nice it is to be on my own, and then you turn up out of the blue and make me realize I needed company all the time!'

'Marjorie's in New York, Ma-in-law. And I'm playing hooky. Thought it was time you saw the rest of the family for a change.' He put his coat on the door hook and went to pour himself some coffee. 'You're back on the caffeine then? No more sickness?'

'Hardly ever. And I've developed this devastating urge to eat greasy food. I can't get enough of pork sausage. Can you believe that?'

'Sounds good to me.'

'Did you just get in the car and come, or did you have a reason to be this far from home?'

'I just got in the car!' He grinned at her across the large mug of coffee he held. 'Thought I'd come and read you the book I've finished editing at last. Before it goes to the editor and she takes out all my glorious adjectives. They have a tendency to do that, you know. Apparently it's part of her job, they tell me. Well I can't throw out my "babies", so I guess someone has to do it.'

She laughed. 'Do you always call words your "babies"? I've heard you say it before.'

'Always. They're the only ones that Marjie pays attention to. Words as babies I mean. Sad as that is.' He smiled ruefully at her, teasing, frivolous, but just for a moment it made Daisy uncomfortable. And she couldn't quite place that feeling.

'Is it sad then? I mean, would you like children? Can't you have them?' She could have bitten her tongue out. 'I'm so sorry, John. That's none of my business.'

'It's OK. Really, I'm OK.' He put a hand out to squeeze hers, small and cold in his warm, comforting man-sized paw. 'I can tell you our business, Daisy. Now, what shall I begin with? I know – Marjie and I had a real blockbuster of a row before she left for New York.' He laughed loudly at the look of worry that flashed across her face. 'Don't imagine things, Ma-in-law. We quarrel all the time. Nothing my wife likes better than a good shouting match. Surprising, huh?'

Daisy stared at him, perplexed. Then she, too, laughed. 'Well, frankly, yes. You're so quiet when you're here. I mean you of course, not Marjorie. She loves to make as much noise as possible – telling us all what to do, that is. I guess she makes a good lawyer, being that way.' She pulled away from him, her face flushed. 'Oh dear, I'm putting my foot in it all round today. First babies, now being not very nice about my own daughter. I don't believe any of that sounds the way a mother should. You must forgive me, John. Things have been very strange around here since I announced my determination to have this baby. Everyone's feathers are badly ruffled, I'm afraid. And a lot of trying to make me feel guilty. It wasn't planned. What must you think of me?'

'The same as I always did.' He stared at her for a moment with such intensity that Daisy thought he was trying to find the right words. Before she could answer, he went on, 'And what a great surprise you are now, after all these years of passiveness. But then, I knew all along, really. You try so hard to hide who you are. But anyone with a grain of sense should see. You can't hide those eyes of yours. Light eyes can't hide secrets. They have to be brown to do that.'

Daisy was embarrassed. 'You really sound like a writer.'

'Good.'

'Was that patronizing?' she asked anxiously. 'What I just said, I mean?'

John roared with laughter. 'Dear me, Mother-in-law, you really do cry out for some decent conversation. My intuition was right.'

'Call me Daisy. Mother-in-law sounds very formidable.'

'You are the least formidable woman I've ever met. Your eyes make you an open book. People should read you more often.'

'Now you're making me blush.'

John stood to pour more coffee. 'Why don't you let me make you lunch?' he said.

Daisy looked up at him. He stood tall beside the coffee pot, at ease in the gingham-decorated kitchen. Bob always said it was obviously a female room from the beginning. 'Done like that to keep the men out!' he had said so many times to friends and visitors, when they came to the house and he wanted to show the changes his wife had wanted. 'Clever woman, my wife! Knows her place, she does!' And he'd patted her on the butt and kissed her cheek, and she'd pretended all along that she knew he was joking, and it was all right for the guests to laugh at his less than funny sense of humour. He'd only been called on to stop that sort of talk when Marjorie had reached her teens. 'Don't embarrass yourself, Dad. I can't bring my friends home if you're going to say things like that. Sounds like you came from the ark, for God's sake!' He shut up then. Daisy believed he was a little intimidated by his clever daughter.

'You don't have to, John. When Dorrie can't get here she leaves me a sandwich in the refrigerator. There'll be a meal tonight. The kids are coming over. Robert and Sharon, I should say. Hardly kids! She's making some sort of chicken cooked with apricots, I believe. Bob will hate it. Not my cup of tea either, I'm afraid.'

'Then you need something warm inside you now. It's cold out there! I'll make some soup, and keep you company until the others arrive.' And he sort of took over from then on.

After lunch he cleaned the kitchen and then sat with her in the living-room.

'I can't remember ever having all this time to talk to you before,' she smiled. It had stopped snowing, and through the window a watery sun was struggling to break the bitterness of the long winter.

'Not time yet,' John said as he pointed at the light pushing through the net curtains, having made its weak climb over and round the leafless trees that stood on the other side of the boundary of their back yard. The pines in the distance were prouder, still fully dressed, catching the snowflakes on their prickly limbs and holding on to them. If you stood outside at that time, as Daisy had often done through many Idaho winters, it would be so quiet she could swear that, if she stayed still enough, she would hear the crystal shapes of the flakes fall to the ground when the trees grew tired of holding them. 'What you just standing there for, woman?' Bob had called to her once from the back door, smiling benignly at his young wife, pregnant with their second child. 'I'm waiting for the pines to let the snow go. Then I'll know that spring is coming.' Bob had laughed, still enraptured with her somewhat poetic English ways. She'd heard his mother sniff behind him. 'Bit fanciful, that wife of yours, son. Get her in here before she catches cold.'

'The pines have been waiting,' she said. And John turned to smile again at her, and said nothing. Which meant he understood, and her heart lifted to his in recognition. It was almost the best moment of the afternoon.

'When's the baby due?' he asked.

'Early June. Well, the date is the fourteenth, but I doubt she'll choose the exact day. They seldom do.'

'I know.'

'Would you have liked children?' she asked at last.

He looked carefully at her, then said, 'I live with the hope that Marjorie will change her mind one day. When the corporate life grows too much for her. When she mellows, and stops seeing kids as a threat.'

'Does she know this? How you feel, I mean.' She looked surprised. 'I thought you and Marjorie had decided quite firmly that any children were not for you.'

John leaned back in his chair, legs crossed, hands clasped behind his head. 'I feel rather guilty about it all. I agreed with her about no children at first. I was under the impression most women change their minds as the years go on – biological – that sort of thing. It's the romantic in me. It was foolish; I should have been straight with her from the beginning. About myself, that is. Wanting a family one day. Now I can't find the right words to discuss it. When your news came out I was extraordinarily excited about the whole thing. Quarrelled with Marjorie driving home that night. After Thanksgiving. You remember? Thought everyone had been appallingly badly behaved to you that day. Not that that was the main thing we fought about. I stupidly asked her if it had made her broody in any way. You know, maybe she'd been so unpleasant to you and everyone because she was jealous suddenly: the thought that her own mother was having a child before *she'd* even considered trying. Well, I don't have to describe the cry that went up after that! My feet didn't touch ground, I'm afraid. I saw a side of your daughter that stunned me when we first met. One I'd only ever seen her perform in court. It had rather "turned me on" when we first dated, I can tell you now. But this was different.'

'What did she say?'

John took his arms from his head and leaned forward to look into her eyes.

'To see, in those windows of the soul,' she thought, 'what my truthful reaction is to my own daughter.' She tried to glance away, but couldn't.

John said, 'You don't want to know.'

'Yes, I do. I know already that, as a child, she hated to watch me breast-feeding. Sharon told me only a while ago. Apparently Marjorie was quite clear, even at that extraordinarily young age, that there was a lot about me she found rather sickening. And I'm afraid my Robert has always been easily impressed and a little intimidated, himself. Not just with his sister, either. I think he has a problem with women.' She bit her lip in sudden consternation. 'Oh dear, I shouldn't have blurted that out. It's just that you make me really want to talk to you. Not like me. Forgive me. Go on with what you were saying about Marjorie. I should know my enemies perhaps. No, that's too brutal. I don't, won't, believe my own daughter hates me. I like to think it's disapproval, and that's all.'

John laughed. 'I think she rather feels that about me these days as well.'

'Go on, tell me. What else did she say?'

'Well . . . I hate this. And I need to see your eyes again, Mother-in-law. If I can see pain in them, I'll stop. I have always seen it in your eyes. Crazy to think that no-one else seems to see it as well.'

'It's not real pain, John. At least I don't think it's that dramatic. Until now, of course, what with the pregnancy, I mean, and the loneliness I've brought on myself, I guess. Except for dear Dorrie. I just can't really talk to her. It would be like putting a notice in the local paper, I'm afraid.' He laughed. She went on, 'My life's been good for the most part. Bob's been a good husband up until now,' and before he could jump in, she said fiercely, 'and yes, I do know about the other women. I've been lazy, I realize that. But I'm not even sure that it bothered me that much. The bedroom stuff was never high on my list of priorities. All that was much more fun when he was stationed in Surrey during the war. That was near where I was born. But maybe you know all this already. Anyway, I really fell for him. The entire Yankee thing, actually. I was a virgin. He was ten years older than me. Experienced. I guess Bob Francken showed me what the back seat of a car was really for! Anyway, it was the excitement of it all: the way he danced, the uniform, the way he stood up when I left the table. I had no idea at the time that all your guys had been warned about their manners by those in command before they even set foot on our little island. It all worked. I got pregnant, he did the right thing, we married with special permission, and then when Marjorie was born, a little while later, he was sent home. I followed. When I got here, with all my poetic dreams in tow, we'd been apart for too long. Too long for us, anyway. Only for those who are truly loved does the old proverb work, I'm afraid. "Absence makes the heart grow fonder." I don't know. I guess it's disappointment you've seen in my eyes all these years. I think I left Daisy at Southampton when I sailed across. I've lived Bob's life, not mine. It's been easier. Not for the best, though. I can see that now.' She looked and smiled again at him. 'I've never talked so much in my life, John Maverick. I'd better shut up and give some other bugger a go! My dad used to say that. I used to giggle until I cried when I was a young girl whenever he came out with it. He's lovely, my dad.'

'Do you still want me to tell you what Marjorie said? Is it worth it? Does it matter? Maybe if she'd heard all that, all those memories you've thrown on my plate, she'd understand you more. Did you ever talk to her? Properly, I mean?'

Daisy shook her head, sad again. Resigned.

'Then leave it, Daisy. It's all too late. I know it's not the American way. We do seem to love delving into our subconscious in this country. It's a fascination with our past, I think. In Europe they seem rather blasé about theirs. Had long enough to take it for granted, I guess.'

Daisy said, laughingly, 'Not round here I don't think! I'd know about it if anyone went to a shrink, I can tell you. Nothing, and I mean *nothing* gets past Dorrie!' On impulse she took his hand and squeezed hard. 'It has been so nice to really get to know you after all this time! I am so pleased you came all this way in this dreadful weather. Well, not glad for your journey of course – just grateful that you took all the trouble to come. And from the song and dance going on inside me, I'd say madam in there approves of you as well. Before we let all the cats out of the bag in our first sitting, (because I'm presuming you'll come again, in fact, I'm insisting on it) I want to hear your story. You promised. It will be this young lady's first fairy story,' and she prodded her stomach as she spoke. 'Is it a fairy story you've written this time? Or is it grim?'

'It's a grim fairy story, I'm afraid. She'll love it. Girls are even more gruesome than boys.'

Chapter Eight

Daisy had never heard him read out loud before, and she found his voice so pleasant, so gentle that, to her later embarrassment, she fell asleep. When she opened her eyes again, Dorrie had arrived. Daisy could hear her talking to John in the kitchen and clattering pots around. Mary was nowhere to be seen, but the television was on in her room, she always put it on too loudly and it played now against the chattering from the kitchen. Someone must have insisted that Daisy was not to be disturbed, so the old woman would have to watch her favourite quiz show in her bedroom. The room was warm, and someone had placed the blanket around Daisy while she slept. It was dark outside. Soon the others would be there, bringing their troubles and their tensions with them. For now, it was peaceful. It seemed to have started snowing again. Maybe John would have to stay the night. For a few minutes, Daisy could believe that only this was her world. And the baby kicked inside her as if to remind her she wasn't alone, and never would be again.

She got up from her sleeping position in the living-room and went to join John and Dorrie in the kitchen.

'Shouldn't be walking around,' John said cheerfully, brushing aside her apologies for falling asleep on him. And without another word, swept her up into his arms and carried her into her bedroom. 'Where you will stay to have supper, and where you can receive the rest of the family, when they arrive, like the queen of your castle!'

Dorrie laughed, and said it reminded her of *Gone with the Wind* and Clark Gable.

'Except Scarlett wasn't pregnant at the time!' Daisy called over her shoulder. It made her feel silly, and rather romantic. It also made her blush.

John did stay that night. Bob came home late and Daisy could hear them talking together in the kitchen before sleep overtook her. Sharon and Robert were quite cheerful when they arrived. Sharon had cooked a pot-roast for them all, losing courage over the promised chicken and apricots – a relief to them all, thought Daisy. Sharon was delighted when everyone praised her for her thoughtfulness, especially Mary, even if the old woman did keep calling her Shirley, when no-one else had any idea to whom she was referring. Daisy complimented her daughter-in-law on her new hair colour as well as her cooking, which brought quite a blush to her cheek when she came to collect Daisy's empty plate at the end of the meal.

'It's the new auburn,' Sharon said cheerfully. 'We were so slow at the salon today. It's the early Easter this year, I think. People have already gone for the weekend. Cherilee insisted I try it. Red's great. Makes me feel good that spring is coming.'

'If you want to talk at all, Sharon, I am here for you, you know. I mean—' But Sharon had already made a bolt for the door before Daisy could get the words out. Anything more personal than pot roasts or hair colour was out-of-bounds for mothers-in-law. When she'd gone back to the safety of the kitchen and the men's talk about football, of which she knew little, in spite of hopeful coaching from her dad and then Robert, she felt safer. If she didn't think about the problem, maybe it would go away.

'Like shutting your eyes as a child,' thought Daisy, tucked up in bed with a full stomach and a cold water bottle, 'if I can't see it, it can't see me.'

And there was no way she was ever able to broach the subject again. Neither with her son nor her daughter-in-law. They must have decided to battle on and pretend nothing had changed by the fact they'd told her. A mistake. Daisy kept thinking about it, the peculiarity of it all. She would have liked a wise head, then maybe she would be able to undo the damage she seemed to have done to her middle child all those years ago.

Lying there, for the next month, her younger life came every day to haunt her. They all settled into some sort of routine. Daisy only became agitated when Dorrie went home at night and Bob stayed away until the early hours. She worried about Mary becoming unwell, and herself unable to do anything. But she said nothing to Bob. She no longer believed he would listen, and she pushed from her mind the thought of how he intended to live his life once the child was born. And for the time being, there was John.

The child grew bigger inside her. John told her she should look into the mirror more often and see how beautiful she'd become. He would come over at least twice a week, to bring her small gifts of flowers or chocolates, and prepare lunch, then stay for supper. No-one seemed to mind. At least, they didn't seem to. Sharon, on at least one occasion, as far as Daisy could tell, even began flirting with him in a rather unsubtle way.

'Silly girl,' muttered Daisy, 'what does she think that will prove?'

John laughed about it with her before he made the journey back to Boise that evening. But after that first night, he didn't stay again. The weather got better, and the daffodils started to show up.

'Go back you idiots!' Daisy called to them from the window, pulling the nets to one side when the still weak sun was shining one April morning. 'A frost will come and you'll regret it.'

'Who are you talking to?' Bob asked. He was trying to find his old working jeans that were still hanging at the back of the closet. He was on the way to the next town, 'only a couple of miles down the highway', to do a friend a favour and look at his car. They metaphorically danced around each other these days, as if the swelling of her body wasn't happening. He would stare at that part of her when he believed she wasn't looking, as if by casting malevolent glances the whole thing would disappear. 'As grim as one of your fairy tales,' she told John later.

'I'm talking to the daffodils, if you must know,' Daisy said, turning from the window. 'Telling them to get the hell out of here if they want to go on living. Every year it's the same. Too early a warm spell, and it's curtains for them when the frost comes back. You'd think they'd have got the hang of it by now.'

Bob laughed, as he'd always done when she got what he used to call 'fanciful'. Daisy raised an eyebrow at him as he turned towards her.

'You needn't look like that, woman. I can still find something to laugh at these days,' he said gruffly.

She got quickly back into bed to warm her feet. There was still a real nip in the air, despite the signs of spring. She felt a pull inside her suddenly, and placed both hands across her belly and looked down. Bob didn't notice, his back to her as he struggled to pull up the zipper on his old jeans.

'Shit!' His expletive was harsh, irrational for the circumstances. A broken zip? A spreading waistline? Daisy's turn to laugh.

Her cramp had gone as quickly as it had arrived, making her think it was just a reminder that even now it wasn't wise to jump quite so vigorously in and out of bed. 'What is it?' she said.

'I can't get into these jeans. Did you wash them?'

Daisy was irritated. 'In case you hadn't noticed,

I've scarcely moved from this room lately, let alone do the washing. There was some talk of plumbing the washer and dryer in here. Save you the trouble of too long a search for clean socks. But Sharon and Dorrie have been taking turns, I believe. To do the washing, that is.'

Bob grunted, then swore again, tearing off the trousers and throwing them in disgust on the floor.

'You've put on weight,' Daisy said bluntly. 'And don't leave those on the floor. Dorrie's not your wife.'

'Why remind me?' He was searching inside the closet for another pair, tossing clothes around fiercely, finally settling on a pair of loose overalls she hadn't seen him wear for years. 'And before you think you're right yet again, I never put on weight. I've been the same since the day we married. I could still get into that uniform if it was around.'

'It's in the attic. It'd be far sexier than those overalls, I can tell you. It must be the guys tonight, I guess. Definitely not going into town. Not in those. Not if you want to get laid.'

It was Bob's turn to raise his eyebrows. But he didn't answer her. Just snorted, in the way he would when he had nothing to say, and 'she got too mouthy for her own good'.

But Daisy hadn't finished. Spring in the air had made her quite perky.

'I'd be surprised if you *weren't* putting on weight these days,' she said. 'All the extra beer you're drinking. To say nothing of the dinners you're buying out so you don't have to come home to a houseful of women.'

'Do you blame me?'

'Not really. I should have done that years ago. Maybe I will yet.'

'What're you blabbing on about now, woman? I'm late already.'

'I'm blabbing on about maybe leaving home.'

'Who's leaving home? What in Christ's name are you talking about?'

'ME! I'm talking about ME. Leaving home. When the baby comes.'

He turned and went to the door. His back to her, voice like gravel, as if he wasn't sure he wanted her to hear, he said, 'Maybe you'll have to.'

And with that he left, leaving her to yell after him, 'What the hell does that mean, Bob Francken?' But she heard the front door open, then Dorrie coming in cheerily at the back door, and Mary shouting something about 'They're fighting again. And blaspheming. I told him not to marry her. Wait till I tell his dad.'

'Take no notice of her,' Dorrie said as she came through to Daisy's room with coffee and doughnuts in her hand. 'She's in another world. Talks to old man Francken all the time these days. How long has he been dead?'

'What d'you think he meant?' Daisy asked John later that same morning. 'Is he going to kick me out when the baby's born? He can't do that, can he?'

She was still in bed and John had brought soup from a diner he'd stopped at on the road from Boise that day. He didn't tell Daisy about Marjorie's impatience when she'd realized how often he was visiting, and then getting home too late to cook supper for the two of them, which he'd done willingly for years, if they weren't dining out. 'You're supposed to be starting on your new book,' his wife had said, barely hiding her irritation. 'If you don't get on with it we'll have no time for a decent holiday this year because you'll be behind with it. What's with my mother all of a sudden? Is it still your *own* need? She won't even begin to fill that cavern inside you. She had little idea of how to be a mother. Mothers, or so I'm told, are strong for their kids, protect them, push their husbands into following their dreams. There was very little of that in our house when we were growing up, let me tell you. She just stood there when we were in trouble. Left all the real discipline to Dad. I don't know what went on in her mind. None of us did when we looked back on it. She always had that quiet look of disappointment on her face, as if none of us pleased her. And she managed to kill all Dad's dreams as well, according to Gran. Those were the days when Gran was more lucid, so I'm inclined to believe her. Mom hardly said a word. Ever. Just cooked and cleaned, and agreed with everything and everybody. That's why Dad took his frustration out on us kids. Someone had to be in control, and it most definitely wasn't going to be her. That's my reading of it, anyway.' And she'd pulled away from him impatiently. 'God knows what the pair of you talk about all day.'

John had not answered. He knew what pulled him back to Daisy's all the time, but it was nothing he could confess to his wife.

That particular day he was late. If he'd got into a real fight with Marjorie it wouldn't have been worth going to Wellington. Not once they'd both aired their peevish complaints to each other, in case the real reason for their disapprobation came up, and then the day would be ruined, as well as almost over. And Daisy would have been disappointed. He would see that look in her eyes again. And this time he'd be the one to put it there. So he resisted the enticement of a damn good fight, which would only end in the kind of rough wordless sex that Marjorie had come to enjoy of late, and went to see Daisy immediately his wife left, angry and frustrated, for the office. He stopped only briefly on the way, to pick up some soup and dinner rolls at a roadside diner.

'He won't turn you out, Daisy. Bob wouldn't do that.'

Daisy turned and gazed out of the window. 'I know you're right. But I wish I could go. Bring my daughter up in another town, another state. It's a pipe dream. I have very little money of my own. I could go back to England, I suppose. At a pinch, that is. But it's not home any more, not after all this time. I'm sure I'd hate it. And from what Mom has told me, I think this baby will have a better chance in life here more than anywhere else in the world. Even Dad's told me that all the promises after the war came to nothing, whatever government's been in. And the sixties just gave everyone enough pretence to gloss over the slow death of our country that has been going on since the forties. Dad's words, not mine. I was never that political. I guess he'd have dragged me into it by now though, if I'd gone on living there. But my only interest during those teenage years was music and how was I going to get over my shyness for long enough to find myself a bloke.'

John laughed, wondering then what she'd been like all those years ago, and did she have the same sad smile then as she did now, or was she expectant of great things, as all teenagers should be?

Daisy looked out of the window again, unaware of just how much John was scrutinizing her. She was back once more in the present. 'I don't know how we'll ever manage to make our marriage work after all this. I'm so unpleasant to him. I must hate him, the things I say. Does he believe all my anger will just evaporate?' She turned to face John again. 'Sometimes, at night, when I'm lying here waiting to hear him come home, holding my breath in case he comes into this room, praying he won't, I'm frightened for us all. The three of us, I mean. Him, me and this baby. What will we do? We can't go back. *I* can't go back. Not to all that pretending, and turning the other cheek. All those things that kept us going all those years.'

'*Do* you hate him, Daisy? Really hate him, I mean? That's a hard thing to do when you've been married as long as you two. Bob's the child's father, come what may. Sooner or later all this – the lack of communication between you, the reason for the tension – well, you know, when she's older an' all, it might come out. Somebody might spill the beans in a fit of temper.'

'You mean about him not wanting her? About the talk of abortion? I'll make darn sure it won't. I want her loved and cherished every single day of her life. I want her to feel wanted with every breath she takes, for as long as she takes it. I have much to make amends for, I'm sorry to say.' Her voice was fierce, strong. John felt admiration for her strength. 'But no, you're right, John. It isn't hate. I can't hate him. I think he's behaved despicably over all this. I knew he wouldn't be pleased at first. A man of his age seldom wants to start all over again with a new baby. It's going to be hard. But then, the rest of the family never let him behave in any other way. He's wanted an easy life as much as me. And my disappointment, submissiveness, whatever you want to call it, is more simple to deal with than anything else. He's known that for years.'

'It'll work out.' John's words echoed weakly, and Daisy held his hand briefly. The tone in his voice belied the words.

'My dad would always say that whenever Mum got into a tizzy about anything. Something silly, like forgetting to stop the milkman when we went

179

away. She never believed him, of course. So she would fret for the whole holiday, imagining the bottles of milk piling up on the doorstep. And we couldn't telephone the neighbours because no-one else in our street had a telephone in those days.'

'Was your dad ever right?'

'Always,' she laughed. 'The first day after we'd left, our next-door neighbour mentioned it to the milkman when he delivered her milk first. Dead nosey, I guess. Really wanted to know if Mum had actually told the guy where we were going that year. We went somewhere different every year before the war. Always in England, of course. Usually to a boarding house, or a holiday camp along the south coast. We were the only ones in our street who ever went on holiday. Dad was the one man who was working amongst our neighbours. Everyone else was so poor. It was better when the war came. Most of the men went to fight, and the women went out to the factories. Mum never did of course. Wasn't expected to, not with me to look after.'

'You love him very much, don't you? Your dad?'

'Yes. Every girl should have a dad. It's more important for a girl in some ways.' She looked down towards the swelling of her body. A ripple of a movement began inside. She smiled and, on impulse, took John's hand so that he, too, could feel it. The innocence of it took John's breath away. They didn't speak. Daisy looked down at her hand on top of John's.

He kept his eyes on Daisy. His face was still.

'Oh God,' he thought, 'I wish this could all be mine.' The thought came, hung, then fell once more into the realms of impossibility. And at last he took his hand from under hers, and Daisy smiled up at him, her eyes shining, unsure of what was in the air. He was more than glad he'd left the thought unspoken.

'Am I being selfish?' Daisy said, a sudden frown passing swiftly across her face.

'About what?'

'Making you share that with me? You wanting children as you said, and Marjorie against the idea? Maybe I'm rubbing salt in the wound. You must tell me. A pregnant woman gets very caught up in her own world at times. You feel very strongly that the entire world revolves round you for those nine months. It has always been the most important I've ever felt. Every pregnancy. Other times I had someone to share. Now I have you. Well, I've kinda commandeered you, if the truth be known! You have to tell me now that you don't mind at all. Because you must always pander to your mother-in-law! Did you know that? Especially if she's pregnant and going on fifty-one!'

Her eyes twinkled at him. She was trying hard to be serious. At this most devastating crossroads in her life, when at any moment her marriage might explode in her face, when her future had never been so confused, she discovered she was having more fun than she'd ever remembered. John could find no words, and to open his mouth at that moment would be disastrous. The rush of blood to his head, the sudden sweat on his hands, threw him into the state of confusion he'd been trying to avoid for weeks. Or was it years. Could a woman of Daisy's age really be this innocent? This lacking in guile?

'What is it, John? Have I upset you horribly? It wasn't my intention, I promise you. Tell me what you're thinking.'

But it would have been impossible at that moment. Searching her face, hoping that extraordinary openness of hers would be shown to be concealing something, that all this was merely teasing, he longed for his words to be more than thoughts. But not knowing what damage it would do, afraid she would banish him for ever from her side, he held both her hands and wouldn't let them go, his smile slow and tender. There was a long silence between them, his rush of thoughts giddy in his head, so strong he wondered that she couldn't hear them. But to Daisy there was only silence. A silence that for some reason she couldn't break.

'Dearest Daisy,' he thought, the words in his head like liquid within a closed tap. 'What am I thinking? How could I ever speak my thoughts out loud? I could never be so destructive. Not to you. Because I'm afraid it might destroy you. Just when you've built all this splendid armour to keep you and your baby safe. I just want it all to be mine: you, the child, everything you are. When did it start, you'd ask? How horrified you'd be. It's been all these years. I've never really been able to face it. Until now. I've put myself in such a dangerous place this time. I'm in a "pickle" as you once said. That might have even been the first time I didn't see you as a mother. It was probably only the third time that Marjorie had invited me to your home. We wanted to get engaged, I believe. I really think that up until then, until that moment, I'd always thought of you as the mother I lost when I was young. We were all here, at this house, and it was Easter. You'd said it was your favourite holiday, because you loved the spring. And before I went down into the town with the others, leaving you as usual to cook the lunch, I came running back into the kitchen because I'd forgotten something. I can't remember what it was. And there you were, wrestling with the turkey, basting it or something, down on your knees with the oven door open, talking away to yourself, as if you'd just been waiting for everyone to go before you spoke. You kept me there for a few moments, ignoring the screeching of the car horn outside that was being relentlessly punched by my impatient peers. That was the day you told me about your father for the first time, and how he had always called you poppet when you were a child, and even now, three grown children later, he still did at times. Especially the times he suspected you might well be disappointed with the life you'd found yourself a part of, when over the years of visiting, he had seen it in your eyes when your guard was down, or in the tone of your voice when you spoke. "All right, poppet? Is my girl managing all those miles away? If you need anything, my dearest poppet, let your old dad know. That's what dads are for!" See how I can remember what you told me? I hadn't intended to lock it into my memory. I remember thinking how pretty you looked. You were in a gingham apron and the tendrils of your hair were wet round your face. You'd laughed, as if apologizing for your outburst of intimacies, and your impulsiveness had taken you by surprise as well as me, and then you explained you'd been trying to light that old wood-burning stove you used to have, and then you'd remembered the turkey needed basting. You looked so tiny in your big old kitchen: like a child playing house. And I can remember thinking to myself at that moment, "I'd far rather stay here with you. I have no interest in seeing what Bob has done to the body shop, or the new tables in the diner. No interest in going to the bar afterwards and struggling to down as many beers as I can get in before it's time to come home. I want to stay here, and you can tell me about your life in England. Because you never do. Talk about it, I mean. It was as if you didn't exist before Idaho. And what would you have done with your life if you hadn't come here? I remember feeling quite appalled at the thought that I wouldn't know you. That we would never spend holidays together. And you'd have another family somewhere." And then I realized that my first thought should have been that I would never have met Marjorie if there had been no you. And I was frightened suddenly with the rapidity that my soon-to-be wife could slip so easily from my thoughts and leave *you* there, in my head, in my heart. I said the others were waiting for me in the car, and could I bring you anything, or could I help you with the stove before I left. And because I must have had that look on my face which said this is not what I should be doing with my Easter, talking to my mother-in-law when my new fiancée was waiting outside, you smiled that smile of yours again. Generous. And, what's that word? Oh yes, "gracious". And there was that twinkle in your eye you only showed very seldom. And you said, "You can help me with this stove, Son-in-law, the old man's gone off without lighting it, and left me in a right pickle, I can tell you." I had no idea what you were talking about but I was so entranced with the possibility it might have been me that had made you laugh for once, that I didn't ask, I just helped you, and then ran off as quickly as I could to drink too much beer with the others. I fell in love with you then, Mother-in-law. I believe I did. Anyway, what you did, what I believed happened, was that you captured my heart. And you seem to have had it ever since, I'm afraid. I don't know what to do about it. Especially as you have never had any idea what's been going on all these years; and because of Marjorie you might be very angry with me and send me away to "grow up". All I do know is, that if I say anything at all we will *all* be in a right "pickle". And hurting you is not on my agenda. Even if I had one. I just want this feeling to behave itself. As it has been doing all these years. Up until now. If perhaps you didn't look quite so vulnerable, or weren't being quite so brave . . . But there you are. And if I could hold you in my arms just once before all this explodes in our face, I believe it might be enough. My darling Daisy.'

'What?' Daisy said, breaking the silence at last, interrupting his reverie. 'Is something wrong, John?'

'Nothing.'

Chapter Nine

And so the days passed. Most of the time slowly, but sometimes fast. That was when John was there. Bob knew he came. They bumped into each other once or twice, when John was leaving, and Bob came home early. Dorrie teased her a little. Said she'd be making her own daughter jealous. Daisy got quite upset over that remark, then angry.

'Is that the gossip?' she said one day to her friend. 'Is that the story for the town? That I'm having an affair with my own son-in-law?'

'Goodness girlfriend, no-one would have the balls to just come out and say that. Besides, they don't really believe it. It's just that nothing really happens in this town, and you have to dig deep and use your imagination occasionally. When everyday events get more boring than watching grass growing. You know that. I mean, you having a baby is discussed most of the time, and most days. You surely didn't expect anything different did you?'

'What do they say? Tell me Dorrie.'

'Just rubbish. Not even worth repeating.'

Daisy narrowed her eyes. If Dorrie refused to gossip, she was hiding something.

Daisy said, 'Don't even think it.'

'What?' Dorrie had gone over to the window and was pretending to straighten the lace curtains. 'Think what?' she said, without turning. Then, 'Why don't I go and put more coffee on? I'll bring the pot in here and you can help yourself when I leave. Need to go a bit earlier this evening. I want to pick up some logs for home. We've got through more than usual. Darn these long winters. It's not far from the end of April.'

'. . . Think that you're going to get away without spilling the beans.' Daisy sat upright in the bed. 'Dorothy Danson, get over here. I need to know. When I push my pram down Main Street later this year, I want to know my enemies.'

Dorrie turned and came over to the bed. 'I've wanted to tell you, Daisy. I *should* be telling you. I've been battling with it for weeks now. It's not easy. Problem is, you're going to find out sooner or later, and I'd rather you heard it from me. I'm just afraid for you and the baby, that's all. You're not supposed to get upset.'

Daisy frowned. 'What? Is it Bob? Are you going to tell me he's out and about? Like some old tomcat? If you are, don't bother. I've known it for years. I can't say I really care any more. He's not the first husband round here to stray, you know that as well as me. Even if your old man keeps his butt at home.'

'That's 'cos he's scared to do anything else! I'd knock his head off. He knows that, as well as knowing where his bread is buttered.'

Daisy smiled. Her body felt uncomfortable

over the past few days, and she'd slept restlessly the night before. She was putting on too much weight, according to the doctor. 'What d'you expect Douglas? I'm in bed all day! It's where you put me!'

Dorrie was serious. And Daisy leaned her head back against the headboard of the bed. 'Go on then,' she said, 'tell me what they're all saying.'

In spite of everything, all the years of occasional betrayal, and slow-dying love that only now she would admit to herself, when Dorrie at last told her about Bob, she felt shocked. And rejected. And all the things she thought she'd dropped from her barricaded heart years ago. She listened at last to Dorrie, and was glad it was her, her oldest friend.

'I've been torn about this for a long time. Couldn't believe it had taken so long to get to my ears. You know me! But it was finally the carers in the place old Mary goes to during the week, that came out with it. They'd asked how you were. They're nice broads, most of them. Unpaid volunteers usually, making coffee all day, cutting up lunches or listening to complaints. The old 'uns complain a lot when they're at the centre. Not because it's any worse than home, I shouldn't think. Just having a captive audience for once, I guess. When everyone's sleepy after lunch, the women eat their sandwiches or whatever, and gossip. I'd stayed a while and had coffee. Hell if I know why. Usually I can't get out quick enough. It smells like hell in there. All those wet panties!'

Daisy didn't smile when Dorrie did an exaggerated shudder. 'Get on with it, Dorrie. You don't have to throw in little anecdotes to keep me laughing in case I cry at the punch line. What did you tell them about me?'

'All right, all right. I wanted to paint the picture. I always wanted to be on the stage, you know that. Should have been as well.'

Daisy prodded her, exasperated. 'Are you ever going to get to the point?' she said. 'You'll have to collect Mary soon. And God knows, you'll never get to the diner to cash up if you're going to take this long.'

'OK. Listen to me. I said you were well. Stuck in bed and bored, but you were well. They'd already heard about having a near miss a while ago. That new receptionist with Douglas had kept her mouth shut apparently, but his regular girl's back now, and she lets them know about everyone's health: who's not going to be with us long, and who's got various social illnesses. That sort of thing.'

'I don't believe that! You'd say anything for a laugh. I can't believe that anyone's got a social disease in this town! If they had, they'd go to Boise to see another doctor.'

'Not if they had had no idea what was wrong with them.'

'All right, I give in. I'll let you sidetrack me. Who? And how, for crying out loud? Surely you're not going to tell me that even this is to do with Bob?'

'Good God, girlfriend, of course not. This is just a little titbit going round with the coffee cups. It almost eclipsed your goings-on at one time. If you see what I mean.'

'How could I? You haven't told me anything yet. All you've done is talk! Can't you get a little more focus in your stories?'

'D'you remember that service they dreamed up? Asking for volunteers to use their cars to deliver prepared food for the disabled living on the outskirts? Most have got willing and friendly neighbours, but there's always an exception. Remember the Bailey brothers that lived with their parents on that farm about ten miles out? The youngest one must have been about forty when you first got here. That's thirty years ago at least. And there were three of them. Three grown men, middle-aged then, still living with their parents. There'd been a daughter once. Can't remember much about her. Except she left before the war under some sort of cloud. Pregnant, everyone thought. But you never saw her in the town. Except once in a while when there was a dance up at the old Baptist hall. Not many Baptists round here any more. The hall's still standing. After a few years they just closed it down. Kids go in there these days for a kiss and a cuddle. And the rest of it, of course. Anyway, this Bailey girl was always with her brothers. Never saw her with any other lads. So she left under a cloud, and soon after that the mother popped off. Died, leaving all those men to live in that house and keep the farm going. The father lived till he was ninety, and the sons are still there. All in their late seventies, I should think by now. Never married. One comes into town for orders about four or five times a year. Well, he did, up until about six months ago, then apparently he fell ill like the others. Incapacitated completely. All three of them, the doctor says. He's the only one who'd stepped inside the house for years. Took them medication. Whatever. Anyway, they were finally put on the list to get their meals delivered to them. Furious, they were. Refused to let anyone in the house. Specially a woman. The only person who would volunteer was that woman who's been living on the trailer park since last summer. She's got three filthy kids and not much money. No sign of the father of course, but the odd man shows his face occasionally, stays around a few days, then disappears again. Anyway, she said she'd do the Baileys. Only one who would. They wouldn't let her in at first. The Bailey brothers, that is. Sounds like a Vegas show act, doesn't it? The rumour is they've got a load of money stashed away somewhere in that big house. They don't ever cry poverty. And any liquor they want, they just call and it gets delivered. They like their liquor apparently. So anyway, this trailer lady persists and eventually they let her in the house, and she volunteers to do a little cleaning for them while she's there. Seems nice of her. Last week, the doctor was called out to one of the brothers. Douglas was away on an emergency, and that young kid, the new assistant down the doctor's, went in his place. Now all hell has broken out.'

'Tell me. Tell me!'

'All the brothers have got crabs, apparently! In their private parts. You know what I mean. And last time they were looked at they were clean as whistles. Down there, anyway. And one of them, 'cos with the enthusiasm of the young, this doctor decides to give them all a good going over, one of them has got herpes! Now they're thinking, Christ, what's going on here? It'll be syphilis next! And it was! Or so the story goes. Probably something like it anyway. They've all been carted off to the emergency room, and then to a hospital for geriatrics. And you've probably guessed by now. It was the nice woman from the trailer park. Desperate for money, for her and the kids, she's been selling her favours, so to speak. The old boys were paying her in cash every time she appeared.'

Daisy's mouth had fallen open, and stayed there. 'Good God, Dorrie, I can't believe it. What a story! What a scandal! I'll admit I thought you were going to tell me they'd found the sister and the mother buried in the back yard somewhere.'

'No. But don't rule it out, girlfriend! People now say they believe those boys *and* the father were getting their rocks off with the daughter, nice to keep it all in the family so to speak. Anyway, the story goes, when the sister, daughter, whatever, got pregnant, they killed her and buried her. When they started on the mother she killed herself, and so they buried her as well!'

Daisy roared with laughter. 'Get out of here! I don't believe a word of it!'

'Well the social disease is true. The trailer broad has moved on quickly, before anyone could say she was an unfit mother and get her kids away from her. I guess nobody actually thanked her for her services. They should have, in my opinion. After all, she was giving the old guys something to remember, and getting enough money from them so she didn't have to go on welfare. Sounds like the American way, if you ask me. Good luck to her. But you can see all the exaggerated sniffing going on in town, can't you? All those church ladies with their noses in the air.'

Daisy was wiping her eyes with the tissues by the bed. She had laughed so much she'd cried. Finally, she said, 'No more beating around the bush, Dorrie. I'm in a good mood now. It'll be easier to tell me about Bob. And what they're saying about me, for that matter.'

Dorrie, content with the good cheer and the flushed cheeks that had settled on her friend's face, told her at last. 'Some people in the town think you've taken leave of your senses. About the baby, that is. The guys tease Bob when they gather in the bar. Call him a slave to his loins. Think that's very poetic. Read the line somewhere, no doubt. Not many cowboys round this way come up with the word "loin". Not so sure about "slave", mind you. Anyway, it's the usual crap, as you can imagine. Like always, when the guys get together and try to outdo each other. Who needs it? Called your Bob a right horny cowboy. Asked him if the trick was to keep your boots on when you're over sixty. I presume they mean in bed. I must say, I'm surprised if any of them take them off! They've started to change their tune a bit lately, though. It's my fella that's telling me this of course. I've been sending him down to the bar so he can listen to what's going on. Not that he needs the encouragement. He thinks every night's his birthday these days. Anyway, your Bob's been getting real pissed off at all the jokes, I can tell you. Grandad daddio, and all that. Then, of course, they've started to listen to their wives and discovered you're seeing another guy up here when your Bob is off doing his job, and whatever else men do when they slam out of the house feeling pissed off with their womenfolk.'

Daisy frowned, puzzled for a moment. 'What other guy? There's only Robert. And John of course.' Her eyes flashed suddenly. 'My God, Dorrie, surely they don't believe something's going on with John, do they? Don't they know he's my son-in-law? What's the matter with these people after all these years?'

'I've just told you the story about the Baileys. All that incest, all those years. Where's your brain, girlfriend? John's not even blood. It's a natural conclusion for the fools to jump to. Old men don't beget babies – because no-one ever has before round these parts. Haven't you heard? If it doesn't happen here, then it shouldn't happen anywhere. And if anything murky *is* going on in any of the weirder families, they should keep it between themselves and kill the rumours before they become fact. Your pregnancy is a fact, honey. Can't deny it. Not the size you are.'

Daisy could say nothing. She was too stunned to think of anything. She would sit quiet. Wait for the anger to move in and quell the tears that were too near her eyes to hide.

'Anyway,' Dorrie said, subdued at last, reaching out and taking her friend's hand that lay listlessly on the bedcover and still clenching a wet tissue. 'Anyway,' Dorrie said again, 'they don't blame Bob for carrying on. That's the men's thought on all this. The general conclusion is that they'd all do the same. Not all the women, of course. They've always thought of you as a nice quiet little woman, and even the old cliché about the dark horse seems unbelievable as far as you're concerned. Do you want to hear the rest? I think you should. It'll make you mad. And that's the place you should be. And I'm right here rooting for you, and on your side.'

'So it's about Bob's "carrying-on" is it? I've told you Dorrie, it's not news to me. He's never changed. He just knows now that it's no secret to me. Though I can't say we actually sit down and discuss it, nothing so confrontational as that, I'm afraid to say. And as for me and John, well it's too ludicrous to even give it time for discussion. He's my son-in-law, and the one and only member of my family who has bothered about me through all this. I have no intention of telling him to stay home because of silly gossip.'

'Believe me, honey, I agree. Let 'em talk. But it's Bob I want to discuss with you. No, let me. Don't say anything until I've done explaining. You remember everyone telling you about the girl he left behind during the war?'

Daisy frowned. 'Well, yes. I can't remember her name. But Mary used to go on and on about them being school sweethearts, and everyone had expected them to marry, even before the war. Bob was thirty when I first met him. If he was ever going to marry her, then he'd have done the deed before I came on the scene.'

'I get that. But he didn't. I guess as long as he got his washing done at home, there was a hot meal on the table, and all that kind of thing, he would have gone on with his bachelor ways for ever. There was always the back of a guy's pick-up in those days, when couples had nowhere to go; because you lived at home till you married. And motel rooms were pretty cheap when the weather got nasty.'

'Why are you telling me all this?'

'I've known the Franckens for years, honey. All my born days, so to speak. When Bob came back after the war, no-one round these parts knew he was married at first. He picked up with Mary-Anne again, that's her name by the way, and for a while there everyone waited for the wedding to be announced. He was just past thirty, for God's sake, and Mary-Anne was only two years behind him. Too old for pick-up trucks, and sick to the back teeth with seedy motel rooms on a rainy afternoon, I should imagine. She started to push his buttons, so to speak. Babies, and all that goes with them, that sort of thing. The old biological thing as always.'

'But his parents knew we'd married in England,' Daisy said, perplexed. 'Why didn't they tell the girl? They adored her, apparently.'

'Sure they knew. They just hoped he'd forget you, and the baby. Plenty of guys did in those years; you can't tell me it didn't cross your mind, waiting in England for him to summon you all those months.'

'Well, yes. But he wrote letters. Sent parcels. And we were married. I thought that meant everything when I was twenty years old and a good Catholic. I had to believe in him. What else was there? Besides, I loved him very much. What did my sweet mother-in-law think was going to happen? That Marje and I would just disappear without any fuss?'

'I think she believed there would be a way of getting the marriage annulled. Remember this, Daisy, he had gone away from her and chosen a wife she'd never met, let alone approved of. So she waited, said nothing to anyone, and, because as a married man with a child it would not be so easy to get laid, Bob said nothing at first, either. Then, when Mary-Anne started to finally get all orange blossomy after all those years, he dropped his bombshell. She went into a tail spin and left for Ohio, I believe, married the first man she met after Bob, on the rebound of course, and that was that. For then, anyway. Then you arrived, along with the baby, and everyone round here loved you. You fitted in real nice. Didn't push your weight around, stayed home and loved your man, it seemed. Yes honey, you fitted in just fine. And Mary could do nothing about it.'

'Where's this leading, Dorrie? It was all so long ago. I can't feel betrayed about something that happened all those years ago. And I feel sorry for poor Mary-Anne.'

'Poor Mary-Anne's marriage didn't last. Not even long enough for any children. She became a teacher, moved back to Idaho – Boise actually – and settled down, apparently. But as a career-minded schoolmarm this time. No more marriage for her.'

'How on earth did you find all this out, for goodness sake?'

'Class reunions through the years. I remember her at school. Two years younger, I was. Nevertheless, I've friends who've known her for years. Word travels. And I used to bump into her occasionally when she was in Boise. We'd chat, be pleasant, that sort of thing. I wasn't a bosom buddy, mind you, but she comes from round here, it's a small-town mentality, her parents still live in Chuttlesford, only twenty miles down the highway.'

'Go on. I think I'm beginning to see the point in all this. Are you going to tell me she's held a torch for my husband all these years, and that's why she never married again?'

'That's exactly what I'm trying to tell you, girlfriend. Seems about ten years ago now—'

'Ten years ago?' Daisy said, interrupting. 'Ten years ago! I don't want to hear this.'

'You'd better. I'd hate you to think for one minute you're being unfair to poor old Bob. Can I go on?'

'Go on.'

'Ten years ago she became head teacher at the high school near her parents. Said they needed caring for, her parents, that is, and that it was only fair she should be near them. She had to explain in some way, you see, why on earth she should leave Boise and take a lower paying job out here in the sticks. She didn't mention there was another sister still living with a husband and four children only a street away from their parents, who had been keeping an eye on the old 'uns for the last few years anyway. Plus a brother who runs the hardware store on their Main Street. Plus, she doesn't even move in with Ma and Pa when she gets back to the old home town, but buys a small place of her own a couple of miles away from the family. Just isolated enough to keep any comings and goings still a part of her own business. Want to know more?'

'No.'

'Are you furious?'

'I have no idea. I'm numb. It's unbelievable. I've never even suspected. At least not this. Is she waiting to marry him? Waiting for me to die or something? What is it?'

Dorrie shrugged. 'God knows. She knows he won't divorce you. I guess she likes what she's got. She doesn't have to wash his underwear anyway. There are compensations to being a mistress.'

Daisy twisted in bed. Grimaced. Frowned, as if allowing all this to sink in. 'So I suppose he just slips over to her when he slams out of here. Disgruntled with me, sorry for himself, he knows he's always got an option?'

'You got it! Now you know why I decided to tell you. It's time to stop feeling guilty. Time to lighten up on yourself all round.'

'I must be either very innocent, or just plain stupid, I guess. To think it's still going on. All these years. Amazing. At their age. She must love him. What about Bob? Does he want to leave? I've told him he can. More than once. As long as he takes care of me and the baby. As long as he takes care of us, he can go.' Daisy could feel the anger rising in her as she thought of the subterfuge of the last ten years. That he'd dared to suggest an abortion. All those times in the last months he'd made her feel isolated, stupid to be so stubborn, when he had another home waiting for him. Another 'wife' to commiserate and understand him. Somewhere to go when things got uncomfortable at home. Maybe this was why he was so horrified about having a new baby. Maybe his lady love was mad about it too. After all, hadn't she remained childless all these years so she was still there for him? And now, after everything, he has to tell her that his wife, of all people – after all, Mary-Anne had probably been told and believed that Daisy and he hadn't shared a bedroom for years – that his old wife was having a post-menopausal baby!

'How could he do it? How could I have been so blind?' Daisy said through clenched teeth. 'I think I hate him.'

'Kick him out, honey. Unless he starts pulling his weight, you have every right to kick him out. Maybe he could take his mother with him.'

'After all those years of putting up with her as well. How could he? He's over sixty, for God's sake! What's the matter with him? I don't understand.'

There were so many factors of the story she had to deal with in her mind, she had no idea where to begin. Sure, she could try to kick him out, but what then? The house was a Francken house. Better if *she* went. But it wasn't just her any more. There was a baby. *His* baby. And what to tell a daughter while she's growing up and asks 'Where's my daddy?' He ran off with an older woman? It wasn't supposed to be like that. Surely husbands run off with schoolgirls when they begin to panic over their fading prowess. Isn't that how it's supposed to work? Bob had been far more sensible. He'd found another wife. One where the question of babies could never come up. Another mother, another housekeeper. That was it. His comfort had become, at long last, more important to him than his sex life. Daisy began to laugh.

'Thank the Lord you're laughing,' Dorrie said. 'I was afraid it might pull the world from under your feet. I didn't want you to face it after the baby came. It's the reason I told you. That, and the fact that Mary meets a variety of folk at that senior centre. Who knows, she might be lucid enough to understand when she comes across this juicy bit of gossip. She would just love to have dropped that into your ears at the very worst moment she could think of.' Dorrie squeezed Daisy's hand, which by now was wet with sweat. So, too, was her forehead. Dorrie reached up and put her hand to her friend's temples. 'You're sweating real bad, honey. How're you feeling? Let me get some water.'

Daisy reached to stop her leaving the room, her head tilted towards the window as she heard Bob's pick-up outside. 'He's here,' she hissed. 'For goodness sake go home, Dorrie. He'll start on you if I confront him with it. He'll know you told me.'

Dorrie hesitated. They could hear Bob coming slowly towards the back door. 'I don't care,' she said, 'I'm not afraid of Bob Francken, girlfriend. I was out of diapers before him! Used to pee his pants at Sunday school right up till he was five.'

'Just go, Dorrie! I'll do this on my own. If you make me laugh, I'll forget how furious I am.'

Dorrie stood up from the bed and bent to kiss her friend on the cheek. 'Are you sure you're OK?'

'I have to be. One of us should have done this

years ago. Go home. I'll maybe call you later. I love you, friend.'

Bob came through the back door. He threw his coat across the back of one of the kitchen chairs. Daisy knew every move. He would pour himself some coffee as usual. Today the coffee pot was still full of the dregs from breakfast. Dorrie left the bedroom door open as she went through to exchange greetings. She sounded terse. Bob's voice was brusque, low. The door slammed as Dorrie went home. Mary, asleep in the living-room, woke up with a start, called out, 'Is that you, son?' Daisy heard him go in to his mother, heard the mutter of their voices, heard the television go on. Soon he would be in to see her. She sat upright in bed, shivered again, and reached for the sweater on the bedpost to put round her shoulders, and waited for the sound of her husband's footsteps across the wooden floor.

Chapter Ten

'Dorrie's gone,' Bob said, 'is she coming back?'

'She's gone to pick something up in the town. Didn't she say anything? You passed her in the kitchen.'

'She just said she'd left some soup on the stove, and maybe she'd see us later.' He threw the evening paper onto the bed. 'Thought you might like to read this. We've made the local press. Or rather, *you* have. Oldest woman to have a baby in these parts since records began. You'd think there was something else they could find to fill a paper that size. Christ! Now the world knows!' He turned away, exasperated, and ran his fingers through his hair. He'd been for a haircut. Not before time, either. His ladyfriend must have been complaining, Daisy thought spitefully as she picked up the newspaper and started to look down the columns.

'I thought the world already knew,' she said. Then, 'What page is it on?'

'I don't know, woman. Sharon gave it to me in that salon of hers. I didn't want to start scouring the darn paper in front of all those broads, for Christ's sake. They'd all be round me like flies once they saw me read it.'

'Why did you go in there anyway? Joe would have cut it for you, like he always does. Why pick Sharon's?'

'Joe was closed for some goddam reason. And I had to cut it tonight.'

Daisy found the piece finally in the centre pages. It was a mere ten sentences long. She kept her finger on the place, right alongside the advertisement for the cinema in the next town. Bob was obviously restless, and her interest in reading it trivial.

'Are you going out?' she asked.

'Yup! Just need to change. Do you want some of that soup before I go? And has the old girl been seen to?'

'I believe Dorrie gave her something when she brought her back from the seniors. She'll probably be hungry again soon. You'll have to see to her. Unless Dorrie's definitely coming back.'

'Shit!' He turned his head away from her and buried it busily into the closet so he could find a clean shirt.

Daisy said quietly, 'Is there something else you need to tell me, before you go slinking off into the night?'

'What's with the tone in the voice, for Christ's sake?'

'Well, for one thing, whatever you want or need to do with your life, you needn't worry about the entire world reading about our fourth child being born. I'd be surprised if many of our neighbours will read it, let alone the outlying towns. So you can disappear without fear of humiliation, old man.'

Bob stared at her. 'The snake really has got hold of your tongue tonight. Must have left you hers by mistake.'

'I wonder why men always refer to a snake as a member of the female fraternity? Like a car, or a boat. I can see those two, you can ride them. But a snake? The metaphor eludes me, I'm afraid.'

'Our son-in-law been here today, then? Unless you've swallowed the dictionary of course, all those big, sarcastic words coming out of your mouth suddenly. Doesn't sound like the Daisy I used to know.'

Daisy turned her head away from him, looking out of a window now opaque with darkness. Her eyes had filled with tears: at her harsh words even more than his. She had no idea how to start talking to him. And talk she must. She felt tired, wanted him to go, so that she could be alone with this feeling of being betrayed. Maybe she should leave the confrontation until the morning. But who knew what day and time would be better? She took a deep breath, and prayed that her voice would not betray her feeling that she was walking into a destiny beyond understanding. 'I need to talk to you, Bob. I need you to sit down in here, with the door closed so your mother won't hear, and listen to me. Will you do that?'

She turned her head back towards him. There was a long silence. Then Bob said quietly, 'Let me go and see if Mom needs anything. I have to make a telephone call, then we can talk.'

'Please don't make that call, Bob. Not now. It can wait until we've done.'

He looked at her for what seemed an age. She could hear her heart beating and the baby stirring. Every part of her seemed aggravated, tense, and in some absurd way excited with her own courage to act so decisively. She watched while he went quietly across the room. The television screeched its banality from the other room.

Bob closed the door. His hands were moist against the handle as he turned it. Wiping them nervously down his trousers, he turned to face his wife. There was a stillness in the room, a quiet broken only by his breathing. Daisy sat as if turned to stone, looking at him, into his eyes, searching his face. 'Waiting like a snake now, certain of its prey,' he thought. 'One false word and she'll swallow me. Why have I never seen this side of her? Why now, when there's nothing left for us, does she begin to excite me?' He sighed. It was time.

She said nothing. Only waited. Bob closed the distance between them at last, moved to the bed, sat beside her and took her hand. Still, she didn't speak. 'Go on, Daisy, so tell me, what's so important?'

Bravado. That's all it was. He knew what she was going to say. They both knew. Why had she never seen how weak he really was? To be married to a man for so long, and fear his strength that

208

kept you docile, only to discover, too late, that he was as afraid as you.

'Your turn, Bob. Don't pretend. Not any more.'

His eyes shifted, then back once more to hers. Another sigh. Still she was patient. What did a few moments matter when the point they'd reached now had taken so long to arrive?

'You know what I'm going to say?' he said.

'Yes, I know,' Daisy said, 'but I want you to tell me.'

'About Mary-Anne?' He said it quickly, before the bravado went. Like a small boy taking off a plaster from a scabby knee.

'Yes, for heaven's sake, about Mary-Anne. Don't procrastinate, Bob. Explain. I'm so full of anger at the moment that I dare not move, in case I lash out.'

'You've changed so much. I can't deal with this.' He fidgeted.

'Mary-Anne. That's what this is about, Bob Francken. Mary-Anne. Ten years of it. Going on at a time when I had no reason to change. I believed everything was OK, that we had as good a marriage as most people around here. We'd brought up kids – not perfect ones, but they seemed to be getting on with whatever life they'd chosen for themselves. And if I felt any disappointment within our relationship, I pushed it out of my mind. We seemed to rub along quite nicely together. I did what I believed was for the best. I wasn't always right. In fact I seemed to have made a mess all round. With everything. The kids' lives are not what I'd convinced myself they were. You and I cannot consider ourselves blameless for that, however good we are at hiding. I'd come to believe over the last few months that perhaps it was all my fault. Because I was always more concerned about keeping you happy and the house free of quarrels. It didn't work. I shouldn't have done that. I should have stood up for myself more often. Stood up to you. You got bored, and the kids withdrew. And all this time, all these years, there was Mary-Anne. So what kind of marriage was I protecting anyway? Don't kid yourself that I didn't suspect about the others that were scattered at various times over the last thirty years. But I felt them not to be serious, no threat, no danger to what I'd told myself we had. We even lie to ourselves, you and I. I had this scenario in my head, that if a wife was content at home, if her libido over the years had shrunk to the point of vanishing, then she should understand her man's fantasies still needed feeding. If that was hard for her, then she should turn a blind eye to his wanderings. Weren't we all so well brought up in those days? And besides, you'd always needed sex more than I did. It happens. And if I felt it a weakness on your part, maybe your strength in other ways made up for it. You always came home. You always would. I'm not the first wife in the world to put up with such crap, and I doubt if I'll be the last, even with the feminist stirring we feel in all our souls. Then came the baby: the mistake, the big surprise, the undoing of us all, it might seem. The one here,' and she took his hand and holding it firmly, pressed it to her. Bob remained rigid. 'You feel it?' she went on. 'Her, I mean. *Our* daughter, Bob. The one you refuse to acknowledge. The one you won't talk about. I believed you'd come round, that it was only fear that governed you. Fear of being too old, of having to share me just when it seemed the time to find out about each other all over again. But that's not the point. That's something else. It's *her* now. This little Francken inside here. The one that's moving so forcefully against your hand while you're trying to pull away. The one you wanted me to abort. The one our other children couldn't bear to think about without disgust. That these middle-aged breasts might have difficulty in feeding, that these arms may sometimes be too tired to hold. Feel the arrogance of life in her as she twists and turns inside me. It's your life as well as mine, husband. And you went on with your sordid little affair and pretended that what was growing inside me was not happening. So I grew strong on my own, fighting for her life, realizing that with her birth I might get another chance after all. And all this time, God help you, all this time—' She threw his hand away from her. Turned from him and let the tears come.

'Don't cry,' he said, 'for Christ's sake, don't do that. I hate it when you cry.'

'It's anger, you fool. This time, when I cry, it's anger. I won't cry any more over you, Bob

Francken. I can't waste any more time or energy or pain over you. It's over.'

There, she'd said it. Not him after all. But during her long explanation, probably the most she'd ever said to him at one sitting, feeling him grow bored so easily with her prattle at other times, she realized that if he were to go, if they were to solve all this in any way possible, it would be up to her. He'd never leave of his own volition. He was too afraid of the opinion of others. And in this close community, folk would gather round her, not him.

Bob cleared his throat. 'I didn't tell you about Mary-Anne because when it started again I didn't think it mattered. The move to Chuttlesford was her idea, not mine.'

'But you didn't stop her.'

He remained silent for a moment. Then, 'What d'you want me to do, Daisy? It's up to you.'

'What did you intend to do, Bob? When the baby arrived, I mean. What then?'

'I hadn't thought about it.'

'Good grief, man! Did you think it would just go away? Did you believe somehow that it would all work itself out? That you could carry on as always? That neither one of us, Mary-Anne or me, would have something to say about the way you wanted to lead your life? Were you always this naïve, or is it some sort of belated mid-life crisis men seem to be having these days? Just tell me the truth this once, and tell me how you feel about this poor woman who's loved you for years. This affair that is creeping nearer and nearer our own doorstep with every passing year. Tell me, for goodness sake!'

Her voice had grown louder with her exasperation. Beneath the bedclothes, her legs were hot and sticky. She longed to throw back the covers, get him out of the room, call up Dorrie, even John, and tell them how brave and assertive she was being. It was the first time during the argument that she'd thought about John. He'd just been there suddenly, popping up like that, approving of her anger, smiling at her in that way he did, taking her seriously with his bottomless brown eyes. The only brown eyes she'd ever seen that couldn't keep a secret. And what she saw there suddenly, in her vision, imagination, was not the approval of a son-in-law, or of one of her children, nor even the same as the look in Dorrie's pale eyes, which showed a friend. His were the eyes of a lover. And as swiftly as the revelation crept in, she threw it out. In fear. To go that way was unthinkable.

Bob said, 'For God's sake, Daisy, don't shout. I don't want my mother in here. None of this could be explained to her.'

'I thought she'd always approved of your childhood sweetheart, that she'd been very upset when you brought over this weepy English wife.'

'You're right. She always liked Mary-Anne. I think that's why we lasted for so long, Mary-Anne and me. It was the first time my mother had liked anything I'd done. When Mary-Anne came over, even as a young girl in her teens, she got on well with both my parents. Her grandparents were from Germany. We thought the same, ate the same things, hated the same things. And everything my mother said, Mary-Anne agreed with, even when she was complaining about me and Dad.'

Without bitterness, only curiosity, Daisy said, 'Why on earth didn't you marry her? You would have been marrying your mother. Isn't that what Mary wanted all along? To be so ingrained in you, her only son, that you would marry someone who mirrored her in every way?'

'I don't know what she wanted. Not then, not now. I don't know what any of you want. I only know that I want a quiet frigging life. Like we had before this goddam madness of yours started!' He stood up angrily, pushing her away with too much fervour, so that she fell back against the headboard. The pillows behind her had slipped, and her head hit the headboard, bringing tears to her eyes. Bob was oblivious, and by now, angry as well. He didn't want to be blamed for any of this. All these women taking over his life. It was never what he wanted. Damn them all. 'I never felt I wanted to marry her, darn it! Mother should've frigging married her! The way she carried on when she heard about you. Not Mary-Anne. She didn't know about you at first. The woman living next door filled her in. She cried on my mother's shoulder! Left the town, eventually. I was glad, for God's sake! That's how mighty my commitment was! Listen girl, I didn't want to marry you all that much. I was thirty years old, for Christ's sake, I'd avoided it up till then, was enjoying my life. Had to do the right thing though, didn't I? You being pregnant and all. But when I came back here I was pleased. About you, I mean. Mary-Anne was still here then, and Mom of course, ranting and raving something about an annulment. How the hell she thought I'd got you pregnant, I don't know. Between her and Mary-Anne, you were a bit of heaven when you arrived. You never asked anything of me. You never said a thing. Sure, you cried when I used to go back to Boise after the weekend, but I liked that. You missed me, had no life when I wasn't there. I'd never had that sort of thing before. You were always there, always willing to fall into bed when I'd come home on a Friday. Sex was the only way I knew how to stop the crying. I thought you were unhappy for love of me. A guy likes that. He can deal with that. So Mary-Anne eventually moved away. Nothing stopped Mom complaining of course, but who cared? For me, you were the tops as far as a wife could be. How the hell was I supposed to guess then that it would never be anything else? I made the best job I could. What was I supposed to do?'

'I was crying because I was homesick,' Daisy said quietly, rubbing the back of her head where she'd hit the bedstead. 'I was crying because your mother made me cry.'

For a moment, a quietness fell once more across the room. Already they both knew there was no going back. Too much had been said. No-one should have too many secrets or revelations flung at them by an old love. Daisy was sensible enough to know that a different kind of feeling can find its way into a marriage over so many years. A kind of love provoked by experiences only known to parents of the same children, sleepers in the same bed, lovers in spite of themselves, thrown together by the necessity of their very nature.

Now they had, once more, lost the power to speak to each other with understanding. Daisy was tired. And Bob yearned for a comfort he was unable to find in his wife's arms, even if she had been willing to give it. The day was over. And so were they.

'Now what?' Bob said. 'What do we do now?'

'You'd better go,' Daisy said, 'what else is there?'

'For the night, or what?'

'You've made your bed, Bob. Just as I made mine all those years ago. All our messes are ours to clean up. No-one can do that for you, not finally. You don't want the baby. You've been honest about that. Go to Mary-Anne. At least let one of us come out with something through all this mess and pain. If it has to be her, so be it. She probably deserves it more than either of us. At least she's faced the truth about her feelings and lived her life to nurture them. Which is more than can be said for us.'

'For how long? I mean, how long should I stay with her? Do I come back for the birth? Is that how it goes these days? Where the hell's my life all of a sudden?'

'Good God man, I can't tell you that. You owe her something after all these years! I won't sit here and give you my blessing for a wonderful life. I have little love left for you after all this. It's taken me a long time to admit that to myself. I thought I never would. It never crossed my mind, at my age, that I would have a chance to change my life so radically. Maybe even now we won't be able to, we'll drift back together for the comfort of familiarity. Maybe you'll have to move on even further, God help you. Maybe I will. Neither of us can make that decision right now. I don't know. I only know I want you out of here tonight, and I need some time to myself before the baby comes. Tell me truthfully, Bob, is it love you feel for me right now? Does anything at all flow hot through your veins these days?'

There was a long, long pause, while Bob stared at the tip of his shoes, and then finally, once more, at his wife. 'No. No to both those questions. There, is that truthful enough for you? Nothing hot's shot through my veins for years now! Not that I wouldn't like it, even at sixty. I can appreciate it more than I did at twenty. I'd make sure I hung onto it for longer. Enjoyed it at a slower pace. I'd like to think I could go off and live a single man's life again.'

Daisy laughed. 'You never *did*, for God's sake!'

'I know. That was my second thought. I went

from Ma to the Army, and then to you. Now it'll be Mary-Anne, I guess.'

Daisy began to get out of bed. Her legs were shaking, but she was glad for a moment of the chill in the bedroom. She'd grown so hot and sticky during their discussion. 'I'll pack a bag for you,' she said. 'Just a small one. That way we can tell ourselves there's still a door open. Will that make you feel better?'

'You mean instead of a suitcase?' Bob smiled. For the first time that evening. Daisy saw in his face how glad he was for her to make the decisions. Without commitment to either woman. 'Not even his unborn daughter,' she thought ruefully as Bob went back into the living-room to deal with his mother.

Mary was confused and upset at her son's departure. Neither he nor Daisy told her the truth, of course. As far as she was concerned he was going to Florida on some sort of business. It didn't make sense, of course, but then neither did she.

'What business of yours could possibly take you to Florida?' Daisy asked him as he was putting on his coat. 'She's going to think about that all night and ask questions in the morning.'

'I picked the place that was furthest away. It made me feel safer,' he said. Then, 'You were right, Daisy. I'm beginning to feel a little – what did you call me a while back? Oh yes – pathetic.'

'Don't worry about it, husband. As soon as you reach Chuttlesford you'll feel wonderful again.'

And when she finally shut the door on him, watching his body language change as he got into his car, and realized that at least this particular subterfuge was over, he was on the way to someone who would make him feel good about himself again, and he could kid himself that in some way he really did have his wife's blessing in spite of what she'd said. After all, hadn't it been she who told him to go in the end? Daisy knew that in a few weeks, days even, he would have forgotten that evening's feeling of mutual failure, and it would once again be all her fault. Bob would never stay humble for long. It would never sit easily on his broad shoulders. But for now, there was this breathing space.

What she would actually do with Mary, they hadn't thought about. For now, she would call Dorrie and ask her for suggestions. Dorrie seemed to be thinking straighter than anyone else. Seeing Mary's face at the moment Bob said he was going away, Daisy had felt only pity for her. Age had weakened her more than anyone realized, and in spite of her often cruel tongue, these days she had only the past to hang on to. Even her enemies confused her, she had long forgotten the reason she hated them. So Daisy went back into her bedroom to find her slippers and then to try and settle her mother-in-law. Dorrie would have to wait for the news until the following day. Tonight was hers. A feeling of elation filled her heart. To be alone and not lonely was surely the best of emotions. It was the first time for her, that alien feeling. Most of her married life she'd felt isolated within the overbearing Francken family. There had never been a place to hide in safety. Solitude was a fantasy for which she hungered. Now, for one night, it was within her grasp. Tomorrow she would think again.

'Can't believe he went. Just like that. Why didn't he take his mother with him? How can you manage her on your own? Suppose she falls down in the middle of the night?' Dorrie said. She'd appeared the next morning with paper bags full of groceries. They sat on the front porch with mugs of hot chocolate and cookies: chocolate chip oatmeal eaten straight from the packet, crumbs settling round them as they ate with unabated zest. Mary had felt unwell when she woke that morning, more confused than usual, not even mentioning Bob's absence, and scarcely taking in either Daisy or Dorrie. So Daisy had put her in the old rocker at the front door and tucked blankets round her. She was asleep in no time. The sunshine and moderate warmth had taken them by surprise, and Daisy had longed for fresh air for weeks. Sipping the sweet cocoa instead of her usual morning coffee reminded her somehow of being a child. It had been Ovaltine in those days. Ovaltine or Horlicks. 'Sex for the lonely.' That's what Gary had called it once when he'd seen her on the way to bed one evening with her mug and saucer. She'd laughed at him. 'Much better than that, son. Just you wait a few more years!'

'I felt so sorry for her suddenly,' Daisy said. 'How could we just uproot her like that? Maybe Sharon would stay some nights. If I can find the courage to ask her, that is.'

'What's Sharon's problem? Thought she liked babies. Thought there'd be knitting going on by now. What about that? Have you got anything in yet? For the baby, I mean.'

'I didn't dare. You know. If I'd lost her I don't think I could have borne to look at all those matinee jackets and new diapers. And Sharon wants her own babies, not mine.'

The thought quietened her for a moment. There was still the problem of Robert's marriage, not that it was ever mentioned. 'An inward angst,' she thought to herself, 'which does none of us any good.' She saw the pair of them only on the Friday nights now. She wondered what they'd do now that Bob had left. Would they still be there, every Friday, along with the usual casserole and too-rich dessert? And should she call Marjorie, and tell her where her father was, and what they'd both decided to do for the time being? Surely it was their business now, hers and Bob's, and nothing to do with the rest of the family? But in the cold light of day she knew the secret would not stay at rest for long. Someone would have to be told something. Then she knew. She would tell John. The thought came into her head with such ease it took her by surprise.

'I'll call John in the morning,' she said. 'D'you think the children know about Mary-Anne?'

'Robert must. And would he dare to keep it from Sharon?'

'I doubt it.' They both laughed. Then Daisy said, 'There's more to come, you know. It was all too easy. It's not supposed to be like this. Not the end of a marriage. He won't just go. How can he? I was euphoric last night. The light of day brings reality crashing down. Or, in my case, about four this morning. That was when the birds woke me. The racket they make at this time of year always wakes me early. Bob won't stay away long, however much he wants to go to this woman right now. It won't take him long to realize he's simply swopped one trap for another. And the mess he's left behind won't just disappear. I'm afraid I just don't want him. But do I have the right to make that decision? What with the baby coming and all. It's nice to be free for a while. To think about myself. But what then? The thought of going back to that old life fills me with dread. I just don't see a way out, and I've left it a bit late for that knight on his white charger, wouldn't you say?'

For once, Dorrie said nothing.

'But at least I spoke my mind for the first time,' Daisy said. 'He can't make that disappear. At least he knows there'll be no more wool pulled over my eyes. What to do about his negative feelings towards the baby is beyond me. Besides, how do you live with a man you can't forgive? How will a child survive in a home full of regrets and resentment?'

'God knows, honey. But plenty of women do.

What choice do you have in the end? No money of your own. No home except his. You might come through it by the skin of your teeth and turning your back if something better shows its face, but your daughter will have to get out as soon as she's able if she wants to spend her life free of therapy.'

'Funny isn't it? We can feel as independent as we like, as free-thinking as we want, us women I mean, but unless we have our own money there's little we can do about living the lives we want.'

They both stared in silence down the street, seeing the land stretch out before them once the line of houses had finished. Early blossom on the trees stood proudly, straining for the sun, soaking in its spring rays with unashamed delight, making the most of it before its short seasonal demise as it yielded to the leaves that inevitably followed.

Chapter Eleven

'I guess I'm lucky,' Dorrie said, much later that day, 'being the breadwinner, I mean. And the old man's not too bad: snores at night, but then according to him I grind my teeth so loud it wakes him up! He says it won't be that long before they have to come out, and he'll get a decent night's sleep for the first time in our married life! I told him, grinding one's gums sounds even worse. You should hear them all down the seniors when I pick up the old girl sometimes! I can't see the point of having teeth when you're that age, false ones that is, most of them take them out when they eat. Say it's easier.' She shuddered. 'God help us, creeps up on you, doesn't it? Can't escape it.'

'Old age?' Daisy smiled. 'I have to say, being pregnant pushed all that out of my head. I used to dwell on it for hours. Wondering which one of the kids would ever take either one of us in when the time came. Can you imagine spending your last hours with my Marjorie?' They both laughed. 'I can't just sit here all day. I feel I must let someone in on the change of circumstances. But God, it's great to be my own mistress for a while. I wonder how many men realize how much we love being away from them sometimes?'

'None of them honey. They believe our lives start and stop when they come and go in it. Believing we function on our own scares the crap out of them.'

Daisy thought for a moment. Then, 'I'd better not call John. Marjorie would be furious.' She didn't tell Dorrie how she suddenly longed to hear his voice, or that her son-in-law did not fit the picture of a man that Dorrie painted so often.

'Let her find out for herself,' Dorrie said. 'The news will get to Boise far quicker than you think. Then the shit will hit the fan! Funny, your Marge seems to be one of the few of our sex that's broken the pattern. Got financial independence and a dish for a husband. Doesn't work though, does it? Not the happiest of creatures is she?'

'What makes you think that? She's always been irritated with life. Even when she was in Junior High. Marriage didn't change her one bit.'

'Maybe she knows her old man is not as smitten as she would like.'

Daisy stared at her friend. From the rocker, Mary stirred and cried out in her sleep.

Dorrie said, 'You're going to have to solve the problem of the old girl before long as well. She's already two sandwiches short of a picnic. Things can only get worse, Daisy girl. You can't manage her and the baby, with or without Bob. She'll have to go to the retirement home. Can't put it off for ever.'

'Bob couldn't do it. They left the old man until the doctor threatened to take him there himself. Lucky for us all he died before it became necessary.'

'Well she won't. And believe me, honey, if you move out and leave the Francken home to the Franckens, your Bob won't think twice about having her committed!'

'Where would I go?' Daisy said.

And the pair of them had talked their way back to the beginning of the circle.

Daisy, having given herself one perfect day in limbo, telephoned her daughter the following day. She'd had a harrowing night with Mary, who had called out so many times for her husband, and then Bob, that Daisy finally sat by her bed and tried to comfort her, praying she would go back to sleep. Eventually the old woman did, after screaming, as Daisy entered her room, that she, Daisy, had come to steal her husband, and round these parts, women knew what to do with female home-wreckers. It should have made Daisy laugh, but in some sort of way, the words from the lips of her poor mother-in-law scared her with their violence. The venom on the old woman's face, the wrinkled hands reaching out, witch-like, as if to tear a person's eyes out, made her shudder. 'It was as if she'd often done it,' she would tell John when next she saw him, 'as if we were still living in a last frontier town in the eighteen hundreds, when women were scarce and men were plentiful. She was the wife defending her man from the local whore. I'm told that's all there was back then in the small towns: wives and whores, and nothing in between. It explains a lot about some American men, I must say!'

But, inevitably, Mary calmed down, letting weakness overcome her by weeping into her pillow and hiding her frightened eyes from her daughter-in-law as best she could. By then, she'd recognized Daisy as a friend, if not kin, and was so glad, it seemed, to see her there, in the middle of the night, and in the centre of a living nightmare, that she allowed her poor outstretched hands to be held until she stopped shaking. Daisy's heart went out to her. For all her brashness, Mary was lost when the men in her life left her side. Husband long dead, which seemed to puzzle her when she was told, as if confused that he'd dared to go before her, and without her permission, and now her son, who had gone away and left this strange woman in the house. Her whole life had been centred on the men in it, and her control of them. She'd started to wither when other women moved in. She fell asleep at last, while Daisy lay down beside her on the old feather bed, too soft beneath her to support her back so far into her pregnancy. It was the closest they'd ever been, she and her mother-in-law, and Daisy let her own tears fall silently down her cheeks that this strange kind of comradeship should bind them now, too late, with Mary confused over whose hand she was clutching with such fervour.

Daisy did not go back to sleep that morning. The birds were in full voice. As her mother-in-law snored and loosened the grip on Daisy's hand, the sun came up slowly and weakly through the window of the bedroom; she quietly disentangled herself and went silently to the kitchen to brew some coffee. She felt strangely alienated from her surroundings, even her own movements, as she drifted slowly and with increasing weakness around the familiarity of her own kitchen. She put it down to tiredness, even the giddiness when she got too quickly out of her chair once to pour herself some water. Her mouth was parched. Her lips stiff with dryness, and she was aware of herself licking them constantly with her tongue. She should have gone back to her own room to lie down, called Dorrie. But the feeling of utter weariness kept her in that chair, sipping her glass of water, praying for this black cloud that had suddenly entered her resilient soul to depart as quickly as it had arrived. And she knew it was time to think of another place for Mary, somewhere her mother-in-law could live out her last years with professional carers. People who could share the confused world of the senile with sensibility and patience. Bob would have to be told. Bob would have to deal with it. Daisy sat and thought of all the years of wishing the old woman a million miles away, and now, here it was, the answer to her long, silent prayers. It was strange now how quickly her mother-in-law had reached that point. Oh, Daisy had seen the retrogression over the last few years, but at that moment she seemed to remember having what she'd believed at the time was an almost normal conversation with the old woman – was it yesterday? And now, in the quiet of that spring morning, Daisy realized a whole era in all their lives was about to change, and the frightening thing for her was that she had no idea which direction she could take. For the first time there was no-one to take her by the hand and pull her in a direction she didn't want to go. That morning she wanted no changes in her life; she was too afraid to trust herself. And then, inside her, the baby moved, and there was no time for self-indulgence, no space for indecisiveness. It wasn't the circumstances that had to change. It was her.

At eight a.m. she rang Marjorie. But her daughter barely heard her mother's greeting before she herself started to speak.

'Dad called us last night,' Marjorie said bluntly. 'You two are really something else! Dad's quite obviously taken leave of his senses, and you seem to have pushed him there. You're both behaving like children.'

'That's not why I called you Marjorie,' Daisy said quietly, in spite of the hint of anger she felt immediately at the tone in her eldest child's voice. 'It's about your grandmother.'

'Is she ill?' Marjorie said briskly. 'Have you called the doctor?'

'Not yet. I've been sitting with her all night. She's been very disturbed. The surgery's not open until nine.'

'Do you have Dad's number? He'll have to come

back. Gran will be better if he's around. I thought the pair of you would have realized that, before you made these grand and irrational gestures. For God's sake, Mom, you can't manage in that house on your own at night. If you won't telephone Dad then I will!'

'I don't want him here, Marjorie. I simply want Mary to go somewhere she'll be able to get constant attention. I can do it no longer. Besides, it's time. The rest of it? The stuff between your dad and me is not your business. I'd be appreciative if you wouldn't make it so.'

Marjorie was furious. Daisy waited in silence at her end of the telephone, hearing her daughter's exasperated intake of breath, her mental gathering of the right words to explode into her mother's ear.

At last. 'I will not be a partner in this ludicrous situation between you and Dad. And that doesn't mean I have to stand on the sidelines and say nothing. I've already told him not to be a fool, and to take himself home where he belongs. Whatever problems you both have at this moment will have to be put aside. The pair of you have both reached an age when you must live with your mistakes, and make the best of them. I'm damned if I'll have any part of this stupid behaviour. And neither will my husband, even if you are determined to drag him along with you. Dad will be back. I've warned him. And now, with Grandma completely driven out of her mind, it is even more necessary to have him with you, at least at night.' There was a long silence. Finally, 'Are you there, Mother? Are you listening? Did you hear what I'm saying?'

'Yes Marjorie, I can hear you perfectly. There isn't the slightest reason for you to shout.'

'Well then. Answer me.'

'In what way?'

At the other end of the telephone, Marjorie sighed, as if trying to reason with a stubborn child. 'I'm trying to tell you, Mom, that Dad must come home. Now, before the baby arrives. He will have to put up with the new addition to the family, and you will have to put up with him putting up with it! You are not teenagers. Other people cannot give up their lives to placate either of you in your silly little caprices.'

Daisy couldn't stop herself thinking how much John had seemed to influence even his wife in her choice of language, so easily did his love for words engage you if you stayed around him for long enough. Daisy felt a warm and safe delight when John entered her mind. She wondered if he was standing next to Marjorie as the telephone conversation burned across the wires. She could only hear the sound of her daughter, irascible as ever.

'Will you answer me, Mom? What are you going to do?'

'I'm going to have some breakfast, Marjorie, and then I'm going to ask advice from Douglas about Mary, because quite obviously I'm going to get nothing from you. I merely wondered, which is why I called you in the first place, if one had to sign anything legal before arranging a place somewhere for your grandmother, and whether I had to speak to your father about it first, and if so, do you have the number of this woman he's with? Everyone but me seems to know all about her, so I presumed it wouldn't have got past you that your dad had had a mistress for the last decade.'

'For God's sake, Mom, there is no need whatsoever to get so melodramatic. He's over sixty. He's hardly likely to run off for sex these days. Merely comfort. Even you must see that. It's hardly been what anyone would call "comfortable" at home lately, what with your obsessiveness about having this baby. But what's done is done. Now is the time to be sensible, make the best of it. Get some sort of order in your lives instead of all this drama you're both causing.'

'I sincerely hope that as your father has left me for an older woman, he is at least getting some sexual satisfaction from it! I can't think of any other strong reason that might, in his old-age lust, urge him to want his own child aborted so he can carry on as usual!'

'I can't talk to you when you're being as dramatic as this.'

'Then don't. Give me your father's telephone number and together we will sort out some place for his mother. I can manage myself for the next two months, and afterwards come to that, and your dad can stay where he feels comfortable. With Mary-Anne. I do not see the problem. At least, I don't see *your* problem with the way we want to live our lives.'

Daisy felt very brave at that moment. Words came easily to her. She heard Dorrie let herself in at the back door. She held up one hand to motion her friend to stay quiet. 'Has it occurred to you, Marjorie, that I no longer want to live with your father, and I doubt very much if he wants to live with me. Mary-Anne has quite obviously waited for as long as she is able, and all I can say is, it's her turn now. Do you have anything else you feel a need to say to me?'

But, surprisingly, Marjorie had put the telephone down.

Daisy turned to Dorrie with a smile. 'That's told her,' she said, and then her knees went from under her and she felt herself falling. Someone, and it seemed like her voice, said, 'Oh dear Dorrie, I think I'm going to faint. Can you get me—' And that was all.

The next time she opened her eyes for long enough to be aware of her surroundings, she was in a strange bed, in a room with bright lighting, and a lot of white.

'Oh dear. Oh dear. Am I dead?' she said, to no-one in particular, because she could see no sign of anything human. Then a face came into focus above her eyes, one with a strange-looking hat on her head, which was white as well, and when this unfamiliar irridescent woman smiled, Daisy said with surprise, 'My goodness, even your teeth are the whitest I've seen! It must be heaven.'

'You're in hospital, Mrs Francken. We've been sedating you to keep you resting.'

'Is my baby here? Is she here? It's too early. She must go back.' And as Daisy began to struggle to sit up, the nurse's arms held her firmly down. There was some sort of contraption going into Daisy's arm. 'It's just a drip, Mrs Francken, for your vitamins. You're very anaemic. You must go on resting.'

Daisy sank back onto the pillows, her voice breaking, the tears coming quickly to her eyes. 'But my baby. My baby.'

Beside her, the nurse's smile was still in evidence. 'She's fine. She had a bit of a flutter. Frightened us all, I can tell you, but she's still with you. Determined, that one. You'll have your work cut out when she arrives! She's definitely going to let you all know who's boss.'

Daisy's tears were gone as quickly as they had arrived, and she was smiling. 'Thank you. Thank you.' She felt sleepy again. And as hard as she tried, she couldn't keep her eyes open.

'Dr Hart will be round later, Mrs Francken. Then you can sit up and have some supper this evening. And see your family if you like. They've been worried.'

Daisy wanted to be smart and retort 'That's all you know', but the utterly delicious feeling of drug-induced sleep crept over her again, and for the first time since the pregnancy began, she felt in safe hands. The last thought across her mind was of John. She wondered if anyone had told him.

The next time she opened her eyes, Robert was sitting by the side of the bed reading a women's magazine. She lay still and looked at him. Oblivious of her scrutiny for a brief while, he turned a page, and the quietest of sighs escaped his lips. His eyes shifted and met hers. Daisy smiled, Robert smiled back and took her hand across the white hospital coverlet.

'All right Mom?'

'I feel more with-it this time of waking,' she said, 'they must have reduced the drugs. I was just beginning to enjoy them as well! Can I sit up, son? With this thing in my arm, I mean.'

He helped her into a sitting position and pushed up the pillows behind her.

'Have you been here long?' she asked.

'Not long. John's been in. Said he'll be back later.'

'Where's your dad?'

Robert shifted uncomfortably in his chair. He wished his older sister were here. Abrasive as she was, she was always better at explaining things.

'Dad's taken the trailer upstate. For a little break, he said. With – you know—' He squirmed again, and reddened. He couldn't look at his mother. He almost understood why his father had refused to come back from his trip because of this last event. There was nothing to say to anyone. Like his dad, Robert had never believed that talking about something would solve it. Some situations were best left to find their own level.

And as for his parents? He found himself rather admiring both of them. Not that he said that to Sharon, who was beside herself with embarrassment over the whole situation. 'My God,' she'd said, 'the whole town knows what's happening. I've never been a part of anything so horrid. Some people are saying your mother's having another man's baby, and that's why your dad left. It's disgusting! Just going off with that schoolmistress! And on the same day your gran's been put away. Didn't even come to see your mom. Now everyone'll believe it's not his baby. I can't believe it. I can't bear it! All those people trying to catch my eye in the salon. Trying to see how much I know. I don't know what to say to them. And you're no help, Robert Francken!'

'You know Mom's not been carrying on. Why don't you tell 'em so? Who the hell do they think she's been seeing, for Christ's sake?'

'Well if you must know, that kid that delivers from the store on Main Street, he said there's always that tall fair guy up there when he's taken the order.'

Robert had stared at her. 'What tall fair guy? You can't mean John?'

'Well that's what he said. And you must admit it, he's been up there a lot these last weeks, cooking, and reading to her. And they laugh together. All the time. He's always been a bit soft on your mom. You just don't notice things like that.'

'Maybe that's because it's too gross to even think about. John's her own son-in-law, you crazy

236

woman! Course it's Dad's baby. He just doesn't want it, that's all.'

Of course, Robert relayed nothing of this to his mother as he sat there, by her hospital bedside, and held her hand. He was glad it was just him visiting. That there was no-one else in the family there at this moment.

Daisy was not upset about Bob being half-way across country with his lady love. She still had the baby. No longer did she feel that this child inside her had anything to do any more with her errant husband. And she was glad. 'But what about your gran?' she asked. 'Surely Dad saw her before he went?'

'Yes. Not for long, though. Marjorie had got her into that home just off the state highway. Remember? It's got all those trees around it. We saw it when it was being built, about five years ago. Sharon used to say she'd put me away in there if I didn't smarten up.' He grinned. 'She was joking. I think.'

'It looks a nice place. Will you visit?'

'We're going up on Sunday for the first time, when she's settled in more. The person in charge said it would be better to leave it for the first few days, seeing she's so confused an' all. You know.'

'Yes.' Daisy fell back against the pillows, trying to envisage Mary in those strange new surroundings. She hoped the family had seen to it that she had her old chair with her. Daisy felt quite sad.

Robert didn't tell Daisy the rest of it just then. The screaming that his gran had done when Dr

Hart came with one of the helpers from the home, and he and Marjorie had followed the doctor's car to the big house resting amongst those trees. It was the first time he'd ever seen his big sister cry. Not that it had softened her up when she finally dried her tears. If anything, her unusual behaviour made her angrier than ever. He tried to put his arm round her at one time, and she pushed him off, declaring 'This is not the time for sentiment, damn you.' Robert remembered John staring at her with no expression in his eyes when she'd said it.

'Does she know where she is?' Daisy asked, concerned.

'Gran? I don't think so. The woman that runs the place says she just keeps saying they must get Jenny to the doctor's, and when's the snow going away? I told her we have no Jenny in the family as far as I know. Perhaps Gran is just living some sort of imaginary life. The nurse said they do that sometimes. Perhaps because they don't like the one they're in. But Gran didn't look very happy when she was crying for Jenny, either. I don't understand any of it.'

Daisy squeezed his hand, wishing she could make him feel better about all of it. Instead, she stared out of the window, biting her lip, determined not to cry. Jenny. That had been the saddest story she'd ever heard about the Francken family. It never failed to remind her how tough those women and men must have been in those pioneer days around those parts. She'd often wished that spirit could have found its way into her own very English and 'frightened-of-it's-own-shadow' soul.

She told John the story later that day, after Douglas Hart had been in to see her and ask if she would prefer to stay where she was for the rest of the pregnancy. 'I rather fear this baby of yours is in too much of a hurry to get here at times,' he said. 'I'd be better pleased if you'd let me arrange a bed for you for these last seven to eight weeks. It's the only way I can keep you in bed all twenty-four hours of the day. I can see that now. Even with Mary gone.'

'Goodness Douglas, where on earth d'you think we'll be able to find that sort of money? The insurance would never cover it all.'

She was anxious to get home, but fearful for the baby. There had to be some arrangement she could come up with that would keep her safe at home, and deliver her to the hospital at the right time without any unnecessary dramatics.

So Douglas had gone away muttering about her catching the Franckens' stubbornness, and having managed not to bring up the subject of Bob even once. 'We must just concentrate on the matter in hand,' he'd said while he was there, 'leave everything else on the sidelines, just for now. It will all get sorted later. Problems are often like that. If you leave them alone for a while, they have a habit of disappearing.'

'Not this time,' she thought, nodding happily at him.

★   ★   ★

'So it's quite obvious the whole town knows where Bob's gone,' she thought to herself, lying there as the sun was going down outside the hospital windows. Marjorie had called, and so had Dorrie, just to enquire after her, and send love. 'That'll be from Dorrie,' she thought grimly.

She'd had supper and was beginning to feel sleepy again when John came. Opening her eyes, pulling herself away from the sleepiness, feeling another's eyes upon her, someone's smile to greet her.

'Hello Daisy. Are you awake enough, or shall I come back tomorrow?' And he was there. At the bottom of her bed. Carrying, of all things, a very large box of English chocolates, and what looked like some library books.

'No grapes?' she said, smiling too quickly to hide the delight in her eyes at the sight of him.

'I don't like grapes. But I do like Cadbury's chocolate. We can eat them together, and maybe give that daughter of yours, the one so anxious to get here early, a taste for them too.' And with that he sat next to her on the bed, and leaned across to take both her hands and kiss her swiftly and gently on the mouth, making the hairs on her arms stand up for some extraordinary reason.

'You smell nice,' she said inanely. 'Is Marjorie buying new soap?'

'Well now, Mother-in-law, I think I should tell you it's usually me that buys the soap in the house. I have a passion for the smell of lavender. It reminds me of a history teacher I had a crush on at high school.'

'She must have been a strange history teacher to smell of lavender at such a young age.' And Daisy wondered why they were having such a silly conversation. But she couldn't stop smiling. And all the time, John was holding her hands and stroking the skin between the thumb and index finger.

'Who said she was young?' he said, his eyebrows raised. 'I remember her very well. Sara Dyson was a respectable married woman of forty-two at the time. I believe I was coming up to my eighteenth birthday.' He began to unwrap the chocolates. 'She gave me a taste for gentility at a very young age. Cheer leaders have never done anything for me.'

She would remember for years how her heart jumped at his words. She recognized something in his eyes, something in the pit of her stomach, that made her feel like seventeen again, and with fear and trepidation she tried to push it away. A path lay ahead, one she should not tread, not in any way. The journey would be disastrous for her, the baby, John, and most of all, for Marjorie. And that was the moment she finally accepted it. She turned her head to hide her eyes from him. But there was nowhere to look. Only the tops of the trees through the window, swaying fiercely, as if even nature was working up some kind of fury over the forbidden thoughts of an unseemly mother.

'What is it, Daisy?' John's voice, low, intense, pushing her down that path that every part of her was trying to ignore.

'I was remembering about Jenny,' she burst out,

delighted with the swiftness of her thoughts. She prayed she'd fooled him for the time being.

'Jenny?' he said, pulling back to look at her. 'That's who Mary was muttering about. Is that the same Jenny? What has it to do with you?'

Daisy felt relieved as the proximity between them lengthened, and her trembling began to subside. 'Jenny was Mary's youngest sister. She told me about her once, when I first came to Idaho. I think it was her way of trying to make me count my blessings at that time. I was being particularly weepy round about then if I remember correctly, and Bob was still working in Boise. I felt very sorry for myself, I'm afraid. A milksop, were her words I believe.' Daisy smiled grimly at the memory. 'She sat me down and told me about her early life as a child. I must admit, when she'd finished, I did feel rather ashamed at my own rather lame excuses for crying so much in my room. Seemed I knew very little about real isolation. And she was right. I'd forgotten about Jenny's story until Robert mentioned that Mary was calling her name out loud. Funny, after all these years. Poor Mary.'

'Tell me the story. Talk to me, Daisy.' He held her hand again.

And Daisy was so suddenly full of the tragedy of Jenny and the rest of that young family, growing up in such poverty at the end of the last century, she offered no resistance, despite the way her hand felt as it lay in his. The erosion of common sense had already begun its journey.

Chapter Twelve

'Mary came from a big family. Despite their poverty, her parents managed to bring nine children into the world, rearing them in a one-roomed cabin up in the hills, miles from the nearest town. Her father, apparently, was a very religious man, what denomination she never said, but it seems he believed very thoroughly that most institutionalized churches had got it all wrong, and everyone was well on the way to the flames of damnation. Particularly in the big towns. Even Idaho city seemed enormously sinful to him. He wanted no part of letting his own family be influenced in any way. He earned a little money from the things he sold as he made his way round the state in their large old wagon. Old-fashioned medicines, herbs, that sort of thing. God will provide and all that. You know how it goes. Finally, he found this broken-down old cabin, miles from anywhere or anyone, and settled his wife and children while he went off to raise what money he could. Mary's mother grew potatoes and carrots apparently in the patch of earth out-side their home, and they scraped by as best they could. Most of the time was spent praying and learning lessons from the Bible, told to them by the mother as they sat together in the evenings, when Dad was away. He didn't approve of the Bible. Mary's mother had been a Catholic when she was growing up. Her folk had been farmers, could only speak their mother tongue, German. Their eldest daughter, Berte, Mary's mom, had picked up English from neighbours. But poor Berte, at the age of fourteen, had got herself pregnant by this travelling salesman person who had been passing through one spring, and her upright Catholic German-speaking parents were so horrified they gave her to him the following year when he happened that way again. Can you imagine that? Just giving away one of your children? But it was tougher then, and when a daughter married, it was for the husband to feed her, and take the burden from her father. I should think. So there this man was, stuck with a fifteen-year-old wife, because with a shotgun at his back even *he* was quick to marry, plus a three-month-old son. It was the last Berte ever saw of her parents. Cruel. A lot of punishment for a roll in the hay, wouldn't you say?' Daisy had relaxed again. She leaned her head back against the pillows, and took a chocolate from the box that lay between them.

'Go on,' John said, playing with the heavy gold band that felt loose on her marriage finger. 'You tell a fine tale, Daisy. And no-one ever tells me stories. Not even my mother did.' A shadow passed briefly across his face, and Daisy caught her breath. He never spoke of his parents.

Apparently they had both died some years ago. She would have to ask him one day. Not then. 'So he was not a Catholic?' John went on. 'This passing tinker, I'll call him. Mary's dad.'

'Goodness no! Black sheep from somewhere I imagine. Mary never told me much about him. Except how quickly the family grew. I guess he must have made his poor wife pregnant every time he came home, and then went off again while she struggled with each situation on her own. So much for his weird religious beliefs. He always said, according to Mary, that God had put women on this earth to suffer and atone for the seduction of Adam.'

'Well, that's a convenient way of looking at it. The more places he dropped his seed, I guess, the more he was doing God's work. Quite a thought. Do you realize there's probably siblings of Mary spread throughout Idaho, thanks to his philosophy, that no-one ever knew about?'

'That was my thought at the time. I didn't dare bring it up. Folk round here get very jumpy over the word incest, because in those times, in all that solitude, there were those who had no idea who they were marrying, so long as some pair of feet kept them warm during the long winters.'

John threw back his head and laughed, and one of the nurses, passing Daisy's door, smiled and nodded at them.

'Hear me out,' Daisy whispered. 'I'm expecting Douglas round about this time, and you may have to go. Now I've started this story I intend to finish it. Besides, the more I tell you about poor Berte and the outcome of her life, the more I'm beginning to relate to her. I've never thought of it before. How morbid can one get?' Daisy was intent on finishing her story, keen to blot out the warmth of John's long fingers, the way she felt safe when he just sat there with her. Jenny's tale would stop the ruminating, if only for a little while.

'Mary, I believe, was the fifth or sixth child. Anyway she was ten when Jenny was born, and she was to be the last. Berte was old before her time. The other children looked after the newcomer while their mother recovered from the birth. That time had been the hardest for Berte, and it was the middle of a long and bitterly cold winter. Their dad had been home and was stuck in the cabin all winter without being able to take the wagon out and raise some money to feed them. The snow lasted until almost the end of May, and when her dad eventually hit the trail again, they were all used to going to bed hungry, and listening through the long nights to Jenny screaming for food, Berte's milk drying up almost immediately after the birth. And Mary would hear her mother crying softly as she slept on the old mattress on the floor next to her snoring husband, and holding her hands to her ears to try and block out the cries of her hungry baby. So even when the spring eventually began, and they managed to get some food again, Jenny grew slowly and more weak than the others. But the other children all found her very special somehow. She cried less and less, and later that year, when she began to crawl and pull herself round the cabin, they would play and cuddle with her, making her chuckle and scream with delight. That summer and fall, Daniel, their dad, had had a better than usual year. There were more and more people coming into the small towns, and as his customers grew and the money came in, he would stock up for the oncoming winter. Mary and her sisters scrubbed the cabin from top to bottom so Berte could rest more. They loved to see her sitting with Jenny on her knee and smiling as she rocked her, and letting the baby play with her long dark hair as the other girls chirped and quarrelled their way through the chores. They would pick flowers from the hillsides that summer, and put them round the cabin to make their mother smile even more. Their dad stayed home that winter. They had plenty of dry and canned goods in the cupboard, and logs by the loadful to see them through, however hard it might get.

So they were all together on Christmas day. And the older children stuffed some old stockings with fir cones, and anything else they could find that looked interesting just outside the cabin door, so that each one of them would have something on Christmas day. They said long prayers that day, thankful for the fruitful year which had enabled them to stock up so well before the snow came this time. And the winter did come hard again. So much so that the children heard their dad talking about maybe finding somewhere nearer town before the following winter. Both he and Berte were getting too weary for all this isolation, however much they felt the very toughness of their environment had strengthened the children's characters, and made real men of the boys. 'Making them all strong and resilient enough in body and spirit to withstand the evils of the world once they might be forced to join it properly. How Daniel ever equated his own behaviour with the tripe he obviously served up to his children,' Daisy said, as a quick aside, 'is beyond me. None of them could read properly, in spite of Berte trying to teach them a little. If they had stayed in that cabin until they were adults, God knows what fates they would have met when they finally emerged into the general populace. It makes my blood boil to think of the ignorance of that father of theirs. Still.'

'Go on.'

'I'm nearly finished. And I've painted such a picture for myself, I feel like crying even before I tell you.'

'If you tell me, my sweet Daisy, I can cry with you. I know the same things move us.'

'Yes.' She took a deep breath. 'Berte had put little Jenny down on the floor to crawl around while they sat round the fire listening to Daniel tell stories about his travels. It must have only been a few moments when Berte said, "Where's the little one?" And one of the older girls stood up to find her. "She's got inside the cupboard by the sink," and Berte jumped to her feet and ran to the cupboard with a cry and picked Jenny up in her arms, letting a bottle only half full of some sort of liquid fall from the baby's grasp and spill over the floor.'

'What had she drunk?'

'Can't you guess? Mary told me it was some sort of cleaning material their dad had brought home for when the girls were smartening up the cabin. It was poisonous. Ooh, Berte washed the baby's mouth out, made her drink as much fresh water as she could, but Mary swears her mother knew at once what had happened and what the outcome was going to be. She sat with the baby in her arms and listened to the tears, and felt the writhing of that tiny frame against her heart as she held her tight, and apparently, she said not a word. The other children went about the usual domestic duties, unsure really what was going on. Daniel tried to move the wagon. Making believe for a while that he could get the child to a doctor. But the snow blinded everything within a few feet of the cabin, and the wagon wouldn't budge, the snow almost covering it as he and the boys struggled and froze for two hours or more trying to get it clear. Finally, Berte sent Mary out to her dad. "Mother says you must leave it. You will all die of cold she says. You must come in now, and help make the baby as comfortable as possible." So they did. That's what they did.'

Daisy looked at John then. His eyes were full of tears. She went on, 'It took her three days to die. And they all had to watch her, all those hours, as

249

she slipped away from them. And when she was gone, and their mother had said nothing, and had cried no tears, the ground outside was too hard to bury her, and the girls wrapped her in whatever they could find, and Daniel took her outside and hid that tiny body from his wife's eyes until he would be able to bury her in the spring. And Mary told me that not one of them cried. Not by the third day, or when they were wrapping her, or watching their father from the window burying her temporarily behind the logs outside, while their mother simply lay on the bed and stared up at the ceiling.'

'And did he bury her when the spring came? Did they all bury her?'

'Mary didn't know. She said her father simply said one day that he had seen to Jenny and they weren't to mention it ever again so as not to upset their mother. But one of the older boys said the body had been eaten, and their mother had guessed because she saw Daniel burning the clothing one evening when he thought his wife and the girls were asleep. Mary also said that her brother could have been making that up of course, just to scare them.'

'And then?'

'Then what? I don't know any more. She never told me any more. I'd asked Bob of course, when he got home that weekend, and he knew all about it. Seemed his mom told him years before. She liked people to know how tough she was. How she'd known hardship and all that. Berte died that following fall. She saved all the sleeping pills the doctor had given her in the spring, when the snow had cleared and they could get to town. She saved them until the snow started again, at the very beginning of the next winter, and swallowed them all, and just went to sleep for ever before anyone found her. Seems the thought of another winter finished it for her. So Mary told him. After that the family just split. Mary found herself back with Berte's family somehow, with her sisters. There she was raised a good Catholic girl. And no-one ever mentioned Berte. Her father said once of her, "Your mother conceived you all in sin, and chose purgatory when she killed herself." That was the last time her name was mentioned.'

Daisy took her hand from John's and reached for a tissue. 'Isn't that the saddest story you've ever heard? I expect you're really glad you visited aren't you?'

John laughed, and wiped his eyes.

'Makes my own problems quite insignificant,' Daisy said.

John didn't speak. When he did, he leaned towards her and took her hand again. His voice was gentle, and his eyes didn't meet hers. A strange thing for John. She waited to hear what he was going to say. 'So Bob hasn't been in touch?'

Daisy hesitated for a moment. 'No. I can't make Marjorie understand anything of what is going on. But then, I can't really think that hard myself at the moment. I'm behaving as if all these problems will disappear by magic if I shut my eyes to them.'

For a long moment, John said nothing. She could feel his eyes on her. She could almost hear him searching for words, and once again the shiver of fear went through her, her hands became clammy, her lips dry, and she closed her eyes.

'Daisy—' John began.

One hand outstretched to him, eyes open quickly, a look of glacial indifference attempted and failed across her face. 'Don't say anything John. This is all something that I must work out for myself. If it's upsetting Marjorie, then you must go home and do some mending in the right place. I have no option but to stay here, in the hospital. Douglas will be happy, and my baby will be safe.'

He said nothing, and that was hard. Eventually he stood up and went to stand by the window. It was dark by now. Daisy watched his back, not knowing how to break the quiet that had fallen between them. Afraid that at any moment her mouth would open and all the wrong words would tumble out. But she couldn't say what she already knew within the thinking part of her brain, the words that any sensible woman would know to be the right ones. She'd seen the look in his eyes before he moved to the window. She knew what he longed so much to tell her. Could see that longing even in the tension of his back as he closed himself off from her. She should tell him once again to go home, to mend his marriage, and then to talk his wife into having children, and forget these irrational and dangerous feelings he had for his own mother-in-law.

'John, listen to me,' she began, and as he turned towards her, and she caught for the first time the look of misery and confusion on his face, Douglas Hart tapped lightly on the door and came straight in.

'Daisy, my dear. I'm on my way home. I wanted to see whether you've had a good think about the suggestion I made this morning.' He turned to John with a smile. 'Hello there! And how's that clever wife of yours, my boy? Not with you this time?'

John smiled. A small smile, Daisy thought as she watched him, knowing how wide and warm his smile could be when his heart was in it. 'She's in San Francisco this week, Dr Hart. I guess you could say I'm standing in for her. With much pleasure, I assure you.' He moved towards the bed and stood beside Daisy as if he'd been employed as a bodyguard.

Daisy gave him a gentle shove, and laughed. 'Look at him,' she said, 'he's becoming like an old guard dog these days! As if someone was going to run off with me! He reminds me of an elderly labrador I had when I was a child before the war.' She turned and looked hard into John's eyes. 'Before you were even a twinkle in your father's eye, John.'

He winced, withdrew his hand which had been reaching out to find hers as he sat down next to her on the bed.

'Oh, my darling boy,' she thought suddenly, unable to stop the flood of feelings that washed over her as she watched his face when her words struck home. 'Dearest John, how can you ever forgive me for making you feel silly, and only because I have no idea of how to deal with what you're feeling for me right now, and I'm far too afraid to admit even to myself, that when I look at you, or feel your hand on mine, my own emotions are as confused as the look I see in your eyes.' But of course, the words weren't vocal, and instead, she smiled up now at Douglas Hart. 'I have no choice, do I, Douglas? I must stay here. You've got me cornered. I'll have to remain in this awful place until the baby comes. And there was so much to do at home. Nothing's ready yet, for a baby that is. I guess Dorrie will have to do it.'

'Good,' Douglas said briefly, 'at long last you're being sensible. Complete bed rest for you. Not even trips to the bathroom.'

Daisy pulled a face. 'I loathe bedpans. Serves me right, I suppose. Thinking all this would be easy, I mean. You did warn me.'

John, who'd been listening intently, with a slight frown on his face, said softly, 'If there was a way of keeping her in bed at home, wouldn't that be better for her spiritually, Dr Hart?'

'That I can't deny. But we'll keep her amused and as worry-free as we can for the next couple of months. She might prefer some home cooking, of course. The food in here is not of the greatest culinary expertise. But you can't have everything. She'll be nourished.'

John stood up rather abruptly. 'I can take her home. To *her* home, I mean. And I can stay with her. Round the clock. I'd be pleased to do that for her. Marjorie is far too busy, and I know she'll be happier if she feels her mother is happy these last couple of months before the baby is born. How would that be?'

'No,' Daisy said, too quickly to make out she'd even thought it over. Besides, both the men in the room, towering over her, one each side of the bed, discussing her future as if she wasn't in the room, drowned out her small protest immediately.

Douglas said tentatively, 'Well, John, it would be good to have her own things around her, but are you sure you can be there all the time? I don't want her on her feet at all. No leaping out of bed and dealing with family crises, as I am well aware she has been doing.'

'Exactly.' John turned to face his mother-in-law at that moment, and smiled broadly at her, his eyes happy again. 'Sorry Mother-in-law, but that's true. And I can be a good nurse. I had to nurse my mom at times when I was a lot younger than I am now. I can cook and be amusing as well. But then you know that already.'

Daisy stared at him, speechless.

'Well, if you can square it with Marjorie,' Douglas said, 'it would be the best arrangement. Save your spirit and some money as well! OK with you, my dear Daisy?'

'Well—'

'Good.' He gathered his things together. 'She could be sent home in a few days.' Douglas bent to kiss Daisy on the cheek, and then shook hands with John. 'My love to that wife of yours,' he said. 'Tell her thanks for letting us borrow her husband. If she's anything like my wife, she'll be pleased to get you out from under her feet for a few weeks. I'll be in touch the day after tomorrow probably. Don't hesitate to call me at any time. Daisy has my home telephone. You can use it at all the times she didn't like to. Too polite for her own good, is our Daisy. But I expect you know that already, being family, an' all.'

And with that he was gone. Daisy and John could hear the cheerful acknowledgements to his patients and nurses fade away as he made his way down the hall and out of the building, leaving a strange silence in the room. A silence full of unspoken words.

'Well then,' Daisy said, and realized she had started to sound like her own mother. 'God,' she stared up at John, 'd'you think any member of this family remembered to tell my parents what's been going on?'

'Should we have done?'

'If she's been calling, my mother that is, and getting no reply, she'll think we've all been murdered in our beds by now. And that there's no-one left alive to tell her!'

John laughed. He looked relieved she'd not immediately brought up the fact he'd offered to move in with her. Daisy's jaw tightened. She'd get to that. 'Would you ask either Robert or Marjorie to call them?' she asked. 'They have the number.'

'OK.'

'And I'd be grateful if they didn't mention about Bob not being in the house. They'll have to invent something. Say he's gone off on a business trip or something. I can't deal with my mother's tears when she realizes the truth of the situation. I'll wait till the baby's born. She can scream as much as she likes then. Poor old Mom. Dad'll have to calm her down.'

'OK. Probably better coming from Marjorie. I'll see to it tonight.'

'Is she back from San Francisco then? Already?'

'I lied.'

'Thought so. What is it, John? Is she so furious with me over all this mess that she doesn't want to see me?'

'Partly. I didn't want you to know.'

'Did you imagine I don't know my own daughter? What else?'

John moved restlessly from one foot to another, then said, 'Personal things, Daisy. Nothing for you to worry about.'

'Maybe you'd better go home, John dear. Talk to your wife. Tell her the offer you've made to the doctor about me. Maybe she'll make you change your mind, see some sense. It's not too late to make other arrangements. And besides, I'm not sure it would be such a good idea,' she couldn't look him in the eye, 'what with the gossip and everything.'

But John didn't take up that part of her somewhat weak response to his offer. It was something else. 'That's just the problem, Daisy, Marjorie has always made me see sense. That's most likely why there's been no passion in my life.'

'Don't say any more. Please.'

But John had moved to the bed again, sat down beside Daisy, refused to see her trying to pull away from him to the other side of the narrow bed, had taken both her hands in his, and held on to them as if his very life depended on her nearness.

'Please John,' she said desperately, hanging on to the last margin of common sense she could muster, her voice already weak as he held her hands tight. 'The last thing you should do right now is say anything that you think is on your mind. Things would get more complicated in all our lives.'

'You don't know what I'm going to say, Daisy. There is nothing in this world I would do to harm or frighten you in any way. I'm coming to look after you. At the moment I have nowhere else to go. So if it makes you feel better about the whole situation, you're doing me a favour as well. I need to care for someone at this time. I would like that person to be you. Marjorie wants a break. For both our sakes: hers and mine. To see if things can still be worked out. Maybe they can. She even suggested I come to you. Said it would kill two problems at the same time. Those were her words.'

'I see.' She was silent for a long moment, and then, 'I'm sorry it's bad between you both. I'd hate to lose you, John. From the family I mean.'

She shouldn't have said anything. Not those words anyway. But there was no going back.

John said, 'You won't. Not ever. Don't you know that already?'

She looked down at her hands, spoke softly. 'Don't go this way John. Not now. Don't say another word. If you do, there is no way you can stay at the house. Think of me as a parent. As a loving parent. That's all. Anything else is too big for me to even comprehend.'

Again a long silence.

Finally, 'Then I won't, Daisy. Just one thing. You must know that I stopped thinking of you as a mother many years ago. And now we'll leave it at that. You must get some sleep, and I'll go home to pack a bag and tell my publishers where I will be for the next two months.'

He bent to kiss her once more on the lips, and she turned her head so that his mouth merely grazed her ear. Then he was gone. And the nurse came in with her sleeping pill.

Chapter Thirteen

Two days later she was home. Dorrie had cleaned and polished, and Sharon had filled the kitchen cupboard and refrigerator. Sharon, with her passion for rich foods.

'Yuck!' John exploded with a laugh. 'Does she really believe that's suitable for a pregnant woman?'

'I was brought up on that sort of food, I'll have you know,' Daisy retorted. 'Her heart's in the right place, our Sharon. At least I think so. Hope so. For my Robert's sake.'

John opened the window in the bedroom as Daisy got into her own bed, sighing with great satisfaction as she felt the familiarity of the pillow against her back, and the feather bed beneath her.

It had been strange coming into that empty house at first. No Mary, shouting from her old chair by the stove. No Bob. No mother-in-law and no husband. Nobody but herself to think about, to worry about. Just herself. And John of course, carrying her from the car and up the stairs of the verandah, both of them conscious of neighbours, both determined not to mention those prying eyes and give the homecoming more significance than was healthy. Then old Mrs Trypol from across the street waved and called out, smiling, 'Let me know if you need anything! Good luck honey. You hang in there.' And Daisy waved back, watching net curtains swing back into place, doors opening, ice broken, friendly faces after all. 'Thank God,' she breathed. 'Why did I think they'd hate me? God bless them.' And John opened the windows in the kitchen, wondering if their loyalty was fed by curiosity. The writer, the cynic.

The stillness, the silence, Daisy couldn't find the word, hung strangely on the big old house. The Francken residence, where no Francken dwelled.

But once in bed, and with John in the kitchen making herb tea, because that's what he'd insisted on, she didn't even feel the need for the sound of a radio. Her head against the pillow, she watched the net curtains moving with gentle protest against the breeze through the open window. It was warm for the last day of April. According to Daisy's calculations, the baby was due to be born in eight weeks, a long time to lie in bed. But then, listening to John rattling crockery in the kitchen, hearing a neighbour call a greeting to someone outside, the sound of footsteps on the rough roadway that ran past the house, the prospect of that two-month wait didn't daunt her. There would be little else to do except think, and sort out her future as best she could. Her heart was heavy with regret over her irredeemable marriage, but her spirits were lifting in anticipation of her new life, whatever that was to be. With Mary placed in the home, where

Daisy prayed she would find some sort of strange comfort, Bob had most likely been seduced into thinking that his family duties were over.

Daisy could almost understand. Perhaps he'd grown weary of the family they'd already raised, looked around it, and, not liking what he saw, decided not to run the risk of another failure. She was the strong one, after all. Poor Bob. No, not that. Poor Mary-Anne. All those years of chasing her dream, only to watch it burn itself out.

John came in with the tea, a purple-coloured liquid filling one of her better cups and saucers, a teabag still bobbing in the unappetizing looking drink.

'Yuck!' she said, smiling immediately the sound left her lips, just in case she hurt his feelings. But John laughed. 'It's some sort of hippy drink,' she said at last. Then, taking a sip, 'it's not bad actually. Quite nice in fact.'

'Well, that's a relief. I thought we were going to have our first fight.'

'Come and sit with me, John. Pull that wicker chair up. Bring your own tea in. I hope you're drinking the purple stuff as well. I have no intention of being bullied unless you share.'

'Would I dare do anything else? I've never seen the bad side of you, but you must have one, and I, for one, would not like to be around when it explodes.'

When he'd got his tea, and brought in the brownies that Sharon had left, ('Good God, I married the wrong girl, these are delicious!

Marjorie even makes gravy from a can') he sat on the bed next to Daisy, ignoring the chair. 'What d'you want to talk about, beautiful Daisy?'

'Don't. I'm not in the least beautiful.'

'Be quiet woman. My eyes don't lie!'

'I can see you're going to become a monster now you believe you've got me in your power.'

'You'd be the first.'

'First what?'

'Woman in my power. Under my control.'

'I see.' She smiled at him, seeing he was teasing her. 'What did Marjorie say?'

'About me coming here?'

She nodded.

'You want the exact words?' John asked.

'I think so.'

'She said, and I hope I don't paraphrase, "Let's hope you do more good there than you do here."'

'Oh dear. D'you want me to call her?'

'She'll call you first. She said she would. I think I detected a glint of guilt when I informed her that I was the only one in the family ready and willing to take on this particular job.'

'Don't say that John. Somewhere along the way Marjorie seems to have been badly hurt by me. I'm just not quite sure when and how. Maybe she perceived something in the wrong way, maybe when she was growing up, and felt unable to speak out about it at the time. That's my fault. I should have known my own children better.'

'Other families are no different. Most of them

anyway. Too many secrets, kept by people with good intentions, and often with disastrous results.'

'I'm glad, at least, you admit families have good intentions.'

'Not all of them, Daisy. Not all of them.'

'That's the cynic in you. I've begun to realize the cynical side of you. It's a shame. Must be the writer in you. Does a writer need to see the world through cynical eyes? Does it make him or her a better one?'

John shrugged. 'I don't know. I try to keep it out of kids' books. They have their life before them. They can figure out the bullshit at a later date.'

'I don't believe I ever did. Figure out the bullshit, I mean.'

He smiled at her, and she smiled back. The moment fluttered, tried to take off in a different direction, and then the telephone rang, and Daisy jumped, spilling her tea. It was Marjorie. And as Daisy sat and watched the washed-out purple stain spreading across the bedcover, it was as if it had reached up and flooded into her own cheeks and she could feel herself growing hot as John went to find a towel to dry her off.

'Hello Marjorie. It's so nice to hear your voice. And thank you for the messages in the hospital.'

'I'm sorry I couldn't get in to see you. Did John explain about San Francisco?'

'Yes he told me,' Daisy lied, crossing her fingers. No point in getting John into trouble. She could play Marjorie's game if it was easier for them all. 'I must thank you for sending him to look after me. It was a kind thought.'

Her daughter seemed embarrassed. 'It was the least I could do.'

There was a silence. Daisy said, 'D'you want to speak to him? I'll call him.'

'No, Mom. I've got to go. I just wanted to see if you were settled in. Have you heard from Dad?'

'No.'

'Shit.' The word was spoken with too much elegance to be an expletive. Pointless exercise if the word didn't relieve your anger.

'I'm sure your father has his reasons for behaving like he is,' Daisy said, waiting a moment to see if her daughter could come up with something more expressive. 'But to face me with them at the moment would be less than considerate. We'll wait. Have you been to see your grandmother?'

'Yes. Once. She seems fine. She has no idea where she is and who we are, neither Robert nor myself. Sharon won't go, says it makes her cry. The place, she means. She's so stupid that girl.'

Daisy didn't answer. John had come back into the room and began mopping the bedcover, mouthing something and shaking his head. Daisy presumed he did not want the telephone passed to him. So she glared, for no good reason, except she suddenly felt she was being used as the lever to push the wedge between her daughter and her husband. The wedge that they both seemed to want so badly. To let them out with their dignity intact. It annoyed her.

'John's here now,' she said quickly, 'have a word.'

John threw the wet cloth at her and glared back as she held the telephone out and he had no choice but to take it. 'Marjorie.' It was all he said. He listened for a few moments while his wife talked, then he said, 'I'll call you in a few days, unless you call first. Enjoy the concert.' And he handed the telephone back to his mother-in-law and walked from the room.

Daisy stared after him. She could hear Marjorie's voice, still talking. 'He's taken the cups back to the kitchen, dear. I'm sorry. Had you forgotten to tell him something?'

'No. It's all right. Tell him to behave himself. I'll call in a few days.'

'Why wouldn't you behave yourself?' she asked when John walked back into the room. But Dorrie was behind him so he said nothing.

'I've brought you some magazines,' Dorrie said gleefully. 'That's if you get bored living with a cute young guy these next few weeks. If you do, you can send him over to me.'

'Oh for God's sake, don't be so silly Dorrie.' And the irritation in Daisy's voice took them all by surprise.

Robert came to see her every evening after work during those first few weeks she was released from the hospital, and Sharon came up on a Friday as usual. Daisy wanted to beg her not to keep to that same ritual, as if everything was the same, that Mary sat in the corner, that Bob would come in from work, that she, Sharon, could still bake her rich desserts and bring them. Eventually, even Sharon realized things were very different in the old house. And she hated change. 'Poor Sharon,' thought Daisy, feeling more and more mellow as the baby's arrival drew nearer. Her daughter-in-law was uncomfortable with John, and he seemed to be making fun of her most of the time. Or so Sharon believed. Robert confided to his mother, 'She's afraid of clever people, she says. She thinks they only say smart things to make the rest of us feel stupid.'

So Daisy spoke to John and told him to stop teasing her daughter-in-law, and she asked Robert to explain to his wife that Mary was not coming back, not ever, that she was too old and quite ill, and that if she, Sharon, wanted to see her, she should find the courage to go to the retirement home. And apparently Sharon cried, and said she didn't like things changing, and everyone at work kept asking her whether John and her mother-in-law were sleeping together, and was it John's baby Daisy was expecting?

Robert told John this of course, not his mother, for fear of upsetting her, and, naturally, John went straight away and told Daisy. Robert was furious, and when John said, 'She hates things to be kept from her. The truth, that is. And I feel the same. We've come to tell each other most things, so that we can laugh at them together,' Robert stayed away for a whole week because he was afraid that his mother, in a fit of truthfulness, and a desire to fill a long boring day with some family gossip, would tell John about Robert's 'little difficulty' with Sharon. Eventually, after six days of absence from his mother's bedside, Daisy called him and asked him if he was ill or something, and said she missed his visits. Robert was caught between his two parents. Terrified that the rumour of John and Daisy's dangerous alliance, true or not, would reach his dad any day now, and trying to not confess to his mother that Bob intended to sell the house from under her as soon as he could, split the money, and move on. With Mary-Anne.

'What about Mom? What about Gran?'

'I've told you, I'll see your mother all right. She'll have half the house. Maybe she'll go back to England.'

'Christ Dad! Not after all these years, she won't. Anyway, what about Gran? How can you just go like that?'

'Your gran doesn't even know who I am, son. She hates the sight of me every time I go up there. Calls me Derek, of all things. Name of an uncle she seemed to hate when she was a child. Screams at me, she does, every time I step foot in that home. The woman there said I only upset her, and that perhaps it would be wiser for me to stay away until she was calmer in her mind. She quite obviously hated this frigging Derek. God knows what he ever did to her. Funny family she came from, your grandmother. Funny blood running through that family there was. That story about their sister Jenny dying. Always sounded suspicious to me. Mary-Anne pops in to see her. They got on quite well in the past. That's where she lives these days, your gran, back in the past. Seems a bit happier there.'

Neither Bob nor Robert touched on the subject of the coming baby. Bob was in deep denial. Robert had no notion what to say.

So Robert came back to the fold, so to speak, once Daisy said she missed him, and he kept his secrets, for the time being. His mother was delighted to see him regularly once more, and he avoided the subjects that would destroy the equilibrium that finally seemed to have settled on her. In fact, he lied to her. Even when she asked him once in a private moment whether the problem with Sharon had cleared up. He said that everything was fine at long last, and each month they hoped for signs that a baby was on the way, but would she please not mention it to Sharon herself because it would embarrass her.

'Of course I won't son. Maybe Sharon can help me with your sister when she is finally born. Get some practice in.'

And Robert smiled and nodded, afraid then of something else, that his wife would be so stressed when she saw Daisy with the baby, all the words and emotions about her mother-in-law would spill out of her mouth like so much venom, and destroy the delicate relationship that was acted out every visiting night at the moment. Words like 'disgusting', and 'old breast-feeding women with sagging tits'. Sharon could be quite a shattering surprise these days when she got out of control, what with her 'fairy for a brother-in-law, father-in-law as Casanova, and mother-in-law as a freak!' Robert had even asked Dr Hart whether he could get some sort of tranquillizers for his wife when she had one of her hysterical fits, but Douglas, knowing the rest of Sharon's family background, said he would have to see her first, and that she would probably be much better when the babies started coming, and was there anything else Robert needed to talk to him about.

So Robert fled the surgery, and hoped things would clear up of their own volition.

Marjorie had appeared one Sunday, late afternoon, straight from one of the most depressing visits she'd had with Mary. Daisy found it uncomfortable to sit with her daughter and John in her room. She, propped up comfortably with a mass of pillows that John had found in the other bedrooms and placed firmly behind her to support her back, which these days was giving her more pain than Douglas Hart liked. Not that he mentioned this to her when he popped in most evenings. But John knew. The visit felt strange because he insisted on arranging those pillows while Marjorie sat there and watched him while she drank the coffee he'd made on her arrival. The scenario made Daisy squirm restlessly as she sat upright in bed. There was even more tension between Marjorie and John, something unsaid, or maybe even said already and regretted. Something that John had not told her.

Marjorie stayed for supper, talking about her work, trivia, avoiding the subjects of her father, Mary-Anne, and, of course, the approaching birth. There was little left to discuss, and the evening dragged on, stagnant with innuendo, fraught with subtext. She enquired discreetly about her mother's health. Was she taking her vitamins, getting enough rest? It was like a gruelling visit with an uninterested social worker. The real nitty gritty stuff, that should be of interest to loved ones, like where would they all be in two or three months time, and how could they get everything back to where it was, and why did her mother start all this upheaval in the first place, was deviously and manipulatively avoided.

'Thank you for calling Gran and Poppa in England,' Daisy said at one point.

'Poppa seemed very upset. Did you speak to him?'

'Yes. He's a bit weepy these days. Mum seems to think he had a bit of a stroke when she was out of the house one day. Now she dare not leave him alone.'

'I didn't know. I'll call Gran again. At least she seems fine.'

'Yes. I sometimes feel sure that my mother will live for ever.'

They all smiled. Not because there was a

sudden rush of communication between them, but more out of politeness, believing the remark warranted such a response, so they smiled without looking at one another, and let it fade when they caught each other's eyes again. Daisy felt very tired suddenly. Her back ached, and she wanted to ask John to rub it as he'd taken to doing most evenings, but it seemed inappropriate with his wife sitting there. Almost indecent.

'It was nice of you to lend me John,' Daisy said.

'So you keep telling me, Mother. Believe me, and let me say again, it was a good time for us both. I'm up to my ears with work, and John has finished his book. He's on hiatus so to speak. I hope you've found something to talk about, the two of you. He's not always the easiest of men to live with.'

John got up immediately at that remark, and left the room. Daisy heard him banging about in the kitchen, and she looked long and hard at her daughter once they were alone. 'Why do you do that, Marjorie? Why do you humiliate him like that? What's wrong between the two of you?'

For a moment there was a silence between them. Mother and daughter, estranged for years as they'd been, caught each other's eye for a second. That instant, Daisy believed there was still some hope for them, some understanding that one wants between mother and child, but then it was gone, and Marjorie hung her head and stared at the toe of her well-shined black patent leather stiletto shoes and began to make circles with her foot as she crossed one elegant and slender leg across the other.

'Who are these people?' Daisy thought. 'Who are these strangers that twirl around me calling me Mom, and kissing me insignificantly on the cheek to greet me or say goodbye? Did they really come from my body, did I really feed them and nourish them and watch them grow? Why do I feel so little understanding for them? What is it we're supposed to have which we don't? And how do we get it? If I was supposed to grow up with a degree of excellence in being a mother, why wasn't any one of them born with a book of instructions for me in their hand? Specially Marjorie. Specially the first.' She sighed.

Marjorie said, without looking up, 'John and I will work out our own problems, Mom. You have enough to think about.' She stood up. 'I have to go. Thank you for supper. I suppose I should thank my husband really. I'll do that on my way out.' And she bent to kiss her mother on the cheek, picked up her bag and went for the door.

'Look after yourself,' Daisy said on impulse. And Marjorie stopped while she was struggling into her coat. She stood with her back to her mother. 'You too,' she said. And she was gone, speaking tersely and quietly to John on her way out. Daisy couldn't hear what she said, and there seemed to be no reply from John. Then all was quiet again. Only the creaks of an old house as it settled down for the night invaded her ears, filling the pauses uncomfortably when there was nothing else to say. A strange depression came upon her as she heard her daughter's car pulling away. She wanted to get up, run to the window, call her back, beg her forgiveness for she knew not what. But then the car was gone, revving up with what sounded like anger to Daisy's ears, and it was too late. Too late for everything, Daisy thought. And when John finally came in twenty minutes later, having calmed himself down while he was alone, he found Daisy crying.

He sat down on the bed beside her, wanting to reach out for her, but afraid, knowing with a lover's true instinct that it was a bad time to touch or even speak. So he just sat there, and waited until her tears finally stopped, and he brought her more tissues and held them to her nose while she blew, which made her laugh rather weakly because it made him seem like her father when he was first teaching her how to blow her nose at a very tender age.

And that memory could have triggered more crying, but John came in swiftly with, 'You mustn't let her upset you. You must stay calm. If this happens again, Douglas will say no visitors.'

'All right, all right. But for God's sake let me blow my own nose.'

They laughed, looked into each other's eyes. And Daisy had already lost the key to the door that would lead her back to the safety of a life without passion, without John, who with the words 'my love' finally made her admit to herself that he was more than a carer, a friend, a father to her, and it was time to talk about it.

'Tell me about you and Marjorie. Tell me what's happened between you. It's quite clear I should know.'

Still they didn't touch. There was no need.

'It might be a long tale,' John said. 'I'm afraid you're tired. Maybe we should wait until tomorrow.'

'I'm suddenly more awake than I've been all day. It's now, John.'

'Right then. Where do I begin?'

'Where else?'

'At the beginning you mean? Well, you are most likely correct. I've found out that the women in this family are more than often right, even when they're the silent type.'

She smiled. 'Don't procrastinate. Get on with it. It will be tomorrow at this rate.'

'I'm not in love with her Daisy. It sounds so simple when you say it out loud to another person doesn't it? Funny how the simplicity leaves when you try to say those words to someone you've shared a life with for six years.'

'Did the love just stop then?'

He shrugged. 'I'm no expert on love, I'm afraid. When I have the courage to write my first grown-up novel, I hope to be able to tear the myth apart. The myth of "being in love". At least, that's what I used to think. Until you were there. In your green and white dress, and wrestling with that darn turkey.'

'I have no idea what you're talking about! And we haven't done with Marjorie yet.'

'Ah yes. My wife. Your daughter. Well, I did believe I was in love with her, at the beginning, I mean. She was young and bright, and more clever and focused than any other girl I'd ever met. I wanted, no, needed somebody who was focused. I put a lot of store in that ability. She was ambitious as well. I liked that. Different to me. She would steer our lives right, and I could sit and daydream over my children's books and the great American novel I would write one day, or so I thought at the time. Lust stops us thinking straight. And I won't be coy or untruthful about it, the sex was great! It looked as if, for the first time, I would have the right woman in my life.'

'So what happened? She brought you home as soon as you became engaged, I seem to remember. It was so nice to see our Marjorie – I don't know – "glowing" like that. I guess that's the word I was looking for. She'd never been a "glower", I'm afraid. She even went to her first prom without a date, I recall. You can imagine. Not that I was shaken by that, coming from a "promless" culture, you could say. Thinking boys were silly when one was only just seventeen seemed perfectly normal to me. We had girlfriends at that age, and our crushes were on the sports teachers, or prefects. Never boys. But in America? I soon learned the importance of a date for the prom. But Marjorie said, and she'd already developed that note of scorn in her voice by then, that she had never met a single boy round here that was any more than pathetic. I'm almost positive those were her very words. So her grandad took her. Escorted her, I should say. All done up in his best bib and tucker. Of course, she was the talk of the campus.'

'She never told me that. I like it.'

'She hated sport, you see. Any sort. Never tried out for a cheer leader. Thought it silly. The best and tallest blond footballer at college was of no interest. She always wanted a scholar. That's why I was so pleased when she brought you home. We'd never met any of her boyfriends before then. And there she was, almost married.'

'I know she'd had lovers before me. I'd never met a woman with such a glorious appetite for sex.' John stopped and laughed a little. 'Should I be telling you this? It seems rather indiscreet.'

'Well you've said it now,' Daisy teased him. 'Maybe you just shouldn't harp on it too much.'

'You're right.' It was John's turn to do the teasing. There was a pause, and he looked serious for a moment.

'Go on,' she muttered, 'I'm still listening.'

'It's hard to say this. It's not something I'm proud of. I'm afraid I knew I was going to marry the wrong woman even before the wedding.'

Daisy frowned. 'Then for God's sake, John, why on earth—'

'It was you,' he said quickly. 'How could I walk away from a family that contained within it the only woman I would ever love?'

'Oh John.'

He reached across the bed and held both her hands. 'It's true,' he said. 'It was unforgivable, I realize that. But I could think of nothing else that would keep you in my life.'

Daisy was speechless. He stroked her thumb until the skin beneath his fingers burned as if against a hot flame, and she withdrew one of her hands.

'Don't hate me Daisy. Not now.'

'I don't hate you John. I'm shocked. And very sad for my daughter. To have lived a lie all these years.'

'She didn't. She never knew. I would never have told her, for God's sake! What d'you take me for?'

'Don't get upset. I know that. But do you really believe she hasn't guessed in all these years there was something not right?'

'Of course not. But almost immediately we married she was disappointed with me. I let her down every way she turned. We had shown each other sides of our nature that didn't sit easily upon us as we relaxed into the relationship. We'd lied about ourselves. I don't mean real lies. Just pretence so we would capture each other, the perfect side of us that impresses at a distance but disappears when you move in with someone. You must know what I mean. All lovers do it at first. The mating game.'

'I know.'

'But you didn't. Not with me, I mean.'

'Well obviously. You were my daughter's future husband. It never occurred to me.'

'It was a mess.'

'It *is* a mess.'

He turned her face towards him. She felt his breath on her face as he took in every feature, every line. 'Oh John,' she said again.

'If you say that again I will have to kiss you.'

'I want you too, John. And that's difficult to admit. I should be feeling shame. But I'm not. There's a light in your eyes when you look at me that I've hungered for all my life. I was past thinking it would ever be mine. But, oh dear John, did it have to be you? I'm at a loss at what to do. I have no strength to resist you. I want to be held, and cherished, and told I'm beautiful with child. I want all those things, because I don't believe I've ever had them. Not with passion. I've been with just one man, you see. Bob. And I've known for years it was all a mistake. It wasn't love I felt for him. It was that overpowering urge you mistake for the real thing when all those young and irrational hormones are dancing with such frenzy inside you. But it was a different time. We married because of it. Bob did the decent thing. Well, the decent thing in those days. And it was all romantic. So glamorous to marry an American. I was the envy of all my girlfriends. If it crossed my mind for one instant that we were both being too hasty, I can't remember. I was swept away with all the excitement. I was heading towards the great American dream so many of us longed for, living out our damp, miserable little lives in an England that was already on its uppers, despite the war, and the false glory of victory, followed by the promise of a Labour government that promised an equality we would never have. My dad cried all through the wedding. And then again, later, when it was time for me to join Bob. I can remember Dad standing on the dock when the boat left, and I was holding Marjorie's hand and waving to him. To both of them. My mother too. Except she didn't cry. Not that she didn't love me, she did. It was simply that she loved my father more, and now she would have him all to herself. My dad got smaller and smaller as he stood there, and I, who had been totally speechless with fear for the whole of the previous week, was still speechless, and I began to cry. Great, enormous, childlike sobs. So much noise I made, that other passengers came to help, and wanted to take us to our cabin, wanted to look after Marjorie. But I had to stand there until I could no longer see my dad, until he vanished from my sight. It was as if, simply by turning a corner, I had banished him from my life. Then it was just water all round us. If I didn't move until then, I believed I would be back soon, I would wake up from this strange nightmare I had created for myself, this journey towards a man with whom I had no desire to spend the rest of my life, no desire to be responsible for our child, when I was little more than a child myself. And the first words out of my mouth that day, after the silence of terror I'd suffered the previous week, the first words as some kind lady tried to move me away from the railing, in fear of my suicide I guess, were, "I want my daddy. Get me my daddy." And then Marjorie threw up all over my new shoes. It was, up until then, the worst day of my life.'

John kissed her. Gently and softly on the mouth. And she took one of his hands from her face and placed it so that he could feel the beating of her heart. 'I love you, Daisy. I always have, and I always will. Wherever it leads us, even apart, I will always feel this way about you. You are the first and the last woman I will ever love.'

Chapter Fourteen

Later that evening, when they had stayed close to each other for comfort, hardly able to tear themselves apart, as if it would turn out to be the last night they would be together, when there seemed little else to share about their past, and too much dread of discussing their future, John told her more about the situation between himself and Marjorie.

'She accused me of having an affair. At Christmas, it was, when we were away.'

'And were you?'

'No. Marjorie has always had a much higher sex drive than me – oh dear, I'm at it again.'

'I refuse to comment.'

'It doesn't mean I can't be passionate, it's just that intimacy means something more to me. You and I may never be lovers. Yet we already are. In our eyes, our hands when we touch, the words we say. Coupling can be an over-rated pastime unless you can control it. So I've heard, I hasten to add!'

Daisy was laughing. 'Then you heard right,' she said.

'Don't misunderstand me, my darling. It's not that I don't want to make love to you. I do. But as it's quite impossible emotionally and physically at the moment, I will make love to you in every other way that is in my power. Do you understand?'

She nodded. Still she smiled.

'So, of course, when I was so strange at Christmas, (I was just thinking about you in actuality) Marjorie, being a normal hot-blooded woman, thought the reason for my abstinence in bed was because I was having an affair with someone else.'

'What did you say to her?'

'I told her she was being ridiculous of course. What else does a man do when he's guilty? They shift the blame to the poor woman by insinuating she's quite crazy to even think of such a thing, thereby making himself the victim.'

'That's what Bob does.'

'We learn the lines in the womb, I'm convinced of it. A sort of telepathy between unborn sons and the expectant fathers. Kind of passing on of the tricks of the trade.'

'You're incorrigible,' she said. 'Are you trying to tell me that's why Bob cheats? Because his father did, and his grandfather before that?'

'I must be. What I'm trying to say, in a very clumsy way, is that Bob's behaviour is not your fault, and more than likely, not his. My father loved only one woman all his life. My mother. Which means, my sweet Daisy, that you will have nothing to fear from me.'

'And Marjorie?'

'I've told you. I didn't love her. I behaved badly

by letting her believe I did. I have no excuse, except my youth.'

Daisy threw back her head and laughed.

'Oh dear,' John said, 'that sounded very glib. I refuse to talk about this any longer, in case I drown in all this hot water!'

'Tell me about your parents. They must have died some time ago. You have never mentioned them.'

'Yes they did.' John rose suddenly from the bed. 'Would you like a hot drink?'

Daisy looked surprised. 'OK,' and as he left the room, 'but don't think that will get you out of it.'

But it was a few days before she heard the rest of John's story. After her hot drink that night, she was all at once too tired and too full of all the warm feelings to even keep her eyes open. The rest of his past would have to keep until the following day.

For John, a sleepless night lay ahead of him. The events of the day echoed round and round in his head. A big part of him was glad that everything he'd felt for her for so many years was finally out in the open. At least, as far as Daisy was concerned. Telling everyone else seemed like an insurmountable problem, and he knew in his heart that Daisy had not even considered the future at all. Not of sharing it with him. Going to another state, and starting a new life would be their only way forward. He knew that. The years of dreams he'd nurtured about her stood now in his memory like a mere prologue for the possibilities that could lay ahead. But he doubted that any of those possibilities had yet crossed Daisy's mind.

He lay on the narrow bed in the small spare bedroom at the top of the stairs. Below him, down the long passage that led to the back of the house, Daisy slept. He'd watched her for a while before he went to bed himself. Her face against the pillow was like a child's. Rounder, since she'd become pregnant, the cheeks pink even as she slept, her breathing shallow, and as he bent to kiss her slightly open mouth, her breath was as sweet as a baby's.

'Oh my sweet Daisy,' he whispered to himself, 'thank God that at last you know I'm on your side. Whatever happens, I'll be here for you.' And as he turned to leave her, 'I wish there was a way I could have gone back in time, met you at high school, and made you mine right then. I would never have let you go. You'd have been mine for ever. I would have kept you safe, and your eyes would never have been sad.'

The moon was bright through his window, and he had no desire to pull the curtains across so he could have the darkness. Everything in the room was alive with moonlight. And he didn't mind not sleeping. Every hour, now that she knew the way he felt, was precious to him. In five weeks the baby would be here. After that, Daisy's mother would come from England, leaving Daisy's father in the care of a relative. And then where would John go? He knew already, from Daisy, that her mother was horrified that he was even in the house alone with her, doing all those intimate things that had to be done at a time like this, but not by 'your daughter's husband, Daisy! I've never heard anything as strange as that. The Americans are the most peculiar race of people. Haven't they heard the word protocol?'

Finally, at six a.m., he went downstairs to put on the coffee. From the kitchen he saw Dorrie leaving for work. She waved to him, and started off by foot down the hill towards Main Street. Always said that walking to work was all the exercise she got these days, what with the old man's back playing him up as soon as she put her black nightgown on! John smiled as he watched her hurrying towards the diner. He liked Dorrie. She popped in most days to sit with Daisy so that he could go off for his run. Daisy enjoyed her company. He could always hear them laughing when he got back from the running, calling out that he'd make some coffee and come in to join them. John liked the company of women. More than men, if he was being totally honest. Men never really opened up to each other the way women did, never seemed intrigued about other people's lives. Women seemed to know almost everything about other folks' lives.

John wondered if Dorrie had guessed at the predicament he found himself in, and the way he'd always felt about Daisy. Not that she said anything.

That same day, he and Daisy had very little

chance to be alone. Dr Hart was around, and sat a long time with Daisy, explaining the procedure of the birth.

'Douglas,' she protested, 'this will be my fourth time. It still comes from the same place, doesn't it? Or have the scientists found something easier?'

But Douglas laughed, and said they may well give her an epidural. Not at all like the other times.

Daisy said, 'Will it hurt the baby?'

'Not at all. You are simply numb from the waist down. You don't feel anything. It'll be easier for you, Daisy. And I'd be happier.'

He stayed for some tea, and asked her in private what was happening with Bob, and would she stay put after the child was born. 'I feel we've been friends for long enough for me to poke my nose in,' he said.

'I don't know Douglas. I'll have to deal with that afterwards. Maybe I'll go home. To England, I mean. Funny to call it home after all these years. But my dad's quite ill, and I'd like to see him again.' Her eyes filled with tears as she spoke, at the thought of life without her father. With her, or apart, he had been such a big part of her, and the thought of never seeing that special twinkle in those blue eyes ever again, depressed her utterly. 'Oh dear, I'm sorry. I'm getting a little weepy these days. That, and living too much in the past. Doesn't your childhood seem like it belonged to another person as you get older?'

Douglas patted her hand and nodded.

The same day, Gary called from California,

saying that he would be out to see her before the baby arrived to give her a birthday present.

'Goodness, son, would you believe I'd forgotten my birthday?' John mouthed something across the room to her, and then ushered in two ladies from the Catholic wives' committee at the local church. She recognized them after a moment, having met them at least twice at the annual Christmas party to raise money for the poor of the area. She nodded to them, surprised, and John went to find another chair so that they could both sit down. 'It's my birthday in two days!' she smiled, still into the telephone. 'That's Sunday.'

When Gary hung up, she turned to her two visitors, curious to find them there, sitting smiling broadly at her from chairs at the bottom of her bed, their well scrubbed faces rough from many Idaho winters. The wives committee of the church had been discussing Daisy at their last meeting, and the two who sat around the bed drinking coffee that afternoon, both well into their sixties, had been chosen to bring some gifts to her that had been made by their members, and indeed, some of the Sunday School children.

Daisy was speechless. She simply sat and stared at the two elderly women, smiling and beaming, as they produced, one by one, the small gifts that had been sent. A lot of jackets for the baby, and some tiny bootees. An apple pie from the wife of the man in charge of the choir. Daisy knew none of their names. She'd been so few times to the church in the last years. She was embarrassed, and deeply touched. John brought in more coffee, and she totally forgot the indigestion that would follow and joined them in a cup. John was insistent that they try his fudge brownies, and they simpered and giggled over him as if they were schoolgirls.

Daisy felt so happy at that moment, all she wanted to do was sit there, watching the two of them, one with quite a discernible moustache, laugh at John's jokes, and drink the first cup of coffee she'd had in months.

Finally, they stood up to leave. The one with the moustache bent over to kiss Daisy on the cheek.

'I can't begin to tell you how pleased I am you came,' Daisy said. 'I'm sure poor John grows quite bored with only my conversation all day.'

The John in question shot her a look over the heads of the two ladies, who had to strain quite a lot to look up at his long slim frame. She thought of all they'd said the evening before, John and her. And she shuddered unseen with a wave of guilt. The feminine moustache tickled Daisy's face quite briefly, and something really ridiculous flew into her mind. 'When I have one of these, maybe I'll condition it so that John will still want to put his cheek against mine.'

But Prickly Moustache was saying something, and Daisy wiped the silly grin off her face and listened to her. 'We just wanted to say, all of us that belong to the church, including our beloved Father Harris, that we think you are the very bravest of women, and that we are proud to see you as part of our community. We know it's been hard for you. And we know you had a choice. In this world of such consuming selfishness, it warms our spirit to know you turned to your Father in Heaven for the right decision. We all wish your child safe passage into this world, and may God bless you both.' The other lady crossed herself swiftly at those words. 'Any time we can be of any assistance to you, dear Mrs Francken, please do not hesitate to call. Father Harris will be saying a mass for you this Sunday, and he will be up to see you before the baby is born.'

To her horror, Daisy burst into tears, and threw both ladies into a terrible dither, believing they had offended her in some way, but John said, 'Not at all. She's smiling under all those tears!' And she was.

So the ladies were ushered out, with John forcing on them the rest of the fudge brownies, which they promised to hand out after Sunday School this very week. And Daisy was still crying when he watched them drive off, unable to convince them that, no, he wasn't Mrs Francken's son from California, because he was laughing so much and trying hard to not show it.

Going back into Daisy's room, he sat down on the bed with her to give her some of the indigestion medicine Douglas had prescribed, 'Just in case the coffee comes back to haunt you later,' and they both fell against the pillows on the bed, Daisy smiling through her sobs, and wiping her nose against John's sleeve because she couldn't be bothered to stretch across for the box, and John holding his sides with a laughter that was hurting his ribs.

Then, when they'd been alone together for scarcely a breath, it seemed, Dorrie was there. It was Friday, and she'd brought some food from the diner for their supper. 'And don't turn your educated nose up at it,' she said to John as she handed it to him in the kitchen and went straight to see Daisy before he uttered a word, leaving him with his mouth open. 'God,' Dorrie said when she found her friend sitting up in bed reading, 'you look about twenty-one again. If this is what having a baby does to you in middle age, you'd better tell me the secret and I'll try and get the old man worked up tonight.'

'I've had a great day. You are going to roar when I tell you.'

And Daisy proceeded to tell her about the church's visit, and John came in with even more coffee, and they sat there, on and around Daisy's bed, with the May sunshine pouring through the net curtains, and its light dancing through the first leaves on the trees, through the curtains, and scattering itself all over the room. On the oak floor, shiny from years of hard polishing, on the colours in the rugs that Gary had bought Daisy for Christmas in the year he had finally moved his last possession out of his childhood bedroom, feeling a passing twinge of guilt at the thought of leaving his mother alone in the house with Gran and Dad, on the old perfume bottles, empty now, that she had brought with her all those years ago from England. The sound of their laughter, Daisy's, Dorrie's and John's, and their words interrupting and tumbling over each other, filling the house with its warmth, and Daisy's hair, grown long in the last eight months, tied back with a piece of ribbon from round an old chocolate box that now held her sewing utensils, coming loose with all the fidgeting she was doing and falling around her face, the streaks of grey mixed with the black, dancing like silver tinsel at Christmas time.

And in the midst of their jocularity, John had said, without thinking, and with a lover's desperate need to say everything that came into his head, 'My God, Daisy, you are so beautiful!'

And suddenly the three of them fell silent, and John stood up with the empty coffee cups and left the room. And Dorrie watched as he walked away, and then turned back to Daisy who sat very still, looking intensely at her finger nails, which had lost all power to attract that kind of attention years ago.

'I told you so!' Dorrie said. 'He's getting more obvious now you're alone in this house. What a glorious pickle, as you used to say. Has he said anything?'

Like a fool, instead of laughing it off, Daisy, perhaps for the sheer delight at hearing about John's obvious devotion from another's unsuspecting lips, said guilelessly, 'What d'you mean, you told me so? What are you talking about?' Thereby opening up the whole dangerous area for debate. The last thing on earth she wanted.

'I told you that boy had a crush on you. You pooh-poohed the whole idea. Don't you remember?'

'No. And really Dorrie, John is thirty-six. Hardly a boy.'

Just as she was trying to think of something else to put Dorrie off the scent, she heard Robert open the back door and greet John. 'Hush now, Dorrie. This isn't the kind of thing you should tease John about. Specially when it's all in the family. It sounds most peculiar to a person who doesn't know you're only joshing.'

'Who said I was joshing? No-one said anything about joshing!'

'Hi, Mom.' It was Robert. 'Aunt Dorrie, how y'doing?'

'You've finished early,' Daisy said as he bent to kiss her.

'I got someone to cover for me. I'll come round later with your present. Sharon and me can have a drink, even if you're not allowed. I'll not be able to come round on Sunday. Have you forgotten? It's Memorial Day on Monday.'

'So it is.'

So Daisy had her fifty-first birthday celebration two days early, with what was left of the family, and Dorrie. Sharon came up trumps. She liked birthdays, even when they belonged to someone else, and had brought a cake with her, which had

293

so much chocolate frosting on it, that it sank in the middle with the heaviness.

Sharon was mortified. 'I don't know what went wrong,' she said, 'I've made this cake so many times before. It's always come out right.'

'It'll taste great,' John said, putting his arm round her shoulders and giving her a squeeze. 'Everything you bake is beyond belief. It was probably the oven, that's all. Amazing that a girl can be as glamorous as you, sister-in-law, and cook like this! I hope Robert knows how lucky he is.'

His sudden chivalry made Sharon blush furiously, and Daisy was afraid she was going to cry yet again, which would make them all groan in exasperation, she was sure, so she poked John in the ribs instead, and he leapt into action and started to eat the cake. Funnily enough, it was the most delicious thing Sharon had ever baked, or at least, so it seemed that May evening. The birds seemed to be noisier than ever outside the window, and continued the singing long after the sun went down, and the chill of the night air that blew in through the window was there too quickly, pushing John into closing the window and pulling the curtains.

'They're all mating,' Daisy said, as the family were finding their jackets and gathering up the untidiness in the bedroom.

'Who are?' Sharon said.

'The birds, dear. It's the season for it.'

Sharon and Robert looked quickly at each other, and then away again.

When they were gone, and she and John were alone, he opened a bottle of champagne he'd obviously been hiding at the back of the refrigerator.

'Should I drink champagne?' Daisy asked with surprise.

'Strictly speaking, sweetheart, it's white wine with a sparkle in it. The local liquor store sold it to me as French champagne, and I didn't want to ruin their dreams. And one won't hurt you. It's the first time I've spent your birthday with you.'

'Is it really?'

'No, not really. But this year it's different. We're lovers, and you are sixteen years old. It's our first love, both of us, and all we've done is hold hands and look into each other's eyes. We do a lot of that. That's what it means to be sixteen. And I am thinking how lucky I am that I have found the only woman in the world for me at such a tender age, and there will have to be no searching ever again, and that we have ahead of us just years of being together, and my only ambition will be to make you feel happy, and safe, for as long as we both live.' He handed her one of the glasses of champagne, and saw the light change in her eyes.

'Oh John,' she said quietly, 'we can't pretend like this. We're grown-ups. This will all end, and you and I will never be able to look in each other's eyes again for fear of other people's wrath. How will I bear it? I will wish I never had this feeling. I will wish I had never loved you.'

His hands empty, he took her in his arms and

lay with her on the bed, holding her from outside the bedcover, feeling the heat of her body from beneath the sheets. Slowly, he kissed her face until the tears were gone, quietened her sobs with the gentleness of his fingers on her lips, wiping her nose with the collar of her nightdress, making her smile.

'Don't think of being anywhere else, my darling. Don't dwell on what might happen. I love you. Everyone has the right to that, even if it's only for a moment.' And he pushed her hair from her forehead, seeing the grey turn young again for him alone. 'You healed all my scars,' he said, 'did you know that?' And as he told her, his hands stroked and soothed her. Daisy felt as if she'd never been touched before. 'Did I not tell you about my mother?' John said. 'I wanted to. It's not a kind story. Not that I didn't love her – I did. More than anything in the world. I was the youngest child. Born ten years after my only sister. And there were two brothers before her. She clung to me as if I were to be her salvation. My mother, that is. I never knew she needed salvation. She was loving and generous, and spoiled me more than is decent most of the time. But then those moods would come upon her. From nowhere. She became harsh. Once she even hit me. Picked up one of Dad's big boots and struck me hard with it. I can't even remember what wrong I'd done. I was five years old. And I wanted her smiling again. Mothers should always smile, in the eyes of a son anyway. I never thought of her having grief, let alone anger. But she did. And she would go upstairs and lock the bedroom door. Dad would knock until she let him in. And a few times he even broke the door down. Then there would be screaming and shouting. Then silence, and Dad would come downstairs on his own, and it would be him who'd make us supper that night. Sometimes my brothers would ignore it, later I would hear them swearing under their breath and stalking out into the yard. My sister would cry, and once she was old enough to date, she made sure she was out when all the trouble began. Because they would go on for days, these crying bouts of Mom's, and Dad locking her in the bedroom, and her screaming as soon as he faced her again behind those locked doors. But no-one explained to me, told me what was going on. So I figured it out for myself. As everyone seemed ashamed of it, it must be that my father was brutal to her. He beat her. There were boys at school that told me about their dads doing that. It sounded the same to me. But I kept our secret. If the rest of my family didn't want to talk about it, then I would do the same. But I hated my dad, more and more, as the years went on. I prayed that he would die, and that Mom and me would be smiley all the time once he'd gone. Once he wasn't there to hit her.'

Daisy started to say something, seeing the pain in his eyes, but John put his hand over her mouth, stopping her words, wanting to finish his story. He remained holding her, on the bed, her head on his chest, the baby quiet in her womb as if she, too, wanted to hear John's tale.

'As the years went by it got worse. Once she went away for almost two months. To a hospital, I thought. Still nothing was really said, except mother was sick and had to rest for a long time. I'd lie awake at nights and think of ways to kill my dad. But through all this, the stubborn pride of our family led us to total silence, even between ourselves.' He paused for a moment.

Daisy looked up at him, but his thoughts were not with her that moment. 'What happened John? What happened to your mother?'

'She died when I was fourteen years old. She shot herself with one of Dad's guns he kept in a locked cupboard in the cellar. He had given up the hunting he used to do when I was younger. How Mom knew where the key was, I'll never know. Or how she knew how to load the damn thing. I guess Dad had taught her when they first married, and he would take trips out of town more often, leaving her alone with young children. I never asked him. I barely spoke to him again. I went to live with an aunt, Dad's sister, until I finished high school. Then I ran away. Talked my way into a job on a local newspaper. Small town, up north of here. I wrote to my aunt, told her I was safe, and please to tell Dad not to try and get in touch. And that was that. Until Dad died as well, only two years after Mom. I went back for the funeral. My brothers were there. And my aunt. My sister had married an English guy, and was living in the UK with him. She sent flowers. I couldn't understand why everyone was so upset. I mean, hadn't he been some sort of monster all these years? And now they were burying him beside the woman whose life he'd ruined? My aunt said, after we'd gone back to the house, run down and filthy since he'd been living there alone these last two years, 'Your father was a wonderful man. Don't you ever forget that, son. I hope that one day you will love a woman as well as he loved your mother.' I simply stared at her. 'Doesn't he know?' she said fiercely to my eldest brother. 'For the love of Christ, Dennis, has no-one told him yet? You let that poor man go to the grave with his youngest child hating him?'

They'd forgotten, you see. Forgotten that I was never told. We'd stayed apart for so long. My mother really was sick, you see. With a madness, a manic depression. One that can be held at bay these days they tell me. Could have probably been done even then, if any one of them had had the courage to take her. Dad had hidden it all their marriage, didn't understand it, but refused to tell me because I loved her so much, and they both hoped I'd be her salvation. A kind of ignorance, I guess.'

'Oh John – I'm so terribly sorry.'

'I've lived with the knowledge that my father died believing I hated him, because he was so afraid that if he told me, I would stop caring about my mother, as the others had, impatient with her, spoiling their growing up. So he let me hate *him* instead. I have worked very hard at trying to forgive myself. I doubt I ever will.' He looked down at her. 'But I'm damned if I will live the rest of my life without telling you how much I love and want you. That if it really is to be just these few weeks, then I will find a way of living with that. But right now, right here, we will love each other. And it will have to be enough.'

She untangled her arms, reached up to touch his face, and began to kiss him.

They didn't hear the back door open, or the sound of footsteps in the hall. They heard nothing until the bedroom door was flung open and there was a cry like the howl of a bear from the doorway. It was Bob.

Chapter Fifteen

After a day of sunshine and friends, and then, finally, the melancholy of John's story, and after kissing him with such a tenderness Daisy had never felt before, and after knowing that whatever the outcome, she was as much in love with him as he was with her, Bob's fury jolted her into a state of panic that terrified her from the moment she opened her eyes from holding John and saw her husband standing in the doorway, with that terrible howl still coming from his mouth.

John stood up, rose from the bed, as if in slow motion, as if playing for time, searching in his mind for something, anything he could say at such a moment. He turned to restrain Daisy from getting out of bed. But it was too late. She was on her feet, standing by his side, trembling with such fervour it was doubtful that either John or her husband could not notice.

At last Bob was quiet, and for one brief moment, the silence in the room was as tense as the icicles that remained on the Idaho pines when the first rays of early spring sun shone on them and they tried to stop from falling. Then they did. And the explosion came.

'What in the name of all things holy—' Bob left the sentence hanging.

It seemed that Daisy could only think of clichés at that moment, the ones she'd heard in the afternoon soap operas. Apparently, John was doing the same. 'This is not what you think, Bob. Can we sit down and talk like sensible people? I'm aware of what you must be feeling.'

Daisy said softly, 'Shush John.' She moved across to her husband, who was leaning now against the wall, covering his face with both his hands. She reached out to touch those hands, pull them from his face. She felt surprisingly calm, in spite of the trembling of her body. Both men were rooted to the spot. Before her hands touched his face, Bob's eyes opened and stared at her. 'Don't shout, Bob. You'll have the neighbours in.'

'You can't think that the neighbours don't already know what's going on in here, can you Daisy? Have you got so frigging stupid that you think people don't already know?' He moved, and sat on the stool at the end of the bed. John moved to the window. A few lights had come on from the next house, old Mr Poolridge was standing on the front porch in his pyjamas. His wife, twice his size and in the same pattern of night attire, except three sizes bigger, was holding a rifle.

'They're on their porch,' John said, 'they must have heard you drive up and then yell. Sarah Poolridge has got a rifle. Can she shoot the darn thing?'

'Show your face outside, son-in-law. With a bit of luck you'll find out the hard way!'

'Please don't Bob,' Daisy's voice rose sharply. 'You just sound childish. No-one is going to fight you, so we'd better talk about all this.'

'I know lover lad won't fight, woman. He'll hide behind your skirts the way he's hid behind our Marjorie for years.'

'You know nothing about John, so don't make a fool of yourself. I want to talk to you like a sensible human being.'

'You don't have to defend me, Daisy,' John said from behind her, 'I can do that for myself.'

'You don't need defending, John. This is between Bob and me.'

'You surprise me,' Bob sneered, 'most people in the town think that you're carrying his bastard. I would think he was more entitled to be in on this little scene than most other folk.'

Daisy turned back to her husband, her eyes cold, her look furious. 'How dare you, Bob Francken. How dare you burst in here at this time of night—'

'Into my own frigging house, woman? Is that what you're saying? My frigging house, that you and this kid here are playing doctors in? Is that it? Jesus Christ, now I've heard everything. And don't start in on the blaspheming bit. Not after your carrying on!'

Daisy closed her eyes against the loudness of his voice, let him finish, feeling herself break out in a cold sweat, then she went on with what she'd started saying. 'This time of night, Bob. When you're usually playing mulberry bush with the schoolteacher, while I go to bed alone. That's what it was. For the last ten years anyway. And before that? I didn't know their names. And now, it doesn't matter. You left me, remember? You walked out. The whole town knows. She's had to resign from the school. Remember? It's all gone, Bob Francken. And along with it, the lies and the pretence, and my unhappiness. And all we're left with is our failures. Yours and mine. Failure as husband and wife, and parents. All our children are screwed up. Our fault. Not just yours, not just mine, but ours. I haven't been unfaithful to you. Deep down inside you, you know that. And one day you will turn round to your schoolmarm and say, I've got a daughter somewhere and I lost her because of you. Because by then, you silly man, you'll be as bored with her as you are with me, and you'll be too old and tired to move on, and you will never understand that the boredom in your life is all your own doing. Not mine, not your mother's, and certainly not Mary-Anne's. She knows we can't get a divorce. If she's still willing to take you on after all the pain you've doled out in her direction since high school, I reckon you should go back home to her quick, get down on your knees, and say you're sorry. And then you can forget about me, and your daughter, and John. Because in spite of what your beer swilling pals have told you, this is *your* child I'm carrying, and in spite of all of you, your mother, your family, she will be born, because she's mine! And I WANT her!'

And she put one hand on the chest to steady herself, so out of breath she was. There was one more thing to tell him. 'And most of the town do not believe what you seem to think. That seems to have been kept within the bounds of the local bar. I will be going away when the baby comes, so even if the rumours of John and I are not true now, they soon will be. I wish she was his child. I wish I could have had a child with someone other than you. I wish I'd stood my ground with you and your mother years ago. You and I would have been much better at being married if I had. Maybe. But it's over. And I'm saying nothing else. And you're right of course. About one thing. John is my lover. Now go away. You'll get your house back soon enough. Get out of my sight. Be off with you husband, and leave us in peace.'

She waved one hand in Bob's direction and then the room began swimming before her eyes. She was aware that behind her John was moving forward, saying her name, and it seemed he was taking for ever to get to her, and she wanted to be in his arms, wanted to build again all the bridges she'd so impulsively burnt for both of them in her long speech. But it wasn't his hands on her. It seemed that Bob had moved towards her, maybe he too had seen her swaying dangerously, wanted to reach out and touch her, but she put her hands in front of herself, as if in defence, as if Bob was going to hit her, and seeing that, or not seeing it,

John came quickly, with a shout, which she heard as if in the distance, and put a hand out to him. In the wrong direction. And Bob swung sideways, thinking she would strike him, and he would be unready for John's attack. So Bob struck out. And Daisy, his wife, went down. And there was blood suddenly on the whiteness of her gown, and spreading onto Gary's rug, that she noticed as she heard the front door slam and felt John's hands upon her as he knelt down. But Bob had gone. Blinded by anger, tears, confusion, he'd struck out, believed momentarily that he had felled his son-in-law, then fled into the night. He didn't really see that Daisy had fallen. Didn't hear her say, 'My baby, John. My baby's coming. Be quick.' And he was already back with Mary-Anne when Daisy arrived at the hospital, and was carried swiftly into the delivery room. Her labour started that Saturday morning, and continued until the very early hours of Sunday. And that was her birthday.

They wouldn't let John into the delivery room when he arrived. He would have to wait for Dr Hart. 'But I'm married to her daughter,' he said, 'I've been looking after her. She'll expect me to be there.'

'Mrs Francken is resting,' they said, not caring to see the anguish in his eyes. 'Mrs Francken must remain calm and sedated for the sake of herself and the baby.'

So John waited, sunk down into the large sofa

in the waiting area of the cottage hospital, head in hands, staring at the mud from the Franckens' driveway drying on the boots he'd pulled on in his haste to go with Daisy in the ambulance. 'Let her live,' he murmured, 'dear God, let her live.' And hoped that the God he spoke to, and in whom he had stopped believing the day his sister found their mother with the back of her head splattered against the mirror in the bathroom, would hear him. In his worst nightmares he could still hear his sister's screams. They had lasted, in his head at least, for long after his mother's body had been taken away, and his father's sister had arrived to stay with him. Those sounds from his sister's mouth, echoing and churning in all his nightmares, drowned out his lessons when he was sent back to school the day after – without comfort, without solace, without knowing anyone else's pain. His silence and his tearless eyes leading them to believe he was strong. 'He'll get over it, teenagers get over things quickly. Good job they're selfish. Send him straight back to school the next day. Best thing for him. He'll thank you in the end, Frank, just you see.' His father, Frank, speechless with a misery he could not fathom, his mouth murmuring the name of his mad, dead wife. And there was blood then as well. On the mirror behind the lavatory. It had seemed such an indecorous place for her to choose as the gate to heaven.

And John waited. The night time sounds of the small town hospital sitting unheard at the back of his mind. Stock still he sat, not looking up, remembering Daisy as if she had already died. Then Douglas Hart was there, two legs encased in weekend jeans walked, wandered, and then stood before his gaze, forcing him to look up. He didn't want to see the look on Douglas' face.

'If I lose her now, I'm finished.' But it was just a thought. He stared at the doctor.

'John? Sorry you've had such a wait. Did they bring you some coffee?' Douglas sat next to him on the blue-grey plastic sofa.

'How is she?' But in his head, a teenage voice sounded, just broken, cracking its way into manhood. 'Is Mom dead? Is she? Will someone answer me? I want to see. Let me see.' And the screams again. And the blood, and something else, pieces of something, not to think about, smeared across the mirror behind the lavatory, where he'd looked at himself as he urinated, masturbated, tried to shave. The things men do. There was the place she'd sat. Pulled the trigger. Found her peace, please God. But not the place for him now. Not the place for sexual fantasies, and a youth's first shave.

'She's going to be fine, John. We've slowed her down a little. But the baby can't wait much longer. She'll be born this time, come hell or high water. You'll see.'

'But it's another four weeks. She's not ready.'

'Then we will have to be.'

A young nurse pushed a plastic cup filled with

hot black coffee into his hands. 'D'you want sugar?' She smiled.

'No. Thank you.' And then, 'Can I see her Douglas? She'll want me to.'

'Let me check next time her eyes are open. We've given her plenty of sedation, just to keep her slow, you understand. Just so she'll get enough sleep to make her stronger.'

'Does she know? About the baby, I mean.'

'She knows there's still a heartbeat. It's all she needed.'

'I must call the family,' John said at last, and stood, putting down the coffee. Liquid spilled onto one of his trembling hands, and he winced. 'Too hot to drink,' he said, and went across to the water fountain and opened his mouth against the icy water.

Douglas, behind him, said, 'I took the liberty of calling them myself. Robert's on his way, and I left a message on Marjorie's machine. I asked her to pass the information on to her father as well.'

John laughed shortly, and splashed the cold water roughly onto his face. 'That'll be interesting,' he said.

'Look John, what's going on inside this family is only my concern when it adversely harms my patient. If having them here will upset Daisy, and, indeed, the staff that will be dealing with her, then I need only make a few more telephone calls and tell them not to come.'

'No. Don't do that. Daisy will want to see them. If she's well enough.' He looked the doctor square in the eye. 'It's all a bit of a mess, I'm afraid. But I know that Daisy would be extraordinarily upset if she thought you believed any of the rumours that have been circulating. If you do, I'll ask you to pretend otherwise in front of her if you don't mind.'

'I've known Daisy Francken since the first week she stepped foot in this town, young man. She doesn't have a cheating bone in her body, and, until this child was conceived, I believed she was merely your ordinary woman, putting up with more than she should from a man who did not pussyfoot over his own desires. Enough said. I can't think of her that way any longer. As far as I'm concerned, her child will be born, and will be healthy, if it's the last thing I do in this town. Any other business is not mine. I don't wish to hear it, and I don't wish to talk about it. I'll go and see if she's awake. Wait there.'

And John, water dripping from his face, leaned wearily against the wall to wait for his return.

Daisy was in that soporific state where whatever they chose to do for her at that moment would be fine by her. The next time she opened her eyes, John was there. Her voice was scarcely above a whisper, and John had to lean in close to hear her. She was so deliciously slothful in her sedated state, she could scarcely find the energy or will to do anything but smile, let alone find words that would make much sense. 'The baby's fine, John. Douglas said there was a good heartbeat. Isn't that good?

Are you all right? You have blood on your coat. And your hands.'

He looked down, realizing the stains she saw were hers, as he'd held her close while she was haemorrhaging, waiting for the ambulance.

'It's nothing,' he said, 'just think of yourself.'

'Will they let you stay?'

'For a while, I guess.'

'What will they do? Do you know?'

John hesitated for just a moment. 'They want you to rest. Then Douglas feels the baby should be helped.'

Daisy stared at him. 'It's too early,' she whispered, 'tell him, no. It's too early. She's not ready.'

John brought her hand to his lips, held it there and kissed it. He leaned in even closer to her, his cheek by hers. He could hear her heart beating rapidly. 'Daisy, Daisy – sweetheart, you must do this. You can't carry her any longer. It's time to let go. Leave it in the hands of the doctors and God.'

'All men,' she said. 'They're all men.' And with that, she turned her head from him and shut her eyes.

He looked at the back of her head, and wished he could feel her sorrow, her tiredness, her surrender. Wished her back in her bright kitchen that summer Sunday, all those years ago, soft and full in her gingham apron, her eyes laughing at him, her smile the smile of a young girl. But there was nothing he could say. There was no confidence he could give her, no safety net for the hours ahead, and the uselessness he'd felt so often in his life flooded back to remind him of his own fragility.

So he just sat, one hand on the back of her neck, and the noises of the hospital spun around them, a feeling of unreality nurtured his soul, and soon he heard her breathing change, and guessed she was asleep again. 'Rest sweetheart. Don't give in, my darling.'

But she couldn't hear him. He stood and bent over to kiss her cheek. She frowned in her sleep, moved away from him, a look of exasperation crossed her face and he stood tall by her side, looking down.

And then Douglas Hart was by his side, speaking softly. 'Robert's here. Go and talk to him. Let her rest.'

When John walked back into the waiting area, he saw Robert at the other end of the corridor on the telephone. John raised one hand in greeting. Robert's gaze was grim. Five minutes later he stood awkwardly by John's side at the drinking fountain. He said nothing.

'She's asleep,' John said. 'Have you spoken to Douglas?'

'Not much. Dad called me.'

John sat down on the blue and grey plastic sofa, and leaned his head back, his eyes closed. Outside, through the open window, he heard the birds begin to sing to each other, getting themselves together to find breakfast for their young.

'You heard what happened then? Earlier to-night?' John said at last.

'Yeah.'

Robert's voice was raspy. John opened his eyes and found his brother-in-law glaring down at him. 'For Christ's sake, Robert! You're not for one minute believing what your father said, are you?'

'About you and Mom, you mean? I don't know what the fuck to believe. How would you feel if it was your mother lying in there? Having a baby who seems at this moment to have no claim on any man as a father? Wouldn't you find all this a bit hard to swallow, man?' His voice rose higher with every word he uttered. 'I can't think what to even say. I can't believe it of Mom, but it all fits, doesn't it, you bastard. Dad's not coming anyway. Here, I mean. He seems to have no fucking doubts, that's for sure. My wife's hysterical as it is. Says even if it's not true, it makes more sense than Dad turning his back on his child like that. Anyway, she reckons that will be what most people will want to believe. It'll be talked about for ever. Sharon thinks we ought to fucking emigrate, for Christ's sake.'

John began to laugh, and Robert stared at him, incredulously. And John was still laughing when Marjorie arrived. Not so much arrived really. More, passed through, so to speak. It stopped him laughing, anyway, watching her come out of the elevator and begin to walk fiercely down the corridor to where he and her brother were sitting.

Not a word was said. As she came to rest beside John's chair, he stood up. Their eyes met.

'Marjorie,' John said.

But she said nothing. Just stood there and searched his face. Then, one hand came up, anger controlled, just a glint in the eye that John knew from old. It wasn't the time or place to speak. Marjorie would have her words in any way she chose. And the hand came down, and landed hard on John's right cheek. The sound was like a pistol shot. John heard Robert say quietly, 'Jesus Christ, Marjorie. There's a time and a place.' There was no answer. As swiftly and confidently as she had entered, Marjorie turned and walked out, past the stares of the nurses as they bustled about changing shifts. One of them sniggered. Then she was gone, and the sound of the elevator taking her down once more to the car park faded away.

John held his cheek. Felt the burning. Guessed it was reddening. Robert sank with a groan into the nearest sofa, and glared at the floor between his feet.

John sat beside him, still holding his cheek. Years later, he would say when asked, 'At least my wife and I didn't have one of those long, drawn-out separations!' Just then, in that hospital, the dawn coming up rapidly through the large windows, the situation seemed merely bizarre. At nine a.m. Robert went to call Sharon at work. She hadn't gone in, apparently. He called home, but there was no reply, so he called Sharon's mother, who answered the telephone. As she spoke, Robert could see her, in his mind's eye, standing in the kitchen of her house, wearing the 'I Love Idaho' apron that he and Sharon had given her one Christmas. He'd never seen her without an apron. Not that he could remember, anyway. All she seemed to do was bake. Sometimes, on winter Sundays, she would be just an arm, emerging now and then from a steamy kitchen, holding out platters of brownies and fudge slices and lemon cream cake to the ever-hungry family that had gathered for the day. Her mouth would purse up in disapproval if you ate nothing. He often wondered how Sharon grew up so skinny. Maybe it was the cigarettes.

'Hi, Mother-in-law. Is Sharon with you?'

'Yes, she is, Robert. She hasn't slept all night. We went over to pick her up and I've just got her to stop crying and shut her eyes for a little while.' The voice definitely came from that famous pair of pursed lips.

Robert sighed. 'I won't wake her then. Why didn't she go into work?'

'I would have thought that was very obvious, Robert. The gossip in this town was spreading at dawn this morning. She felt she couldn't face all those stares in the salon. I can't say I blame her. I see it must be hard for you as well, but let's face it, dear, everyone's known about your father for years, maybe it's not such a shock to find out about your mother.'

'Look, Mother-in-law, all this is just at the moment – rumours. Gossip—'

'Are you still at the hospital, Robert? Has the child been born? Is it dead? Maybe it would be a blessing if – well, you know. Your poor sister.'

Robert gripped the telephone until his hand hurt. 'Look, I'm going to hang around until Mom's awake. See what's going to happen. Tell Sharon I'll come by your place later, unless she goes home of course.' And he put the receiver down with a great clatter, so that it bounced up again and hit the floor. The sound echoed down the long corridor. John glanced up and then he saw Douglas Hart walking briskly towards them.

'Your mother's awake, Robert. Go in for five minutes. No longer. Her labour has begun. I will trust you not to distress her in any way. This is supposed to be a joyful event. Let's do our best to keep it that way. John, come with me. You can have a shave and a wash in my office. They're breaking all the rules today; the staff are very excited about this birth, as I suspect you probably know. D'you want to sleep for a while? She could do with some company later on, but I'm not sure you'll have the stomach for it. This is the first time, I presume?'

'I'll have the stomach for it,' John said quietly.

Daisy smiled joyfully at her son, when he slid silently into the room.

'Hi, Mom.'

Daisy put out her hand and motioned him to sit down. She felt the beginning of a contraction, and caught her breath in surprise. It subsided, and Robert stared at her with a terror born of ignorance. It made her laugh. 'Oh dear, son, this isn't the place for you. Go home to your wife. They'll call you when the baby comes.'

Robert sat glumly. 'Are you OK, Mom? What shall I do?'

'I want you to call Gary for me when the baby's here. That's all, son. And don't look so frightened. Everything will be just fine. You run along. Send one of those nurses in. Is John all right?'

He forgot to kiss her in his haste to get out of the room. John was nowhere to be seen, so he turned towards the elevator and decided to go home. He felt confused and alone. It seemed he'd felt this way before. But now he was a man, and there was only himself to heed his feelings. He would close the gas station that day. It seemed fitting.

At ten that Saturday night, Daisy was still in labour. And then the child's heartbeat got fainter and fainter. John was sitting with cold towels on Daisy's forehead to wipe away the sweat. She had stopped cheering herself on quite a few hours before. Now her eyes were closed, and she would fall into small spasms of sleep any time she had a few moments without pain. She wished now she'd chosen the epidural after all. John saw the faces of the doctors. Daisy's grip on his hand was loose after hours of squeezing it.

Douglas Hart bent towards her. He spoke softly. 'Daisy. Daisy, my dear. We'll just give you something to help you to sleep. The baby just needs a little help, that's all. It's been a long day.'

Daisy's eyes opened. 'She's not moving,' she said wearily. 'She can't be dead, Douglas. Not after all this. Just do what you have to.' And she closed her eyes again.

And when she opened her eyes again, John was still there. She was in a different room, and there were things in her arm, and she felt sick. The clock on the wall in front of her said one o'clock.

'Happy birthday, sweetheart.'

'Should I feel sick? I do.' She tried to sit, but John pushed her back. 'Be still,' he said. 'You are quite incorrigible. I see I'm going to have my work cut out with you.'

'Have I had my baby? Is she all right? You needn't look so pleased with yourself, John. *I* did it, you know! Where is she? I want to see her. Tell the nurse. Quickly.'

Again he pushed her down. 'Daisy be patient. You've got your daughter! She's very tiny. Just four pounds. But that's apparently not bad for an eight-month baby. But she's in ICU.'

'What's wrong with her? There can't be anything wrong with her. Tell me.'

'Sweetheart be still. She's as tired as you. Let her sleep. Let them finish checking her.'

But then Douglas was there, in the doorway. And behind him the excited faces of two of the nurses. And in the arms of the plumpest one was the tiniest bundle that Daisy had ever seen. The other girl, red in the face, and crying with excitement, put some roses on the bed. 'Mother and child both fine,' she'd told the local journalist. And the same thing to the disc jockey from the local radio station. 'Mother and daughter are just fine.'

Douglas said, 'We're giving you five minutes with her. No more. I can break no more rules tonight. But have a look at your daughter. She's quite perfect, is our little miracle. And I'm sure she'll grow out of looking just like your mother-in-law!'

Daisy, crying, laughing, held up by John, took her baby in her arms. The three of them were alone. She stared with awe at this tiny human being she held so carefully. 'Hi baby,' she whispered. 'I've been waiting so long for you to get here. Thought you'd given up on me a couple of times, but that's not in your nature, is it?' The smaller than small hands, transparent in their newness, waved for a moment, and then subsided. The tiny face crumpled, as if to cry. But then a snort. And the eyes stayed closed. And she slept. Daisy had to put her face very near to hear her breathing. She said, very quietly, because somebody so new would hate, at first, the noise of the world she'd fought her way into, 'I don't know what's going to happen to you, my darling. But whatever it is, you will be loved. You will be one of the lucky souls, thank God. I'll not let you down.'

Finally, John spoke. 'When you're ready Daisy. When you're both ready, in a few weeks, however long it takes, I'll take you home to Seattle. Both of you. To my dad's house. It's still there: he left it to me. I never could live in it, but now I can. With you. All the old place needs is some love, just to chase away the ghosts. No, sweetheart, don't ask any questions. Not now. It's what's going to happen. I'll take care of it. I'll take care of you. There's nothing so broken it can't be fixed. My aunt used to say that. There's nothing left for either of us here.'

And Daisy smiled. The smile that John had always loved. She'd done it, had Daisy. She said she would. Now it was his turn.

'What are you going to call her?' he asked.

'I haven't thought about it. I've only thought of her. What a fighter she's been from the very beginning. How determined she's been to hang on in there. Who does she get it from? Maybe I should name her after some determined woman in history. But Joan doesn't seem right, somehow. And Joan of Arc is the only extraordinary woman I can think of at this moment. She was full of courage, and determination, and a good deal of stubbornness, which will never go amiss. Have you any suggestions?'

John said, 'Well sweetheart, if that's what you want for her, there's no doubt of her name. You must call her Daisy. After her mother.'

So they did.

THE END